FOR THIS REASON: The Quest for Purposeful Leadership

"Leadership From the Heart, Illuminating Lives, Inspiring Organizations"

By

Kennedy Barasa

E-Book ISBN: 978-1-970894-28-8

Paperback ISBN: 978-1-970894-29-5

Hardcover ISBN: 978-1-970894-30-1

DEDICATION

To **every seeker of purpose**— the mentors who ignite imagination, the quiet servants who labor in love, the vision-bearers who dare to see tomorrow in today— may these pages mirror the light you already carry and multiply it into brighter constellations of hope.

To all who choose to **brighten another's path, leading with heart,** who shoulder community on compassionate arms, who measure success not by applause but by the lives they lift— this journey is written with your heartbeat between each line.

To my beloved parents, the late **Tepla Namalwa** and **Joseph Wanyonyi,** who is still ageing graciously, whose intentional upbringing shaped the compass of my character: your faith, sacrifice, and unspoken prayers still echo as coordinates guiding every step I take toward meaningful leadership.

Your legacy remains the first chapter of any good I accomplish.

And above all, to **my Lord Jesus Christ— the wellspring of purpose, the author of wisdom, and the truest example of servant-leadership**— may this work honor the grace that turns ordinary lives into extraordinary testimonies of love in action.

For this reason, with gratitude and reverence, I place these words in Your hands.

Kennedy Barasa

November 22, 2025

ACKNOWLEDGMENTS

With a heart overflowing in gratitude, I pause to remember every hand that steadied the pen, every voice that whispered courage, and every prayer that lifted these pages heaven-ward.

Rosemary, my beloved wife, and our wonderful children—Brenda, Theophilus, Paul, Moses, and Candy—along with the entire Barasa family, your constant love, joy, and late-night prayers fill my heart with warmth. Every page reflects your support; every word echoes your faith. This book is as much your achievement as it is mine.

To **Pastors Dwayne McCarty and Kelvin Shaw** of Everybody Growing Church: your steadfast prayers turned weary moments into worship. Thank you for reminding me that resilience is simply grace in motion.

I am truly grateful to my colleagues and friends at Trinity Western University's Master of Arts in Leadership—Dr. Imbenzi George and Dr. Hyne-Ju—for your unwavering support and camaraderie, which really carried me through this journey.

To the publishing team—**Jason Stones, Senior Publishing Consultant, and Milli Jones, Project Head of Self Book Publishing**—your expertise transformed a manuscript into a mission. Your tireless dedication ensured this vision would circle the globe.

Special gratitude to **Stones Bob**, a man whose caring heart welcomes strangers as kin. Your gracious "Foreword" lends depth and vitality to these pages, framing the journey with wisdom and warmth.

Above all, **Lord Jesus Christ**, Fountain of grace and Author of purpose, You supplied the wisdom, strength, and peace that breathe through every line. All glory and praise belong to You.

Wishing each of you abundant blessings from our loving God and gracious Lord Jesus Christ! May He keep you and guide you toward new horizons in your lives and callings. Your partnership has truly brought this pursuit of meaningful leadership to life—thank you from the bottom of my heart for your support and dedication.

Kennedy Barasa

November 22, 2025

FOREWORD

In a time marked by rapid global change—where technological disruption, environmental uncertainty, and shifting moral landscapes converge—the need for purposeful leadership has never been more urgent. *FOR THIS REASON: The Quest for Purposeful Leadership* arrives as both a mirror and a guidepost: a mirror that reflects our present challenges and a guidepost that illuminates a path forward rooted in wisdom, integrity, and spiritual insight.

The strength of this book lies in its rare integration of ancient biblical narratives with the modern realities of organizational leadership. Across its pages, the author draws from the timeless lessons of Jesus, Moses, Abraham, David, Esther, Daniel, and Paul—leaders whose courage, clarity of purpose, and unwavering faith shaped the course of history. Their stories reveal that leadership is not merely a position of authority but an expression of divine purpose in action. The author skillfully bridges these narratives with contemporary leadership theories, organizational research, and emerging global trends, creating a work that is both rich in scholarship and deeply grounded in spiritual truth.

This book emphasizes that purposeful leadership begins not with strategy, but with the heart—with intention, humility, and a willingness to serve. It challenges the reader to look inward, aligning actions with core values, cultivating emotional intelligence, embracing adaptability, and anchoring decisions in ethical principles. It also situates leadership within a global context shaped by climate change, artificial intelligence, and renewed conversations about faith, calling leaders to respond with wisdom and moral clarity.

What sets *FOR THIS REASON: The Quest for Purposeful Leadership* apart is its insistence that authentic leadership is fundamentally spiritual. As the book powerfully states, purposeful leaders "lead from the heart and soul," embodying compassion, resilience, and a steadfast commitment to the greater good. This perspective acknowledges that leadership is not simply about achieving organizational goals; it is about influencing lives, shaping communities, and stewarding a shared destiny.

The author's exploration of adaptive leadership for the 21st century is particularly compelling. Drawing from research and real-world case studies, the book argues that leaders must cultivate mindsets of curiosity, growth, belief, and intuition to navigate increasingly complex environments. By weaving together biblical lessons and modern leadership frameworks, the text offers readers an actionable roadmap for building agile, ethical, and purpose-driven organizations.

Yet, this work is more than theory—it is a call to action. Each chapter invites leaders to reflect on their purpose, examine their motivations, and embrace the responsibility of leading with courage and integrity. It challenges organizations to integrate purpose into culture, systems, operations, and vision—not as a slogan, but as a lived reality. And it encourages every reader, regardless of background or role, to consider how their unique purpose can illuminate others' lives.

Ultimately, *FOR THIS REASON: The Quest for Purposeful Leadership* is a testament to the transformative power of purpose. It reminds us that leadership is not about titles or achievements but about answering the deeper question: *For this reason, why have I come?* Through its blend of biblical insight, academic research, and practical application, this book equips leaders to respond to that question with clarity, conviction, and hope.

May this work inspire you to lead with heart, to act with intention, and to pursue purpose that transcends time and circumstance. In doing so, you join a long lineage of leaders who understood that purpose is not simply what you achieve, but what you illuminate in the world.

Stones Bob

November 21, 2025

Table of Contents

Page left blank intentionally

PART 1: PURPOSE AND THE ESSENCE OF PURPOSEFUL LEADERSHIP

Part 1 explores the context of the book's theme, purpose and leadership, a unified perspective—and the three dimensions of leadership: eyesight, heart, and shepherd.

CHAPTER 1: THE CONTEXT OF THE BOOK'S THEME

Setting the Stage

Have you ever read something that made you pause and ask, "What does that mean?" That moment of wonder often ignites a curiosity that drives us to seek deeper understanding. One powerful example is in Mark 1:38, where Jesus underscores the importance of purpose in leadership.

Biblical Foundations and Reflections

In Mark 1:38, Jesus told His disciples, "Let us go somewhere else into the next towns, that I may preach there also because I came out for this reason."

Many Bible versions render this phrase as "for this purpose." Each repetition deepens the mystery and underscores that purpose is not a casual remark but a life-defining principle—one intended for His original audience and still relevant to us today.

Consider the account in Luke, where Jesus' parents traveled to Jerusalem for a festival. Assuming He was with extended family, they were surprised to find Him in the temple, immersed in discussion. When questioned, Jesus explained that He was "about His Father's business." This response connected His actions to a divine mission and demonstrated that a clear, guiding purpose can shape decisions and destiny.

Similarly, early in His ministry, after reading from the scroll that prophesied about Him, Jesus declared to His congregation,

"This prophecy is fulfilled right in your eyes." Later, during His encounter with Pilate, when confronted by Jewish leaders about His kingship, He affirmed, "You rightly say I am a king," and then added,

"For this reason, I came to bear witness to the truth." Each of these instances reinforces the idea that when purpose is clearly understood and embraced, it becomes a driving force behind impactful leadership.

Questions for Reflection

The recurrence of purpose in Jesus' teachings naturally raises some key questions:

Can there be leadership without a purpose?

Imagine a leader operating without clear intent—how much potential remains untapped? Now, envision the transformative power of leadership driven by unwavering purpose.

Why are corporations and leaders striving to integrate purpose into their operations?

This book explores these critical questions, unraveling the essence and potency of purposeful leadership in an increasingly fast-changing world.

Why This Book?

In today's environment, where leadership can feel disconnected or adrift from purpose, I wrote this book to offer practical principles derived from biblical narratives—principles that can transform contemporary leadership practices. This book takes you on a transformative journey, bridging historical insights with emerging themes such as artificial intelligence, climate change, and faith. By integrating timeless biblical wisdom with contemporary, actionable frameworks, it empowers leaders to navigate today's uncertain and turbulent environment with both purpose and integrity.

FOR THIS REASON: The Quest for Purposeful Leadership offers a comprehensive blueprint for heart-centered leadership that transforms lives and inspires communities. It combines time-tested principles with innovative insights, providing a rich, multidimensional approach to redefining leadership in our dynamic world.

Drawing on over two decades of experience in diplomacy and international affairs, as an instructor and advisor in the Business Global Program at Trinity Western University- through my faith, as well as being a published author and consultant—I selected this book's title to reflect a meaningful fusion of foundational spiritual insights and forward-thinking leadership strategies.

I chose the Bible because it reveals truth without hiding anything. Since God created everything with intention, every human endeavor carries purpose—a cornerstone of effective leadership.

A Collective Journey Forward

The quest for purposeful leadership is not an isolated journey but a collective challenge that invites us to reflect, act, and inspire. As you delve into the chapters ahead, ask yourself:

How can I embody purpose in my leadership?

How can I inspire those around me to discover and embrace their inherent purpose?

Let us commit to fostering a culture of purpose that goes beyond mere ambition. By integrating clarity of purpose into our decisions and actions, we align ourselves with a higher calling and empower others to follow. In doing so, we not only lead but also construct a legacy of impact that resonates through generations.

Embrace this journey with conviction and integrity; let us lead with purpose.

CHAPTER 2: PURPOSE AND LEADERSHIP - A UNIFIED PERSPECTIVE

This chapter examines the biblical interpretation of purpose and leadership, juxtaposing it with the viewpoints of contemporary corporate leaders. By examining foundational texts, we gain insights into human nature and its implications for leadership. The literature review highlights the importance of purpose-driven leadership in addressing the challenges that organizations and society currently face and are likely to encounter in the future. Biblical perspectives serve as a lens, revealing how the past, present, and future are interconnected and illuminating the continuity of purpose-driven leadership.

THE BIBLICAL VIEW OF PURPOSE AND LEADERSHIP

To fully comprehend leadership, we must first understand human nature by asking, "Who am I, or who are you?"

The Concept of Man in Leadership

Genesis 1:26, 27 (KJV) states, "Let us make man in our image, after our likeness .... God created man in His own image, in the image of God created He him; male and female created He them." Genesis 2:7 (KJV) further adds, "And the LORD God formed man of the dust of the ground and breathed into his nostrils the breath of life; man became a living soul." These scriptures introduce two aspects of humanity: the physical form created from the dust of the earth and the living soul infused with God's breath of life.

Man Formed from the Dust of the Earth

The creation of man from the dust signifies the physical aspect of human beings, embodying potentiality and the capacity for growth and fulfillment (Alter, 2004). While representing the basest form of human existence, this earthly aspect also holds the promise of ascension (Brueggemann, 1982). It symbolizes the potential to rise from life's lowest points, instilling hope and optimism in our leadership journey.

Man, the Living Soul

The divine act of infusing God's breath transformed the earthly form into a living soul capable of thought, emotion, and self-awareness. This transformation elevates man to reflect God's image, which is not a physical likeness but a spiritual potentiality (Von Rad, 1961).

Duality of Man and Its Significance

The Hebrew term "Adama" (earth) and its relation to "Adam" (humanity) encapsulate the potential for life to spring from the ordinary (Sacks, 2005). This duality encompasses the earthly tendencies towards destructive impulses and the spiritual call to leadership and greatness (Kass, 2002). Rabbi Doniel Baron illuminates the duality inherent in the word "Adam." The Hebrew letters spell "dam" (blood), symbolizing the baser elements of the soul, while the prefix "aleph" represents the potential for teaching and leadership (Baron, 2010). This linguistic nuance underscores humanity's capacity to transcend its base instincts and embody the divine image (Levenson, 1988).

Despite Adam's historical yielding to temptation, the narrative continues to promise human potential for greatness, as seen in God's counsel to Cain in Genesis 4:7 to master his impulses (Wenham, 1987).

The scriptural journey through the nature of human beings underscores the importance of overcoming base desires to align with the higher calling of service and leadership. This choice is pivotal in fulfilling one's purpose and caring for others rather than pursuing selfish ambitions.

Implications for Purposeful Leadership

The biblical portrayal of man offers valuable insights for purposeful leadership. Leaders who acknowledge their dual nature can navigate the challenges of their roles more effectively. By embracing growth and self-discipline, leaders can set an example for others, fostering an environment of empathy and cooperative effort. Purposeful leadership, grounded in self-awareness and a commitment to a shared vision, can drive transformative changes within organizations and communities.

DOMINION OVER GOD'S CREATION ON EARTH – A CASE FOR LEADERSHIP

Biblical Foundations of Dominion

Genesis 1:27 reveals God's initiation of dominion by bestowing human beings the authority over the earth and all its inhabitants. This dominion, granted to humanity in its pure, spiritual state, implies an intended harmony between man and nature. Despite man's fall from grace, the essence of this divine calling persists, filled with the potential to realize God's original intentions (Wright, 2004).

Understanding Dominion

The biblical concept of dominion is encapsulated in the Hebrew word "radar, " which signifies a form of rulership. Ancient Hebrew expert Jeff A. Benner associates " radar" with descending, wandering, and spreading, indicating a guiding rather than an oppressive form of leadership (Benner, 2002). This interpretation aligns with the idea that humans are to lead the animal kingdom as benevolent stewards, fostering a mutually beneficial relationship (Davis, 1984).

Stewardship as Service

Tom Gilsong, exploring dominion, concurs with Justin Holcomb's view that dominion equates to stewardship, service, and responsibility (Gilsong, 2015). This view is rooted in the belief that humans are caretakers, not owners, of the earth's resources, a role entrusted to them by God (Bauckham, 2010). Stewardship is characterized by responsible management, care for creation, and accountability to the Creator, in contrast to the destructive tendencies of man's perceived ownership (Berry, 2015).

The Challenge of Human Governance

Humans' struggle to control base impulses often leads to misuse of the dominion mandate, resulting in environmental degradation and social injustice (White, 1967). This misuse underscores the need to reassess the meaning of dominion. It is not an endorsement of exploitation but a call for responsible, compassionate stewardship that aligns with God's purposes (Schaeffer, 1970).

Dominion over God's creation is a call to leadership rooted in stewardship, service, and responsibility. It requires a delicate balance between governance and care to ensure that all of God's creation thrives. As societies grapple with environmental and ethical challenges, the biblical concept of dominion is a potent reminder of our responsibility to lead with wisdom and compassion.

Implications for Purposeful Leadership

The biblical concept of dominion has profound implications for purposeful leadership. Leaders should exercise their authority not as tyrants but as stewards who serve and nurture those they lead. This perspective encourages leaders to foster relationships built on trust and mutual respect, recognizing that their role is to guide and support rather than to dominate.

Furthermore, understanding dominion as stewardship underscores the importance of accountability. Leaders must recognize that their decisions have a direct impact on their immediate environment, the broader community, and future generations. By prioritizing responsible resource management and compassionate care for others, leaders can foster a culture of sustainability and ethical responsibility.

Purposeful leadership rooted in the biblical understanding of dominion can catalyze transformative change. By embodying stewardship principles, leaders can inspire those around them to pursue a shared vision of growth, care, and mutual benefit, thereby fulfilling the divine purpose intended for humanity.

THE CONCEPT OF STEWARDSHIP AND ITS IMPORTANCE FOR PURPOSEFUL LEADERSHIP

Biblical Foundations of Stewardship

The concept of stewardship, deeply embedded in biblical teachings, is introduced in Genesis 2:15 (KJV). The mandate given to man, "And the LORD God took the man and put him into the garden of Eden to dress it and to keep it," employs the original Hebrew words "abad" (to serve or cultivate) and "shamar" (to keep or guard). These terms underscore the importance of care and maintenance, which are fundamental to stewardship (Hamilton, 1990). They are also intrinsically linked to the roles of management and leadership (Northouse, 2016).

Stewardship involves valuing the task or object of care, infusing actions with meaning, executing tasks intentionally, and embracing responsibility.

Dual Dimensions of Leadership

Leadership operates on both personal and corporate levels. The divine mandate to steward the earth's resources necessitates individual and collective commitment (Wright, 2010). It encompasses physical, mental, emotional, psychological, and spiritual work, reflecting a holistic approach to leadership (Fry, 2003).

Purpose and Partnership in Leadership

Matthew 19:3-5 (KJV) metaphorically illustrates the necessity of leaving familiar grounds to fully unite with one's purpose. This departure symbolizes the transformative journey toward purposeful living (Burns, 1978). Likewise, the quest for a suitable partner, illustrated by Eve's companionship with Adam, is vital for achieving one's purpose (Collins, 2001). Purposeful leadership is a dyadic, mutually beneficial relationship with transformational leadership (Bass & Riggio, 2006).

Integrity and Obedience

Integrity is a non-negotiable trait in purposeful leadership (Kouzes & Posner, 2012). Disobedience, as seen in the fall of Adam, poses a direct threat to integrity and purpose. The narrative of Adam's redemption underscores the possibility of restoring integrity and purpose through grace (Piper, 2012).

Servant Leadership as an Ideal

Genesis 2:5's use of "dress" and "keep" suggests that the primary role of leadership is to serve and care, which Greenleaf (1977) identifies as the essence of servant leadership. This form of leadership prioritizes the needs of others and fosters community growth (Greenleaf, 1977).

Relational Leadership

In Genesis 3:8, the emphasis on fellowship over mere cultivation suggests that leadership is fundamentally relational, built on unconditional love (Patterson, 2003). This relational aspect is akin to the nurturing responsibilities of a shepherd, a metaphor often used to describe the caring dimension of leadership (Kellerman, 2004).

Contemporary Stewardship

Today, stewardship extends beyond the biblical context, encompassing environmental, social, and corporate responsibility (Laszlo & Zhexembayeva, 2011). Modern leaders must strike a balance between progress and sustainability, reflecting the stewardship principles of care, service, and love (Elkington, 1997).

The concept of work, as it relates to purposeful leadership, underscores the enduring importance of care, service, and love. These principles, rooted in ancient texts, continue to inform and guide contemporary leadership practices.

Hypothetical Comparison of Stewardship Between Adam's Days and Today

The hypothetical infographic below compares stewardship between Adam's time and today, focusing on climate change, pollution, and deforestation.

The infographic uses hypothetical data, represented in percentages, to illustrate the contrast between the two periods.

Interpretation of the Infographic

On the left side of the image, representing stewardship in Adam's time, we see a lush, green, and pristine environment. It symbolizes a time when nature was largely untouched by human activity. The percentages indicate a high focus on climate change (90%), with minimal concerns about pollution and deforestation (5% each).

On the right side, representing stewardship today, we see a barren, polluted, and deforested landscape. It symbolizes the current state of our environment, shaped by human activities. The percentages indicate a more evenly distributed focus on climate change, pollution, and deforestation, with each accounting for approximately 35% of the total.

This stark contrast highlights the pressing need for improved stewardship of our planet today. The increased focus on pollution and deforestation in today's stewardship reflects the significant environmental challenges we face.

Comparing stewardship from Adam's time to today highlights the dramatic environmental changes and the growing importance of addressing climate change, pollution, and deforestation. It serves as a reminder of our responsibility to care for our planet and the urgent need to take action to mitigate these environmental issues.

References

Alter, R. (2004). *The five books of Moses: A translation with commentary*. W. W. Norton & Company.

Baron, D. (2010). *The aleph-bet book*. Feldheim Publishers.

Bass, B. M., & Riggio, R. E. (2006). *Transformational leadership* (2nd ed.). Psychology Press.

Bauckham, R. (2010). *Bible and ecology: Rediscovering the community of creation*. Darton, Longman & Todd.

Benner, J. A. (2002). *The ancient Hebrew lexicon of the Bible*. Virtualbookworm.com Publishing.

Berry, R. J. (2015). *Environmental stewardship: Critical perspectives - past and present*. T&T Clark.

Brueggemann, W. (1982). *Genesis*. John Knox Press.

Burns, J. M. (1978). *Leadership*. Harper & Row.

Collins, J. (2001). *Good to great: Why some companies make the leap... and others do not*. HarperBusiness.

Davis, J. J. (1984). *Biblical numerology: A basic study of the use of numbers in the Bible*. Baker Book House.

Elkington, J. (1997). *Cannibals with forks: The triple bottom line of 21st-century business*. Capstone.

Fry, L. W. (2003). Toward a theory of spiritual leadership. *The Leadership Quarterly, 14*(6), 693–727.

Gilsong, T. (2015). *A biblical view of dominion: Stewardship*. Thinking Christian. Retrieved from [source website].

Greenleaf, R. K. (1977). *Servant leadership: A journey into the nature of legitimate power and greatness*. Paulist Press.

Hamilton, V. P. (1990). *The book of Genesis: Chapters 1–17*. Eerdmans.

Kass, L. (2002). *The beginning of wisdom: Reading Genesis*. Free Press.

Kellerman, B. (2004). *Bad leadership: What it is, how it happens, why it matters*. Harvard Business Press.

Kouzes, J. M., & Posner, B. Z. (2012). *The leadership challenge: How to make extraordinary things happen in organizations* (5th ed.). Jossey-Bass.

Laszlo, C., & Zhexembayeva, N. (2011). *Embedded sustainability: The next significant competitive advantage*. Stanford Business Books.

Levenson, J. D. (1988). *Creation and the persistence of evil*. Princeton University Press.

Northouse, P. G. (2016). *Leadership: Theory and practice* (7th ed.). Sage Publications.

Patterson, K. (2003). *Servant leadership: A theoretical model*. Servant Leadership Research Roundtable.

Piper, J. (2012). *Future grace: The purifying power of the promises of God*. Multnomah Books.

Sacks, J. (2005). *To heal a fractured world: The ethics of responsibility*. Continuum.

Schaeffer, F. A. (1970). *Pollution and the death of man*. Tyndale House Publishers.

Von Rad, G. (1961). *Genesis: A commentary*. Westminster John Knox Press.

Wenham, G. J. (1987). *Genesis 1–15*. Word Biblical Commentary. Word Books.

White, L. Jr. (1967). The historical roots of our ecological crisis. *Science, 155*(3767), 1203–1207.

Wright, N. T. (2004). *The last word: Beyond the Bible wars to a new understanding of the authority of scripture.* Harper San Francisco.

Wright, N. T. (2010). *After you believe: Why Christian character matters.* HarperOne.

CHAPTER 3: THE EYESIGHT DIMENSION OF LEADERSHIP

This chapter examines the dual aspects of physical and spiritual eyesight. Our objectives are to:

- Define physical and spiritual eyesight.
- Investigate the connection between physical and spiritual eyesight and purposeful leadership.
- Emphasize the key attributes of eyesight that are essential for effective leadership.

Physical Eyesight: An Explanation

The process of writing this book serves as an example of conceptualizing and crafting a vision. In Chapter 1, a verse from Mark 1:38 piqued my curiosity, prompting me to consider the more profound meaning Jesus Christ conveyed. This curiosity sparked a series of questions, triggering a visualization process that gradually formed a mental image of a book. As this mental picture expanded, excitement surged, sketching out the book's title, chapters, topics, and themes. This initial sketch, further enriched by meticulous research, data gathering, analysis, categorization, and interpretation, crystallized into a clear vision for the book. As Annalisa Ponti (2020) suggests, vision is the driving force behind significant decisions and actions, providing clarity and direction.

Historical examples underscore the importance of keen observation and perception. Isaac Newton's observation of an apple falling from a tree prompted him to question the forces at work, leading to the discovery of the universal law of gravitation (OpenStax, 2024). Similarly, King Hieron of Syracuse's suspicion about the purity of a golden crown led him to request that Archimedes verify its authenticity without causing damage. While bathing, Archimedes observed a floating object, which led to the discovery of the principle of buoyancy (Britannica, 2019, 2024).

These examples emphasize the interplay of curiosity, imagination, perception, and vision in shaping purposeful leadership. They illustrate how curiosity initiates the exploration journey, leading to the visualization of possibilities. This imaginative process fuels the creation of a vision, refined through meticulous research and analysis, yielding a clear and purposeful direction. The transformative power of curiosity, imagination, and vision in guiding the creation of a comprehensive and impactful vision is evident in their correlation with intentional leadership.

The insights from these examples highlight the importance of integrating curiosity, imagination, perception, and vision in purposeful leadership. This holistic approach equips leaders with the tools to navigate complexities with depth and insight, fostering purposeful and impactful leadership.

Spiritual Eyesight: A Description

Spiritual eyesight is the ability to perceive beyond the physical world and to gain a deeper understanding of the spiritual realm. It often involves receiving divine revelations or visions about future events. This God-given capacity enables individuals to perceive God's vision for a people or a nation, often called a spiritual vision.

This form of perception enables individuals to transcend ordinary sensory experiences and gain a deeper understanding of divine will and spiritual realities. When acted on by faith, this spiritual reality becomes concrete. It is often associated with religious or spiritual experiences that provide individuals with a heightened awareness of the divine purpose and future events as envisioned by God.

In a spiritual context, vision represents the substance hoped for and the evidence of things yet to come (Hebrews 11:1). It reveals purpose, provides guidance and direction, and inspires individuals to turn a vision into reality, potentially urging others to join them in their pursuits.

References

Britannica, T. Editors of Encyclopaedia. (2019, June 26). What is Archimedes' principle? Encyclopedia Britannica.

https://www.britannica.com/science/Archimedes-principle

Britannica, T. Editors of Encyclopedia. (2024, July 2). Archimedes' principle. Encyclopedia Britannica.

https://www.britannica.com/science/Archimedes-principle

Jonassen, C. (2018). Seeing vs. perceiving—how we interact with the world. Retrieved from

https://claesjonasson.medium.com/seeing-vs-perceiving-how-we-interact-with-the-world

OpenStax. (2024). Newton's Universal Law of Gravitation. Retrieved from

http://cnx.org/contents/031da8d3-b525-429c-80cf-6c8ed997733a/College_Physics

Ponti, A. (2020). The difference between visualizing and having a vision. Retrieved from

https://www.annalisaponti.com/food-for-thought/the-difference-between-visualizing-and-having-a-vision/#

CHAPTER 4: THE HEART DIMENSION OF LEADERSHIP

This chapter delves deeper into the heart's leadership dimension, exploring the interplay between biological and spiritual aspects.

The Heart: A Biological Perspective and Its Role in Leadership

From a biological standpoint, the heart is an organ that pumps blood throughout the body, supplying oxygen and nutrients to tissues and removing carbon dioxide (Cleveland Clinic, 2020). However, this perspective is limited, focusing solely on the heart's physiological role and overlooking its broader significance.

The Heart's Intelligence

Neurocardiovascular research has shown that the heart functions as a sophisticated information-processing center, akin to the brain. This "heart brain" communicates with the cranial brain through various channels, including the nervous and hormonal systems, with heart rate variability serving as a dynamic reflection of an individual's emotional and cognitive state (HeartMath, 2015).

The heart and brain communicate bi-directionally. The brain sends signals to the heart via descending pathways, regulating heart activities. Conversely, the heart sends signals to the brain via ascending pathways. Interestingly, the heart sends more information to the brain than the brain sends to the heart, suggesting that the heart can significantly influence our cognitive functions. The heart's neural network, consisting of ganglia, neurotransmitters, proteins, and support cells, enables it to independently perform functions such as learning, memory, decision-making, and sensing (HeartMath, 2015).

The Heart's Hormonal Influence

The heart also communicates with the brain through hormones, significantly impacting our emotions, behavior, and resilience. Emotions play a crucial role in physiological processes related to energy regulation. For instance, atrial peptide hormones can trigger emotions that influence our motivation and behavior. Oxytocin, known as the "love" or "social bonding" hormone, affects our ability to form and maintain healthy relationships. Estrogen can induce emotions associated with happiness, motivation, fear, stress, and depression, significantly impacting our engagement, focus, and performance (HeartMath, 2015; Marion Gluck Clinic, 2022).

Resilience, a critical trait for effective leadership, depends on the energy level generated by emotions. Therefore, emotional regulation is essential for preparing for, recovering from, and adapting to stress, adversity, trauma, or challenges.

The Heart's Role in Purposeful Leadership

Understanding the heart-brain connection can profoundly impact purposeful leadership. Leaders aware of the influence of emotions on cognitive function and well-being can foster environments that promote emotional stability, resilience, and overall wellness. By acknowledging the importance of emotional regulation and cultivating a favorable emotional climate, leaders can optimize performance, engagement, and well-being within their teams.

The Heart: A Spiritual View on Leadership

The Bible's View of the Heart

The Bible refers to the heart over a thousand times, not as a physical organ, but as a person's cognitive and emotional state (Evans, A., July 1, 2024). For example, Psalm 19:14 states, "May the words of my mouth and the meditation of my heart be acceptable in thy sight, O LORD, my strength, and my redeemer" (KJV, 2013, p. 842). It raises the question: Can a heart reflect, contemplate, or deliberate? Isn't this the mind's function? Does this suggest that the heart possesses a mind? Jeremiah 17:9-10 declares, "The heart is deceitful above all things and desperately wicked; who can know it? I, the LORD, search the heart, test the mind, and even give every man according to his ways and the fruit of his doings" (NKJV, 1982). This verse and Luke 6:45 suggest that the heart is a seat of thoughts and emotions.

In the biblical context, the heart is not merely a physical organ but is portrayed as the seat of a person's cognitive and emotional state. It reflects, contemplates, and deliberates, akin to the functions associated with the mind. This portrayal suggests that the heart encompasses mental and emotional aspects, suggesting a deeper significance beyond its physiological function. The scripture underscores the heart's role in shaping a person's character and actions, highlighting its profound influence on human behavior, spiritual life, and, more importantly, leadership.

The concept of heart intelligence, rooted in diverse cultures for centuries, regards the heart as the source of love, wisdom, intuition, and courage, often referred to as the intuitive or spiritual heart. This understanding predates the 17th-century Cartesian view of the heart as a mechanical organ, with ancient civilizations like the Egyptians believing the heart to be the center of wisdom, intellect, and emotions (Doyle et al., 2023; HeartMath, 2015; Talley, R. 2024).

Recent scientific research has supported the concept of the heart's intuitive intelligence, acknowledging its powerful energetic connections and role in fostering physiological coherence and intuition (HeartMath, 2015). Heart intelligence, as described by HeartMath, refers to the flow of higher awareness and intuition experienced when the mind and emotions align with the energetic heart (2015). It enables individuals to self-regulate their thoughts and feelings effectively, resulting in a stronger connection to their inner, more resonant voice. This empowerment enables a person to become more perceptive, conscious, alert, attentive, focused, relational, and attuned in decision-making (HeartMath, 2015).

The Impact on Purposeful Leadership

Heart intelligence and its impact on purposeful leadership lie in its ability to enhance decision-making, emotional regulation, and relational attunement. By tapping into intuitive intelligence through heart coherence, leaders can make more creative, wise, and conscious decisions, fostering a deeper connection with their inner wisdom and balanced discernment.

Furthermore, the heart's intuitive guidance can help leaders align their thoughts and emotions, fostering more authentic and empathetic leadership. This alignment with the heart's wisdom can contribute to a leadership style that is more attuned to others' needs, fostering a more inclusive and compassionate approach to decision-making and interactions (Doyle et al., 2023).

In conclusion, integrating heart intelligence into leadership practices can potentially lead to more authentic, empathetic, and inclusive leadership driven by a deeper source of wisdom and balanced discernment.

References

Cleveland Clinic. (2020). Blood flows through the heart. Retrieved from

https://my.clevelandclinic.org/health/articles/17060-how-does-the-blood-flow-through-your-heart

Doyle, E. A. (2023). The heart as our source of true wisdom and intuition. Retrieved from

https://www.anuttara.org/post/the-heart-as-our-source-of-true-wisdom-and-intuition

Evans, A. (2024). What does the Bible say about the heart? Retrieved from

https://biblereasons.com/the-heart

Lane, R. D., & Smith, R. (2021). Levels of emotional awareness: Theory and measurement of a socio-emotional skill. *Journal of Intelligence, 9*(3), 42.

https://doi.org/10.3390/jintelligence9030042

Marion Gluck Clinic. (2022). Hormones and mental health – What's the connection? Retrieved from

https://www.mariongluckclinic.com/blog/hormones-and-mental-health-whats-the-connection.html

Nelson, T. (1982). New King James Version. Retrieved from

https://www.biblegateway.com/passage/?search=Jeremiah%20173A9&version=NKJV

Talley, R. (2024). Discovering the intuitive intelligence of the heart. Retrieved from

https://bahaiteachings.org/discovering-the-intuitive-intelligence-of-the-heart/

CHAPTER 5: THE SHEPHERD ASPECT OF PURPOSEFUL LEADERSHIP

The Shepherd Metaphor: An Explanation

The shepherd metaphor is a powerful representation of purposeful leadership. The term "shepherd" is derived from the Old English "sceaphierde," combining "sceap" (sheep) and "hierde" (herder or guardian). Thus, a shepherd guards and tends sheep, symbolizing guidance and protection (Harper, D. 2024).

In biblical literature, Jesus employs the shepherd metaphor to illustrate the relationship between a leader (the shepherd) and his followers (the sheep). The sheep rely on the shepherd for sustenance, safety, direction, and healing. The shepherd's rod and staff are tools of correction, support, and guidance, not harm (Thebiblesays.com). A shepherd's primary concern is the welfare of the flock, demonstrating a commitment to their interests.

John 10:1-18 provides a comprehensive depiction of a shepherd. The shepherd enters the sheepfold through the gate, and the sheep recognize his voice, indicating a close relationship. The shepherd leads the sheep, who follow him because they trust his voice. A good shepherd is willing to sacrifice his life for the sheep, showing a commitment to their total protection (NLT).

Contrarily, a hireling, paid to tend the sheep, lacks a genuine connection with the flock and is motivated by self-interest. When danger approaches, the hireling abandons the sheep, akin to a thief who intends to steal, kill, and destroy.

The Shepherd Metaphor: Its Significance in Leadership

Psalm 23:1-3 further emphasizes the shepherd-leader metaphor, portraying the Lord as a shepherd who meets our needs, keeps us safe, and guides us. The shepherd is caring and visionary, providing for the sheep, healing the weary, and leading them to a place of rest and hope.

Biblical texts highlight the sheep's tendency to wander and the shepherd's duty to retrieve the lost, feed them, heal the injured, strengthen the weak, and treat them fairly (Isaiah 53:6; Psalm 119:176; Jeremiah 50:6; Ezekiel 34:11-16). In Matthew 9:36, Jesus' compassion for the confused and helpless crowd is likened to a shepherd's care for his sheep (NLT).

The shepherd metaphor extends to human leadership in Psalm 78:72, where David is portrayed as a shepherd who led with integrity and guided with skill, emphasizing the importance of these qualities in purposeful leadership.

In summary, the shepherd metaphor in purposeful leadership underscores care, guidance, protection, and sacrifice. It highlights the leader's ethical and compassionate role, emphasizing their responsibility to nurture, protect, and guide their followers. This metaphor highlights the importance of a profound understanding of those being led, a dedication to their well-being, and a willingness to make personal sacrifices for their benefit.

References

Harper, D. (2024). Shepherd. *Online Etymology Dictionary*. Retrieved from https://www.etymonline.com/word/shepherd

Nelson, T. (1982). *New Living Translation (NLT)*. Retrieved from https://www.biblegateway.com/

Thebiblesays.com. (n.d.). The shepherd's rod and staff. Retrieved from https://www.thebiblesays.com/

PART 2: DECODING PURPOSEFUL LEADERSHIP: INSIGHTS FROM MODERN THINKERS AND PRACTITIONERS – A LITERATURE REVIEW

This section examines the perspectives of contemporary thinkers and practitioners on purposeful leadership. It builds on the spiritual perspectives discussed in Part 1, focusing on biblical insights into purpose and leadership. We transition from traditional to modern views of leadership, weaving the past into the emerging future and integrating the timeless wisdom of the Bible with practical insights from contemporary literature. It is organized as follows:

- Views of faith-based thinkers and practitioners.
- Insights from experts and corporate leaders on purpose and purposeful leadership.

The comprehensive perspectives from Parts 2 and 3 of the literature review offer valuable insights into the concept of purposeful leadership in Chapter 8, particularly in its definition.

CHAPTER 6: FAITH-BASED THINKERS AND PRACTITIONERS – A LITERATURE REVIEW

Understanding Purpose, Mission, and Vision in Leadership

Dr. Myles Munroe defines purpose as the original intention behind an entity's creation, the fundamental reason for its existence, and the specific role or task it serves. His teachings emphasize:

The Impact of Unrecognized Purposes

Dr. Munroe underscores that a lack of understanding of an entity's purpose can lead to misuse or abnormal use, potentially causing harm.

Unveiling Purpose

Dr. Munroe proposes that the creator of an entity is the most reliable source for understanding its purpose. The creator often symbolizes the purpose through a logo or image and provides a 'manual' for optimal use.

The Link Between Purpose, Mission, and Vision

Purpose gives rise to mission and vision. Mission encompasses an organization or individual's goals and strategies, while vision is a future-oriented aspiration aligned with the organization's or individual's purpose.

The Role of Mission and Vision

Dr. Munroe characterizes a mission as a comprehensive task that fulfills a purpose, outlining what exists and why.

Vision, conversely, is the tangible manifestation of purpose and mission, detailing the desired outcome and necessary components to achieve it.

Dr. Munroe's insights provide a framework for understanding purposeful leadership. Purpose is the core of existence, mission is the action plan derived from the purpose, and vision is the explicit depiction of the intended result.

The Intersection of Faith and Science in Defining Purpose

Wang, an advocate for purpose-centered living, contends that faith, particularly in Jesus Christ, is essential for a life of purpose, despite the significant role of science. He exemplifies this by using his scientific expertise to develop treatments for blind orphaned children, considering this his mission. His vision is a world where all such children regain their sight.

In conclusion, leadership is rooted in purpose and guided by a clear mission and vision is essential for achieving optimal outcomes and enhancing productivity.

References

Ming Wang, MD, PhD. (n.d.). *The eye convinces me there is a God.* YouTube.

https://youtu.be/IFI0a1k3mU?Si=9d52-2SRZaZa7BJ

Purpose, mission, and vision: Understand the difference. (n.d.).

http://www.youtube.com/watch?v=yourvideoid

The power of purpose. (n.d.). Wisdom for Dominion. https://bit.ly/tpofpurpose

CHAPTER 7: MODERN CORPORATE EXPERTS' AND PRACTITIONERS' VIEWS ON PURPOSE AND PURPOSEFUL LEADERSHIP

This section examines the perspectives of experts and corporate leaders on purpose and purposeful leadership—concepts that have garnered considerable attention following the COVID-19 pandemic and amid the escalating effects of climate change. The review addresses the following issues:

- Understanding the Meaning of Purpose in a Corporate Context
- Integrating purpose within an organization
- What it means to lead purposefully – embracing empathy and authenticity.

Examining these questions provides a comprehensive understanding of the perspectives, challenges, and strategies associated with purpose and purposeful leadership.

UNDERSTANDING THE MEANING AND IMPORTANCE OF PURPOSE IN A CORPORATE CONTEXT

Personal vs. Organizational Purpose

The discourse on purpose often revolves around its personal and organizational dimensions. Dhingra et al. (2020) define personal purpose as a deep, enduring sense of significance derived from life's endeavors, while Joly (2020) highlights its transformative nature and emphasizes its role in enhancing others' lives. In contrast, corporate leaders view purpose as the core reason for an organization's existence, a guiding principle that shapes strategic decisions (Aaron, 2024) and contributes to societal betterment (Nuttal, 2022).

Purpose goes beyond profit-making to encompass societal welfare, as evidenced by customer satisfaction, employee well-being, reduced turnover, and improved community relations (Joly, 2020). The synergy between personal and organizational purposes is essential, fostering collective success and individual fulfillment.

The North Star Metaphor: Illuminating Purpose

The North Star metaphor serves as a powerful tool for explaining purpose. It acts as a steadfast and inspiring guide, directing individuals toward their destined path (Dhingra & Schaninger, 2021). In both leadership and personal development, the North Star represents a firm vision or goal that guides decision-making and fuels motivation during challenging times (Vance, 2024).

Purposeful leadership embodies this metaphor by transforming a leader's personal 'why' into an organizational 'what.' It promotes a broad vision that mobilizes teams toward meaningful change (Oesch, 2017; Gast et al., 2020). George (2023) and Joly (2020) highlight the significance of leaders aligning their purpose with their organization's mission. George's "true north" concept encapsulates one's core values and beliefs that emerge from life's narrative and challenges, culminating in a leadership purpose.

The North Star metaphor reflects the enduring nature of personal purpose, guiding individuals toward their aspirational goals. Integrating personal purpose in the workplace is essential for employee satisfaction and organizational success.

The North Star, a radiant beacon in the deep indigo sky, is a natural compass for travelers—this serene sight, where nature's beauty meets celestial wonder.

The Role and Importance of Purpose in Organizations

The Role of Purpose in Organizations

Purpose plays a crucial role in shaping a company's collective identity, influencing its management, and guiding its decision-making, planning, and strategy (Dhingra et al., 2020). Similarly, Leke (2021) emphasizes the significance of purpose in establishing a network united by common goals.

As individuals seek purpose in their lives and work, they are increasingly attracted to organizations that incorporate purpose into their roles (Dhingra et al., 2021). This leadership style is gaining recognition as a viable solution to the productivity crisis within organizations.

Creating Value and Progress Through Purpose

When a company's purpose aligns with its capabilities, it can drive value creation and progress in environmental, social, and governance (ESG) themes (Gast et al., 2021). The goal is to stimulate topline growth, cultivate loyal customers, build trust, retain the customer base, and lower costs by adopting environmentally friendly technologies.

Additionally, it can help attract and retain top talent, thereby enhancing the company's financial performance.

INTEGRATING PURPOSE WITHIN ORGANIZATIONS

Aligning Individual Purpose Within Organizations

Aligning individual purpose with organizational goals is crucial for achieving productivity, maintaining health, fostering resilience, and cultivating loyalty. A study by Naina Dhingra et al. (2021) found that 70% of employees believe their work defines their purpose. However, there is a disparity across employee levels: 85% of executives and upper management report alignment with the purpose at work, compared with only 15% of frontline staff. Addressing this gap is vital to fostering a harmonious, purpose-driven work environment.

The bar chart below illustrates the percentage of employees who feel their work defines their purpose, broken down by employee level.

1.1 Bar Chart: Purpose Alignment at Work by Employee Level

Employee Level	Percentage of Employees Feeling Purpose Alignment
All Employees	70%
Executives & Upper Management	85%
Frontline Staff	15%

This focus on employee purpose alignment is mirrored in the broader corporate world, where there is a growing emphasis on Environmental, Social, and Governance (ESG) factors.

Purpose-Driven Leadership in Organizations

Leaders like Kathy Warden, CEO of Northrop Grumman, increasingly recognize the importance of purpose in their organizations. Warden has effectively integrated purpose into her company's operations by clearly defining the corporate purpose and its guiding values, aligning these values with leadership behaviors, equipping leaders with the essential tools and training to instill these values in their teams, and empowering employees to operate within this value system (Padhi, 2022).

Experts such as Dhingra, Samo, Schaninger, and Schrimper (2021) suggest that purpose can be instilled in an organization by fostering a shared identity. This process involves leaders actively listening to employees and stakeholders to understand their concerns, recognizing their organizations' unique capabilities, and empowering line managers to commit to the purpose with conviction. Furthermore, leaders can enhance purpose integration by engaging employees in discussions about their purposes and how they align with the company's mission, and by sharing personal experiences of living their purpose at work.

Leadership is vital for integrating purpose. It begins with recognizing and applying the purposes and ethical values that are crucial for internal alignment, market effectiveness, and stakeholder responsibility. The organization's vision, mission, and values steer strategic and operational decisions, ensuring alignment (OpenStax, 2019a).

Executive leaders, such as Warden, play a vital role in acquiring and expanding the talent pool. They also significantly tackle industry-specific challenges, including the STEM crisis and mentoring new CEOs (Gartner, 2019).

In terms of organizational change, influential leaders set clear objectives, outline specific activities to achieve them, and define indicators of success. Both planned change processes, which involve large groups and occur over time, as well as incremental changes and minor refinements in existing practices can facilitate the integration of purpose within an organization (OpenStax, 2019b).

Aligning Environmental, Social, and Governance (ESG) Within Organizations

The corporate world is shifting from profit-centric to ESG-based investments, driven by stakeholder demands. Environmental efforts focus on mitigating climate change by energy-efficient technologies and sustainable production methods. Social considerations involve the impact of corporate actions on individuals, with diversity, equity, and inclusion as key factors. Governance is closely tied to ethical decision-making and its broader societal implications.

ESG-based investment is gaining momentum, with $74 billion in global ESG Exchange-Traded Fund assets focused on climate action. Vena (2024) reports that 42% of global investors prioritize client expectations and reputations in ESG decisions, and 87% of global assets under management are allocated to sustainable funds. Furthermore, 75% of business leaders worldwide consider ESG criteria essential to their business strategies, and 99% of investors consider ESG disclosures in their investment decision-making process. Anderson (2022) notes that 97% of executives prioritize ESG within their organizations.

The diagram below highlights the key statistics and insights.

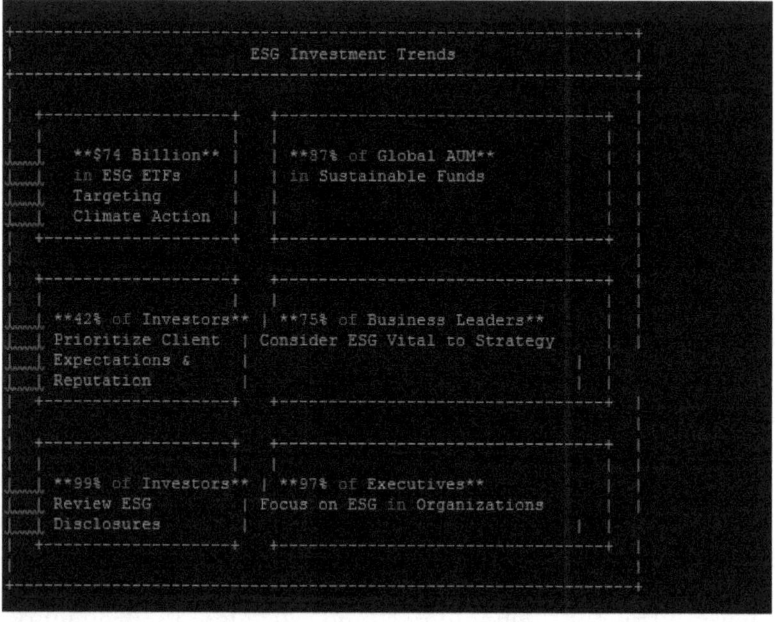

Key Points:

- $74 Billion in ESG ETFs: This represents the global assets in ESG Exchange-Traded Funds specifically targeting climate action.
- 87% of Global Assets Under Management (AUM) in Sustainable Funds: A significant portion of global

assets under management is in sustainable funds, indicating a strong trend towards ESG investing.

- 42% of Investors Prioritize Client Expectations and Reputation, highlighting the importance of client expectations and reputation in ESG decision-making.
- 75% of Business Leaders Consider ESG Vital: Most business leaders globally consider ESG criteria crucial to their business strategy.
- 99% of Investors Review ESG Disclosures: Nearly all investors consider ESG disclosures part of their investment planning, showing the critical role of transparency and reporting.
- 97% of Executives Focus on ESG: Most executives concentrate on ESG within their organizations, underscoring its importance in corporate governance.

The diagram clearly and concisely captures current trends and priorities in ESG-based investing, reflecting the growing emphasis on sustainability and responsible investment practices (CFA Institute, 2024).

Consumer behavior reflects this shift, with 44% of consumers selecting brands based on the company's values and 50% willing to pay a premium for sustainable brands (Hastwell, 2023). These trends underscore the importance of integrating purpose into corporate frameworks and aligning them with ESG principles for sustained long-term success.

WHAT IT MEANS TO LEAD PURPOSEFULLY: EMBRACING EMPATHY AND AUTHENTICITY

Understanding and Responding to Emotions

Purposeful leadership requires a profound understanding of emotions and feelings, much like tuning into a radio. These innate responses to our environment significantly impact our decision-making, interpersonal relationships, and reactions to various situations. Accurately interpreting these emotions can foster a clear and confident grasp of our challenges (Nielsen et al., 2020).

Nielsen, D'Auria, and Zolley (2020) emphasize the importance of leaders' ability to connect with and effectively respond to their emotions. This necessitates awareness of one's own feelings and emotional needs, as well as those of others. By attuning ourselves to our emotions, we enhance our ability to listen, alleviate fears and anxieties, and empower others to move forward. Leaders can cultivate a sense of community by showing vulnerability, authenticity, and inclusivity, which in turn inspires hope and confidence.

Prioritizing People

Joly (2020) states that prioritizing people is fundamental to purposeful leadership. Prioritizing people involves actively listening to employees, understanding their challenges, and incorporating their ideas into decision-making processes.

Demonstrating Care

Gregg, Aimee, and Perrey (2020) note that purposeful leadership involves caring for people, customers, and communities. In times of crisis, this means helping to alleviate suffering, investing in people, and supporting them through challenging times. Purpose-driven customer journeys can foster trust, loyalty, and a unique experience (Gregg et al., 2020).

Embracing Learning

Chawla, CEO of FairPrice, views learning as a crucial aspect of purposeful leadership. Learning involves working closely with employees, listening to their perspectives, and understanding their challenges. Chawla emphasizes the importance of serving, leading empathetically, and bringing authenticity to work daily (Razdan, 2023).

References

Aaron. (2024). *Lead with Purpose: Strategies for Purposeful Leadership.* Leader Navigation. Retrieved from

https://www.leadernavigation.com/lead-with-purpose-2/#

Anderson, K. (2022). Embed sustainability with an ESG scoreboard. Retrieved from Mercer.

Brown, S., & Nuttal, R. (2022). The role of ESG and purpose. Retrieved from

https://www.mckinsey.com/capabilities/strategy-and-corporate-finance/our-insights/the-role-of-esg-and-purpose

CFA Institute. (2024). What is ESG investing? Retrieved from

https://www.cfainstitute.org/insights/articles/what-is-esg-investing

Dhingra, N. et al. (2020). Activate purpose to create shared identity. McKinsey & Company. Retrieved from

https://www.mckinsey.com/capabilities/people-and-organizational-performance/our-insights/the-organization-blog/activate-purpose-to-create-shared-identity

Dhingra, N. et al. (2020). Help your employees find purpose – or watch them leave. Retrieved from

https://mckinsey.com/capabilities/people-and-organizational-performance/our-insights/help-your-employees-find-purpose-or-watch-them-leave

Dhingra, N., Samo, A., Schaninger, B., & Schrimper, M. (2021). Purpose: Shifting from why to how. *McKinsey Quarterly.* Retrieved from

https://www.mckinsey.com/business-functions/people-and-organizational-performance/our-insights/purpose-shifting-from-why-to-how

Dhingra, N. et al. (2021). The power of purpose: How organizations are finding their way. McKinsey & Company. Retrieved from [insert URL].

Dhingra, N., & Schaninger, B. (2021). The search for purpose at work. Retrieved from

https://www.mckinsey.com/capabilities/people-and-organizational-performance/our-insights/the-search-for-purpose-at-work

Gartner. (2019). CEO talent champion Q&A | Kathy Warden-Northrop Grumman – An interview. Retrieved from

https://www.gartner.com/en/human-resources/insights/ceo-talent-champions-kathy-warden

Gast, A. et al. (2020). Purpose: Shifting from why to how. Retrieved from

https://www.mckinsey.com/capabilities/people-and-organizational-performance/our-insights/purpose-shifting-from-why-to-how

Gast, A. et al. (2021). Purpose and progress: Driving value creation through ESG. McKinsey & Company. Retrieved from [insert URL].

Geroge, B. (2023). Leading with authenticity: A conversation with Bill George. Retrieved from

https://www.mckinsey.com/capabilities/strategy-and-corporate-finance/our-insights/leading-with-authenticity-a-conversation-with-bill-george

Gregg, B., Aimee, M., & Perrey, J. (2020). Leading with purpose: How marketing and sales leaders can shape the next normal. McKinsey & Company. Retrieved from [insert URL].

Hastwell, C. (2023). Workplace ESG: How Environmental, Social, and Governance Factors Impact Employee Experience. Retrieved from Great Place to Work.

Joly, H. (2020a). The heart of business: Leadership principles for the next era of capitalism. Harvard Business Review Press.

Joly, H. (2020b). Leading with purpose and humanity: A conversation with Hubert Joly. Retrieved from

https://www.mckinsey.com/capabilities/strategy-and-corporate-finance/our-insights/leading-with-purpose-and-humanity-a-conversation-with-hubert-joly

Leke, A. (2021). The importance of purpose: An interview with Acha Leke. Retrieved from

https://www.mckinsey.com/capabilities/people-and-organizational-performance/our-insights/the-importance-of-purpose-an-interview-with-acha-leke

Nielsen, N. C., D'Auria, G., & Zolley, S. (2020). Tuning in, turning outward: Cultivating compassionate leadership in a crisis. McKinsey & Company. Retrieved from [insert URL].

Oesch, T. (2017). Developing Purposeful Leaders: The Organization's Northern Star. Retrieved from https://trainingindustry.com/articles/leadership/developing-purposeful-leaders-the-organizational-northern-star/

OpenStax. (2019a). Leadership: Ethics at the organizational level. In *Principles of management.* Retrieved from

https://openstax.org/books/principles-management/pages/5-4-leadership-ethics-at-the-organizational-level

OpenStax. (2019b). Organizational change. In *Principles of management.* Retrieved from

https://openstax.org/books/principles-management/pages/10-2-organizational-change

Padhi, A. (2022). Leadership rundown: Finding power in purpose with Kathy Warden. McKinsey & Company. Retrieved from

https://www.mckinsey.com/capabilities/strategy-and-corporate-finance/our-insights/the-strategy-and-corporate-finance-blog/leadership-rundown-finding-power-in-purpose-with-kathy-warden

Razdan, R. (2023). 'Before skills set comes mindset': FairPrice CEO on breakthrough leadership. McKinsey & Company.

Vance, T. (2024). Finding Your North Star and Moral Compass. Retrieved from

https://www.coaching-focus.com/blog/finding-your-north-star-and-moral-compass

Vena. (2024). ESG Statistics. Retrieved from Vena Solutions.

CHAPTER 8: DEFINING PURPOSEFUL LEADERSHIP

In this chapter, we consolidate insights from previous chapters to offer a comprehensive definition of purposeful leadership. We highlight the transformative nature of purposeful leadership and focus on collective well-being, outlining its key characteristics and components, and its impact on individuals and organizations.

Critical Characteristics of Purposeful Leadership

1. **Stewardship:** Purposeful leaders prioritize the common good by placing collective interests over individual self-interest.

2. **Values-Driven Leadership:** Effective, purposeful leadership is rooted in values, authenticity, and adaptability.

3. **Promotion of Diversity, Equity, Inclusivity, and Ethical Decision-Making:** Purposeful leaders are dedicated to promoting these principles within their organizations.

4. **Alignment with the North Star:** Purposeful leadership entails aligning the organization's vision, mission, and operations with its ultimate goal, often referred to as the North Star.

5. **Inner Wisdom and Strength:** Purposeful leaders tap into their inner selves to showcase care, compassion, creativity, insightfulness, and innovation resilience.

6. **Transformational Impact:** Intentional leadership has a profound impact on both the leader and the broader community.

7. **Leading from the Heart and Spirit:** Purposeful leadership involves leading with heart and soul, drawing from spiritual insights and wisdom.

Components of Purposeful Leadership

Purposeful leadership comprises four primary components:

1. **Cognitive:** This relates to the leader's capability to think critically and strategically, crafting an inspiring framework that encapsulates the organization's vision and purpose.

2. **Emotive:** This refers to the energy and passion required to propel the organization toward its envisioned destiny, emphasizing the importance of intuition and emotional intelligence in leadership.

3. **Aligning Actions with Core Beliefs:** Purposeful leadership means aligning actions with core beliefs, inspiring others, and building a strong organizational culture.

4. **Effective Communication**

Empathetic listening, following instructions, and communicating messages clearly and respectfully are vital to effective leadership.

Biblical Narratives

Throughout the Bible, numerous examples of purposeful leadership can be found. Moses led the Israelites out of slavery in Egypt, guided by his unwavering faith in God's plan. Jesus Christ exemplified purposeful leadership through his teachings, emphasizing love, compassion, and service to others. The Apostle Paul, in his letters, encouraged early Christian communities to live purposefully, aligning their actions with their faith and beliefs.

These biblical narratives illustrate the enduring nature of purposeful leadership and its capacity to inspire and transform lives across generations. By drawing from these timeless examples, modern leaders can develop a deeper understanding of purposeful leadership and its potential to foster lasting positive change in their organizations and communities.

Purposeful Leadership Defined

I emphasize that purposeful leadership is a transformative process that directs individuals and organizations toward meaningful goals by embodying stewardship, authenticity, and value-driven decision-making. It involves aligning vision and actions with a higher purpose, fostering an inclusive and ethical environment, and drawing from inner wisdom to inspire care, creativity, and resilience. This leadership style not only transforms the leader but also empowers others to seek collective betterment, creating a positive impact on both individuals and the broader community.

PART 3: UNVEILING PURPOSEFUL LEADERSHIP: CASE STUDIES OF ABRAHAM, MOSES, DAVID, DANIEL, ESTHER, AND PAUL

In Part 3 of this book, we explore purposeful leadership by examining the lives and experiences of six historical figures from biblical narratives: Abraham, Moses, David, Daniel, Esther, and Paul. These individuals are renowned for their exemplary leadership and resilience in the face of adversity. By providing contextual details about their lives and times, we aim to draw meaningful parallels between these ancient stories and contemporary perspectives on corporate leadership.

The Bible is an enduring source of wisdom and leadership lessons, offering profound insights into the nature of purposeful leadership. These narratives transcend cultural, religious, and temporal boundaries, providing universal lessons that remain relevant today. It is crucial to recognize that these biblical figures were human, with their strengths and weaknesses. Their stories offer valuable guidance on navigating life and leadership challenges while maintaining authenticity and integrity.

As discussed in Chapter 2, modern literature complements these biblical insights by addressing contemporary leadership challenges and trends (Smith, 2020). This integration of ancient wisdom and current viewpoints provides a comprehensive exploration of purposeful leadership, enabling readers to understand this essential concept holistically.

In this section, we aim to inspire current and future leaders to embrace purposeful leadership by drawing on the experiences of these extraordinary individuals. By applying these insights within their spheres of influence, readers can positively impact their organizations and communities.

We invite you to join us on this enlightening journey as we uncover the essence of purposeful leadership through these compelling case studies.

Reference

Smith, J. (2020). Contemporary Leadership Challenges and Trends. Journal of Leadership Studies, 15(2), 45–60.

CHAPTER 9: THE CASE STUDY OF ABRAHAM

Embrace Adventure by Letting Go of Familiarity

In Genesis 11:31, we read, "And Terah took his son Abram and his grandson Lot, the son of Haran, and his daughter-in-law Sarai, his son Abram's wife, and they went out with them from Ur of the Chaldeans to go to the land of Canaan, and they came to Haran and dwelt there" (New King James Version). Terah and Abram envisioned reaching Canaan, but they became comfortable in Haran and lost sight of their original destination. After Terah died in Haran, God spoke to Abram, saying, "Get out of your country, from your family and your father's house to a land that I will show you. I will make you a great nation" (Genesis 12:1-2, New King James Version).

Abram's country, family, and father's house symbolized deep-rooted traditions and a past that stood between him and his promised destiny and purpose in life. God spoke to Abram only after his father died. Although Abram obeyed, he still clung to some of his traditions by bringing his cousin Lot.

Upon arriving in Canaan, God spoke to Abram, saying, "To your descendants, I will give this land" (Genesis 12:7, New King James Version). However, Abram was still with Lot, and God had not yet revealed the land to him. Only after Lot separated from him did God reveal the land to Abram. In Genesis 13:14-15, the LORD said to Abram, "Lift your eyes now and look from the place where you are—northward, southward, eastward, and westward; for all the land which you see I give to you and your descendants forever" (New King James Version). Only after Abram broke free from his traditions and past did he truly see his purpose.

In this context, "seeing" extends beyond physical sight; it represents a profound understanding of one's purpose and destiny, unencumbered by past influences. It is about shedding the scales that prevent us from seeing clearly and embracing a new perspective, worldview, and life philosophy. This transformation often requires letting go of familiar behaviors and attachments that obscure our vision. Our mindset, worldview, and life philosophy are shaped by what we see. If your vision is clouded, how dark is your understanding of your purpose and potential?

Haran: The Crossroads of Faith and Transformation

Abram faced a significant challenge at Haran: he had to let go of things close to his heart, but he struggled to do so. God had told him to leave behind his familiar way of life and embrace a new path he did not yet understand. This inner conflict left him grappling with deep life issues. He was "pregnant with nations in his loins," symbolizing the vast potential and purpose within him. His decision at this crossroads could lead to the death of his dreams or the birth of a great legacy.

The pain of letting go may feel unbearable, but despite this pain, it is necessary to endure it to bring forth your purpose. This journey calls for perseverance. As Paul writes in Romans 5:3-5, "And not only that, but we also glory in tribulations, knowing that tribulation produces perseverance; and perseverance, character; and character, hope. "Hope does not disappoint, because the love of God has been poured out in our hearts by the Holy Spirit, who was given to us" (New King James Version).

We need character, that is, the right mindset, to fulfill our purpose, which often emerges from the sufferings we encounter in our life journey.

Obstacles on the Journey to Fulfilling Purpose

Abram left Haran and traveled to Canaan, accompanied by Lot. After their separation, God showed Abram the land. For Abram to become the father of a nation, he needed a territory to call his own, fulfilling the first condition. The second condition was that people needed to occupy the land. However, Abram's wife, Sarai, was barren, and both Abram and Sarai were biologically past the age of having children.

A purpose may seem out of reach or impossible to fulfill because, humanly, you may lack the ability. God promised Abram that he would have a son, but Abram struggled to comprehend this promise and had difficulty believing in God. To help Abram understand His promise, God took him outside one evening and asked him to look at the sky and count the stars. Abram looked at the stars and realized he could not count them as they were far too numerous (Genesis 15:5, New King James Version).

Harnessing the Power of Imagination: The Role of Visualization in Purpose and Belief

Understanding your purpose in life can be difficult until it becomes clear in your mind and heart. Cognitive understanding and emotional connection need to align for someone to grasp a meaningful purpose. Hebrews 11:1 emphasizes that "faith is the substance of things hoped for, the evidence of things not seen" (New King James Version), underscoring the power of imagination to visualize one's purpose.

How can you pursue something you cannot see, understand, or believe in? Your belief is born from what is not seen by your physical eyes, but you perceive through your mental vision. Jesus spoke about the importance of sight, and Moses asked Hobab to be their eyes, highlighting the need for guidance in seeing beyond the immediate (Numbers 10:31, New King James Version).

Abram, who became Abraham, represents a transformational journey. This transformation signifies a profound change in identity and purpose. Until an individual undergoes this transformation, fulfilling their purpose can be difficult.

Purposeful leadership is inherently transformative, involving a comprehensive 360-degree transformation. A 360-degree transformation entails a mindset shift that alters how you perceive the world, leading to a profound change in your worldview and behavior.

The Power of Believing: Abraham's Journey of Faith

Abraham's journey to fulfill his purpose of becoming the father of nations lasted twenty-five years, demonstrating the long-term nature of purpose. Purposeful leadership requires a leader to maintain a long-term vision and patience to endure such a lengthy journey (Taber, D., 2024). As Habakkuk 2 illustrates, purposeful leadership involves three key steps: seeing the vision, writing it down, and waiting for it to come to fruition.

Believing is crucial for a leader to progress from seeing the vision to waiting for its fulfillment, empowering them to navigate uncertainty and ambiguity.

Abraham's strong relationship with God, built on trust and integrity, translated into unwavering loyalty. Belief plays a vital role in guiding leaders through uncertainty, fostering trust, and building steadfast loyalty, the core values of purposeful leadership.

Test of Faith

After two decades of waiting for the promise of a son, Abraham faced the ultimate test of faith when God asked him to offer Isaac as a burnt offering. Abraham's willingness to obey and preparation to sacrifice his only son demonstrated his reverence for God. The Apostle Paul writes in Romans 4:18 that "contrary to hope, in hope he believed," which ultimately made him the father of many nations (Taber D., 2024).

On the way to Mount Moriah, Isaac asked his father, "Where is the lamb for the burnt offering? I see the fire and the wood" (Genesis 22:7). Abraham's response, "God will provide the sacrifice," demonstrated his unwavering faith in God (Taber D., 2024).

Hebrews 11:17-19 vividly captures Abraham's mindset: "By faith Abraham, when he was tested, offered up Isaac, and he who had received the promises offered up his only begotten son... concluding that God was able to raise him, even from the dead". This experience marked a profound transformation in Abraham, enabling him to believe in God and undertake the unimaginable act of sacrificing his son. It is a life-changing leadership lesson about the power of faith and obedience (Taber D. 2024).

A Shift in Perspective: Abraham's Journey to Purpose

Initially, Abraham was preoccupied with the immediate concerns of daily life, unable to see God's purpose for him. Despite God's promise, Abram focused on his limitations, such as his age and his wife Sarai's barrenness. Biologically past the age of having children, Abram struggled to fulfill the promise of becoming a father of nations, focusing on his inadequacies, burdens, and impossibilities, which nearly led him to nearly forfeit his life's purpose.

In frustration, Abram turned to substitutes, such as Hagar, as a wife and Eliezer as his heir, which could have undermined God's purpose for his life had God not remained faithful to His promise. Abraham's example underscores the need for a profound shift in perspective to appreciate and fulfill one's purpose fully. This shift involves moving from the familiar to the unfamiliar, from insufficiency to sufficiency, from seeing challenges as opportunities to perceiving impossibilities as possibilities, from seeking certainty to embracing uncertainty, from unbelief to belief, and from focusing on the present to envisioning the future. Breaking self-imposed barriers is crucial to this transformative process.

Lessons Learned from the Case Study of Abraham: Implications for Purposeful Leadership

Abraham's journey underscores the importance of faith, long-term vision, and the necessary mindset and perspective adjustments required to discover and fulfill one's purpose. His story serves as a powerful reminder of the transformative journey individuals must undertake to realize their destinies.

The story of Abram's journey to Canaan is a powerful metaphor for the human experience of abandoning familiarity for adventure and purpose. It illustrates the necessity for individuals, organizations, and nations to undergo fundamental change and embrace purposeful leadership to fulfill their destinies. This change often requires leaving behind the familiar, enduring tribulations and developing the character necessary to bring dreams and visions to fruition.

Abram's journey and the hurdles he encountered highlight the necessity of overcoming obstacles, transforming one's mindset, and embracing a clear vision to fulfill one's purpose. His experiences emphasize that purposeful leadership is about having a vision and the resilience and adaptability required to navigate challenges.

Abraham's evolution from being the father of a nation to the father of many nations exemplifies the concept of 360-degree transformation. This transformation involved leaving the familiar, embracing a new identity, establishing a covenant relationship, demonstrating persistent faith, making sacrifices, and experiencing transformation through grace. This comprehensive approach to change can be applied across various aspects of life, emphasizing holistic growth and alignment with a higher purpose (Taber D. 2024).

The lessons from Abraham's case study highlight the importance of belief, vision, and a willingness to embrace change in effective leadership. Leaders can draw inspiration from Abraham's journey, recognizing that authentic leadership involves guiding others and undergoing personal transformation to fulfill a greater purpose.

References
1. New King James Version. (1982). *Thomas Nelson.*
2. Taber, D. (2024). *Unwavering faith: Lessons from Abraham's life journey.* Retrieved from

https://answeredfaith.com/bible-character-study-abraham

CHAPTER 10: THE CASE STUDY OF MOSES

Moses: The Man of God and His Staff

Moses is one of history's most pivotal leaders—a figure whose life embodies the complexities of authority and the profound impact of compassionate guidance. His journey, marked by early missteps and transformative encounters, is exemplified by the symbolic importance of his staff, which came to represent divine authority and comfort.

Moses' Early Attempts at Liberation

In Exodus 2, we encounter Moses as a man ready to challenge injustice. When he witnessed an Egyptian beating a Hebrew, Moses intervened and, in an act he deemed just, killed the Egyptian. The next day, however, his attempt to mediate a dispute among the Hebrews was met with skepticism regarding his authority. This rejection forced Moses to flee to Midian—a pivotal moment in his life that set the stage for a profound transformation following his encounter with God at the burning bush.

The narrative emphasizes that genuine leadership stems not from impulsive acts but from a deeper understanding of one's responsibility to serve others.

The Symbolism of the Staff

Moses receives a staff during his divine encounter—a tangible symbol of divine authority and comfort. This symbol is later echoed in Psalm 23:4, reminding us, "Your rod and your staff, they comfort me." Here, the staff serves as an instrument of power and a reminder that proper authority rests on guidance rather than punishment.

This symbolism teaches a valuable lesson: leadership is grounded in empathy and support rather than coercion.

Authority Versus Coercion

The ethos of the Egyptian system influenced Moses' initial approach to leadership —a realm where coercion and force were prevalent. His early reliance on such methods ultimately proved ineffective. His experience reveals that authoritarian leadership, grounded in coercion, is more likely to fail than an approach that values nurturing and protective guidance.

By recognizing the pitfalls of forceful authority, Moses gradually adopts a leadership style that prioritizes his people's genuine welfare.

The Shift from Staff to Shepherd: Transforming Leadership

After his dramatic act against an Egyptian and subsequent escape from Pharaoh, Moses found refuge in Midian. There, he spent many years as a shepherd under his father-in-law, Jethro's guidance. This period of isolation and simplicity marked a departure from the luxury of the Egyptian palace and revealed the contrasting worlds Moses navigated:

- **From Palace to Wilderness:** A transition from luxury to the stark desert landscape.

- **From Abundance to Simplicity:** Transitioning from a life of privilege to one focused on survival and reflection.

- **From Companionship to Solitude:** Evolving from a life surrounded by courtly figures to one defined by solitude—accompanied only by his sheep.

This dramatic contrast reveals how adversity and isolation can shape a leader who is aligned with the needs of those they later serve.

The Leader as Shepherd

Understanding the dynamics between a shepherd and his flock becomes essential in examining Moses' transformation. Like a shepherd who guides and protects vulnerable sheep, Moses needed to cultivate a shepherd's mindset to lead the often wayward children of Israel—a people known for their vulnerability and resistance to authority. This theme recurs in other biblical figures, such as David (a shepherd before becoming king) and Jesus, who is often referred to as the Chief Shepherd in the Gospel of John. Their examples demonstrate that effective leadership is grounded in care, guidance, and protection rather than domination.

God's Call and Moses in the Wilderness

When Moses began to embrace his true potential, God called him to undertake the monumental task of liberating the Israelites from Egyptian bondage. Despite his initial struggles to accept this divine directive, Moses' time in the wilderness proved indispensable. He underwent significant personal growth in solitude—a period marked by deep introspection and transformation.

Embracing Solitude for Growth

The wilderness becomes a powerful metaphor for every leader's internal journey. During this time, Moses was encouraged to:

- **Look in the Mirror:** Engage in honest self-reflection by acknowledging both your strengths and weaknesses.

- **Embrace Reflection:** Dedicate time to meditate on his experiences, reassess his past decisions, and set a clear path for the future.

- **Clear the Mind:** Eliminate distractions and mental clutter to see challenges and opportunities with clarity.

The Path to Transformation

Solitude in the wilderness presents a choice: stagnation or growth. Moses' journey teaches us that letting go of the past, addressing unresolved issues, and embracing change are essential steps toward personal growth. This transformative process enabled him to transition from a reluctant shepherd to a bold leader who eventually guided his people with compassion and determination.

Strongman Leadership: Single Leader Authority

Throughout his journey from Egypt to Mount Horeb, Moses initially exemplified what might be called **strongman leadership**—a solitary approach in which a single individual bears the weight of all leadership responsibilities.

Solitary Leadership

- **Independent Decision-Making:** Moses often resolved disputes independently, embodying the qualities of a solitary leader. Loneliness, privacy, and intense independence marked his leadership style.

- **Work-Life Balance:** His single-minded dedication sometimes left little room for personal relationships, even with his immediate family.

Prioritizing Goals Over Relationships

Moses prioritized setting and achieving goals. While this focus earned him respect as a tireless leader, it also meant that significant personal relationships, such as those with his wife and children (who lived with his father-in-law), took a back seat.

Public Perception of Strength

Moses was seen as a rock—a steadfast figure admired for his endurance and unwavering work ethic. His seemingly tireless efforts solidified his reputation as a resilient leader. However, relying solely on public favor can be perilous, as popular opinion is fickle and can swiftly shift from admiration to disapproval. This highlights the importance of balancing public perception and personal integrity, ensuring leadership is grounded in principle rather than mere popularity.

Influence of the Egyptian Mindset

Moses' early leadership was steeped in the Egyptian tradition in which he was raised. He was immersed in a culture that favored strongman tactics and centralized, one-person rule. This background initially constrained his ability to lead collaboratively.

Evolution Toward Empathy

Over time, as Moses faced increasingly complex challenges, his leadership evolved. He shifted from an isolated, strongman approach to one that celebrated empathy, connection, and understanding. Ultimately, Moses emerged as an authentic leader—humble, faithful, and true to his mission.

From Holding on to Power to Sharing It: The Lesson of Delegation

A Pivotal Moment in Exodus

In Exodus 18:13-22, Moses reaches a turning point. Overwhelmed by his solitary workload of judging disputes from morning until evening, he was on the verge of burnout. His father-in-law, Jethro, recognized that this approach was unsustainable.

Jethro's Counsel

Jethro observed, "What you are doing is not good" (Exodus 18:17), warning that Moses would exhaust himself if he continued alone. Rather than a critique, this was a gift of practical wisdom to foster a more effective leadership model.

The Importance of Delegation

- **Empowering Others:** Jethro advised Moses to delegate routine matters to capable men, reserving the most challenging cases for himself (Exodus 18:22).

- **Implementing Change:** Moses responded positively to this advice, transitioning from an isolated leadership style to one that embraced shared power and responsibility.

This shift alleviated Moses's burden and empowered community members, laying the foundation for a more sustainable leadership structure.

Hobab: "Be Our Eyes" – Embracing External Expertise

In Numbers 10:29-32, Moses calls on Hobab, saying, "Be our eyes." This request underscores the importance of seeking guidance from others when internal knowledge is limited.

- **Internal versus External:** When facing challenges, leaders must decide whether to rely solely on their own experience or to seek the expertise of others.

- **Critical Skills:** Recognizing the need for external help is crucial, as it ensures that broader perspectives inform decisions.

Essential Qualities for Effective Leadership

- **Adaptive:** Adjust your approach according to changing circumstances.

- **Open-Minded:** Welcoming new ideas and perspectives leads to more comprehensive and practical solutions.

- **Receptive:** Valuing the input of those with specialized expertise enhances decision-making.

- **Humble:** Acknowledge that you do not have all the answers and be willing to learn from others.

How to Respond to a Crisis: Managing Difficult People

Throughout his leadership journey, Moses faced continual crises. His responses provide timeless lessons for managing adversity.

Trusting in God at the Red Sea

In Exodus 14:1-31, Moses urged the Israelites to remain calm as Pharaoh's army closed in. Rather than succumbing to panic, he inspired trust in divine salvation, demonstrating his unwavering faith in God's intervention.

Exercising Humility Amidst Conflict

When Aaron and Miriam confronted him in Numbers 12:1-2, Moses chose not to respond defensively. Instead, he remained silent and later intervened on Miriam's behalf. His humility—remarkably noted, given his unique relationship with God—is echoed in the wisdom of Proverbs 3:7 and Romans 12:3, which counsel against exalting oneself.

Intercession During Rebellion

After the spies' negative report in Numbers 14, Moses again interceded for his people despite their rebellion. His persistent role as an intercessor, even in the face of potential divine punishment, characterizes his enduring commitment to the people's welfare.

A Moment of Rashness

However, at Kadesh (Numbers 20:10-12), a moment of impulsive action on Moses' part proved to be a critical misstep. This lapse ultimately curtailed his leadership journey, a powerful reminder that even great leaders are vulnerable.

Lessons from Moses' Leadership Journey

Moses's journey from a solitary strongman to an empathetic, collaborative leader offers timeless lessons in effective leadership:

- **Adaptability:** Leadership evolves when we are willing to grow and share power.
- **Delegation:** Empowering others eases personal burdens and fosters collective strength.
- **Seeking Guidance:** Knowing when to ask for help reinforces sound decision-making.
- **Humility in Crisis:** Maintaining composure and trust in the face of challenges is essential.

- **Compassionate Authority:** True leadership stems from empathy, self-reflection, and a willingness to transform—not from coercion.

Moses's life is a compelling study of balancing personal strength with collaborative leadership. His transformation from relying on coercive power to embracing compassionate guidance illustrates that authentic leadership uplifts rather than oppresses. The symbolism of his staff reminds us that effective leadership is rooted in offering comfort, nurturing community, and fostering growth.

Final Reflections

Moses's case study teaches us several critical lessons for purposeful leadership. By embracing adaptability, fostering collaboration, evolving leadership styles, and maintaining a humble, service-oriented approach, leaders can navigate challenges effectively and inspire those they lead. Moses's journey remains a timeless testament to the power of personal transformation and the importance of uplifting others through compassionate and inclusive leadership.

The thoughtful integration of personal transformation and the symbolism of the staff enriches our understanding of leadership, making Moses' story timeless and widely relevant.

Reference

Liberty University. (2013). *The King James Study Bible (2ⁿᵈ Edition)*. Thomas Nelson.

CHAPTER 11: THE CASE STUDY OF DAVID

Justice: The Foundation of Leadership

The David case study emphasizes the foundational role of justice in leadership. In 2 Samuel 23:2-4, David emphasizes the importance of rulers being and ruling in the fear of God, which enables leadership to flourish and bear fruit. This emphasis on justice and righteousness was a fundamental aspect of David's leadership, as reflected in his last words. The Spirit of the LORD spoke through David, indicating divine inspiration behind his emphasis on just leadership.

Shepherd Leadership

The passage from Psalm 78:70-72 emphasizes the qualities of a shepherd-leader, highlighting the importance of shepherding the people with integrity of heart and skillful hands. It underscores the significance of leading with the heart and mind of a shepherd.

The heart of a shepherd embodies care, comfort, and safety for the people they lead, while the mind of a shepherd seeks opportunities for provision, growth, development, and protection. It aligns with Benson's commentary, emphasizing the care, diligence, and self-denial necessary for effective leadership. In his commentary, Benson stated, "From following the ewes with the great young – by which employment he was inured to that care, and diligence, and self-denial which are necessary qualifications in a king or governor; and instructed to rule his people with all gentleness and tenderness" (Bibblehub.com, 2024).

Integrity of Heart and Skillful Hands

David exemplified leadership with a sincere heart and the ability to act wisely. His pure intentions and righteous actions instilled confidence in his followers, while his skillful execution of leadership responsibilities demonstrated competence and sound judgment. Authenticity and ethical principles were the pillars of his approach.

David's Passion for a Cause

In *1 Samuel 17:29*, David's exclamation, "Is there not a cause?" reveals his determination and the purposeful drive behind his actions. Rather than relying solely on his physical prowess to confront Goliath, David's deep faith and trust in the Lord—further illustrated in 1 Samuel 17:45-46—underscore the importance of authenticity, courage, and conviction in leadership.

Led by Conviction

The account of David sparing Saul's life on two occasions, as depicted in 1 Samuel 24:4-7 and 26:7-12, reveals David's remarkable integrity and sensitivity in his actions. Despite being pursued by Saul, who sought to kill him out of fear that David would usurp his throne, David chose not to harm Saul when he had the opportunity to do so. Initially, David refrained from harming Saul when he found him vulnerable in a cave, recognizing Saul as the Lord's anointed and respecting God's authority.

Similarly, David spared Saul's life in the second instance, acknowledging that harming the anointed king would be a sin. David's actions demonstrate a deep reverence for God's anointed and commitment to righteousness, even in the face of persecution.

These events in David's life, particularly his experiences in the wilderness, shaped his character and exemplified the importance of leading with the integrity of the heart. David's attentiveness to his conscience and willingness to repent, as well as his trust in leaving matters in the Lord's hands, showcase essential leadership principles.

This case study of David serves as a powerful example of how listening attentively to one's heart and obeying its convictions can prevent actions that, while appearing logical, contradict one's values.

Approachable, Quick to Listen, Learn, and Grow

A notable feature of David's leadership was his willingness to listen and learn. When Abigail advised David against taking vengeance on Nabal in 1 Samuel 25:23-35, he demonstrated his openness to counsel—even though his initial response to Nabal was less than ideal.

Moreover, when confronted by the Prophet Nathan about his adultery with Bathsheba, David did not deflect blame; instead, as seen in *Psalm 51*, he responded with genuine contrition and humility. This readiness to acknowledge mistakes and seek correction illustrates a growth mindset that strengthened his leadership [Doohan, 2018].

Dark Side of Leadership

The story of David's affair with Bathsheba is a stark reminder that, despite their positions of authority, leaders are human and susceptible to moral failings. This narrative highlights the significance of acknowledging one's humanity and the challenges that accompany it, even for leaders. It reveals the darker side of leadership and the danger of succumbing to evil if we are not conscious of our own temptations. The abuse of power and the subsequent attempts to cover up his transgressions highlight the potential for moral failings even in the most esteemed leaders.

The consequences of David's actions, including the loss of life and the turmoil within his family and kingdom, further underscore the far-reaching impact of leadership failures. These insights shed light on the complexities of leadership and the ethical considerations that leaders must navigate.

The story of David's affair with Bathsheba serves as a cautionary tale, reminding leaders of the importance of acknowledging their humanity and the potential for moral failings. It underscores the importance of humility, accountability, and adherence to ethical and moral standards in leadership.

Believing in and Developing Others

David was a leader who believed in others and molded them into outstanding leaders. The story in 1 Samuel 22:2 illustrates how David transformed distressed, indebted, and discontented individuals into a formidable army, demonstrating his inclusive, visionary leadership. He created an environment where others could grow and excel, fostering a culture of mutual success and selflessness.

The story provides insight into David's leadership qualities and principles, including accountability, care for those led, and the ability to adapt to challenges. They also highlight the importance of seeking guidance from a higher authority and being open to change. David's leadership teaches us the importance of believing in others, creating growth opportunities, and fostering a culture of mutual success. It highlights the importance of humility, accountability, and concern for those under one's leadership.

Aware of His Weakness

His awareness of his weaknesses characterizes David's leadership and trust in God for guidance and strength. He devoted much of his time to quiet reflection, meditation, and prayer, acknowledging his limitations and yielding to the

Lord to search and test his heart and thoughts, as exemplified in Psalm 51. This principle of quietness, both in personal life and leadership, is a critical tool for learning from mistakes, fostering growth, and developing as an individual and a leader. The principle of quietness also serves as a means of seeking clarity, strength, resilience, and spiritual growth, fostering a deeper understanding of divine wisdom.

Conclusion

David's leadership is characterized by unwavering faith, humility, integrity, competence, authenticity, reflection, and a relentless pursuit of personal growth. His story is a powerful reminder that effective leadership requires staying true to one's values while remaining vigilant against moral failings. By listening to one's inner convictions and seeking divine wisdom, leaders can build trust, inspire those they serve, and navigate the complex challenges of leadership with grace and accountability

References

Bible Hub. (2024). *Benson commentary*. Retrieved from

https://biblehub.com/commentaries/psalms/78-70.htm

Doohan, B. (2018). *The heart of David: Committed to our calling*. Retrieved from

https://wholeheartedwoman.live/2018/03/01/the-heart-of-david-committed-to-our-calling/#

CHAPTER 12: THE CASE STUDY OF DANIEL

In this chapter, we examine the life of Daniel—a young Israelite taken into captivity—and explore how his experiences provide timeless lessons on purposeful leadership. Daniel's story illustrates adaptability, integrity, and excellence, which are essential for modern leaders navigating complex and multicultural environments.

Background and the Selection Process

Daniel was among the young Israelites taken captive by Nebuchadnezzar, the king of Babylon, after the conquest of Jerusalem (Daniel 1:1-2). This pivotal event forced many of Jerusalem's nobility and skilled individuals to relocate.

Nebuchadnezzar ordered Ashpenaz, the master of his eunuchs, to select young men of royal lineage and nobility who were intelligent and capable of understanding various sciences to serve at the king's court (Daniel 1:3-4). Daniel's inclusion among these chosen individuals underscores his exceptional abilities and intellectual promise.

The intent was to train these selected youths in the Chaldeans' language and literature, preparing them for leadership roles in a foreign cultural setting while challenging them to maintain their heritage and identity.

Resilient and Purposeful Leadership

One of the most striking elements of Daniel's early experience was his determination to remain faithful to his cultural and religious values. In a situation designed to change him, Daniel consciously decided not to defile himself with the king's rich food and wine (Daniel 1:8).

Instead, he respectfully requested an alternative diet, which the prince of the eunuchs granted.

The act of intentional discipline highlights two key points:

- **Commitment to Integrity:** Daniel's refusal to partake in food that may have been offered to pagan gods demonstrates his steadfast adherence to the dietary laws and religious customs governing his faith.

- **Purposeful Decision-Making:** By prioritizing his beliefs over personal comfort, Daniel demonstrated how leaders can—and sometimes must—navigate compromise while holding firmly to their core values.

Divine Talent and Wisdom

Daniel was not only resilient but also exceptionally talented. God endowed him and his three friends with extraordinary wisdom and understanding. Daniel's unique ability to interpret dreams and visions distinguished him from his peers. His divine gift led King Nebuchadnezzar to acknowledge that Daniel and his friends were ten times more capable in wisdom and understanding than all the astrologers and magicians in the kingdom (Daniel 1:20).

Key leadership lessons from this episode include:

- **Recognizing and Nurturing Talent:** Just as Nebuchadnezzar valued exceptional qualities in his chosen advisors, modern leaders should actively identify and cultivate talent within their teams.

- **Seeking Guidance Beyond Human Understanding:** Daniel's reliance on divine wisdom reminds leaders to pursue knowledge and insight from diverse sources, such as spiritual, intellectual, or mentorship.

Leadership Excellence and Overcoming Opposition

Daniel's later achievements further underscore the intersection of excellence and personal conviction in leadership. His ability to interpret King Nebuchadnezzar's dreams earned him significant favor in the Babylonian court. After successfully interpreting the king's first dream, Daniel was elevated to the chief of the governor's staff, overseeing the province of Babylon (Daniel 2:49).

Later, under Darius the Mede, Daniel was appointed as one of three presidents responsible for managing the kingdom's affairs, a testament to his exceptional qualities (Daniel 6:1-3).

However, Daniel's prominence also sparked envy among his peers. Unable to find fault in his diligent and trustworthy governance, his adversaries manipulated religious laws and persuaded the king to issue a decree that prohibited anyone from praying to any deity or human other than the king (Daniel 6:4-17). This decree directly challenged Daniel's faith and underscored the difficult choices leaders sometimes face when personal convictions conflict with political pressures.

Implications for Modern, Purposeful Leadership

Daniel's story offers profound lessons for today's leaders:

- **Integrity and Consistency:**

Daniel maintained an unwavering commitment to his values—from dietary discipline to navigating complex court politics. Modern leaders, too, must demonstrate moral courage and consistency, even when external pressures tempt them to compromise.

- **Intentional Decision-Making:**

By making deliberate choices aligned with his core beliefs, Daniel earned respect and influence. Today, leaders can inspire trust by ensuring that every decision reflects their fundamental principles.

- **Adaptability and Cross-Cultural Sensitivity:**

Daniel successfully adapted to a new cultural environment while retaining his identity. In an increasingly global and diverse world, leaders must strike a balance between cultural sensitivity and adherence to personal and organizational values.

- **Recognition and Cultivation of Talent:**

Nebuchadnezzar's selection of gifted individuals serves as a reminder of the importance of identifying and empowering team members with exceptional skills. Fostering an environment that values diverse talents enhances both organizational effectiveness and innovation.

- **Continuous Learning and Wisdom:**

Effective leadership involves seeking insights beyond conventional boundaries—whether through spiritual guidance, professional mentorship, or lifelong learning. Daniel's reliance on divine wisdom underscores this principle.

- **Courage in Adversity:**

Daniel's willingness to face the possibility of death without hesitation underscores that authentic leadership often requires making tough, value-driven choices, even at great personal risk.

- **Resilience Against Opposition:**

Confronted with conspiracies driven by jealousy, Daniel remained steadfast in his purpose. Leaders may similarly encounter resistance; his resilience teaches the importance of staying focused despite external pressures.

- **Being a Role Model:**

Through his consistent adherence to his faith and practices, Daniel set a powerful example for others. Leaders who embody strong values and lead by example foster a culture of integrity and purpose within their organizations.

This case study of Daniel not only reinforces the timeless nature of his example but also serves as a practical guide for modern leaders. **Today's leaders can inspire trust and drive transformational success in their organizations by holding steadfast to core values, displaying courage, and leading with unwavering integrity.**

Reference

Liberty University. (2013). The King James Study Bible (Second Edition). Thomas Nelson.

CHAPTER 13: THE CASE STUDY OF ESTHER

Background of Esther's Case Study

During a lavish feast hosted by King Ahasuerus of Persia, the splendor and wealth of his kingdom were on full display. The king summoned Queen Vashti to exhibit her beauty before the assembly. However, Vashti's refusal to comply led to her removal from the throne. This decisive act marked the end of an era and paved the way for a new era. In a divinely orchestrated turn of events, Esther was later chosen as the new queen, signaling that her appointment carried a profound and purposeful destiny (Esther 1–2).

Time and History: Importance for Leadership

Moshik Temkin emphasizes that truly transformative leaders, like Esther, must be understood within the context of their historical environment. He argues that the crises they face, and the timing of their actions are crucial in shaping their leadership. According to Temkin, effective leaders often embody various roles—those of warriors, rebels, saints, and teachers. From this perspective, being a "teacher" means that a leader operates within history, clarifying the circumstances, challenges, and importance of their role. This view highlights the importance of timing in shaping the character and outcomes of leadership (Moshik Temkin, McKinsey, 2024).

Haman's Rise and Mordecai's Defiance

Haman the Agagite had been exalted by King Ahasuerus above all other princes, receiving rapt attention and respect from the royal servants. In stark contrast, Mordecai, grounded in his Jewish faith and adherence to the commandment "Thou shalt have no other gods before Me" (Exodus 20:3, KJV), refused to bow or show customary reverence. In Persian culture, bowing was regarded as an act of homage akin to worship.

Mordecai's steadfast defiance was not merely a personal stance but a profound expression of his sincerely held religious beliefs. Enraged by Mordecai's noncompliance, Haman resolved to eliminate all the Jews from the kingdom—a plan he cunningly secured the king's approval to execute.

Mordecai's Challenge and Esther's Response

Esther's Initial Hesitation

Upon learning of Haman's genocidal plot, Mordecai publicly mourned per Jewish customs—tearing his clothes, donning sackcloth, and lamenting alongside fellow Jews. He then urgently informed Esther of the unfolding crisis and implored her to intercede with the king on behalf of her people. However, Esther was initially hesitant, acutely aware that approaching the king unsummoned was a violation of court protocol and an act punishable by death. Despite her reluctance, Mordecai's determination underscored the urgency of the situation and the need for decisive action.

Esther's Courage

In a pivotal moment, Mordecai challenged Esther by asking, "Who knows if perhaps you were made queen for such a time as this?" Mordecai's query was a call to action, reminding her that her rise to queenship might have been divinely orchestrated to serve a crucial purpose during this crisis.

Inspired by her potential destiny and the dire needs of her people, Esther summoned the courage to risk her life by boldly approaching the king without summons. With extraordinary tact and wisdom, she pleaded for the salvation of her people, ultimately thwarting Haman's genocidal scheme.

In the aftermath of these events, Esther and Mordecai established Purim as an enduring memorial of divine deliverance.

Lessons Learned: Implications for Purposeful Leadership

The story of Esther offers several profound insights into effective and purposeful leadership:

1. The Role of Timing:

Effective leadership often hinges on recognizing the precise moment to act. Mordecai's acute sense of urgency and Esther's timely response demonstrate that understanding historical context and decisive action are crucial in leadership.

2. Courageous Action:

Esther's willingness to approach the king despite personal risk exemplifies the courageous, sometimes sacrificial decisions leaders must make for the greater good.

3. Intuitive Intelligence:

Leaders should cultivate the ability to read complex situations and discern the underlying significance of the moment—an intuitive intelligence essential for navigating crises.

4. Collaboration and Support:

Esther highlighted the importance of collective action and support in overcoming significant challenges by calling for communal fasting and unity.

5. Historical Awareness:

Informed by history and tradition, leaders who understand the broader societal and temporal context can make decisions that address immediate crises and resonate with future generations. This notion echoes the biblical portrayal of the men of the tribe of Issachar, who were renowned for their wisdom in understanding and responding to the signs of their times (1 Chronicles, NLT).

Conclusion

The case study of Esther reveals that purposeful leadership is deeply intertwined with historical awareness, courageous decision-making, intuitive intelligence, and a sense of collective responsibility. Leaders who remain attuned to the context of their times and are willing to make bold choices can inspire transformative change. Esther's story is a timeless reminder that thoughtful, timely leadership can profoundly impact communities and shape the course of history.

References

Liberty University. The King James Study Bible (Second Edition). Thomas Nelson.

Temkin, M. (2024). *Understanding transformative leadership in historical context*. McKinsey & Company.

CHAPTER 14: THE CASE STUDY OF PAUL

Paul's Influence

Acts 17:6 describes Paul as one of "those who have turned the world upside down." Renowned for his bold teachings, he was recognized for his courage, daring spirit, and passionate pursuit of truth. His actions challenged the established order, catalyzed paradigm shifts, and ultimately transformed entire movements. As a profound thinker and innovator, Paul is remembered among history's great disruptors—individuals who introduced fresh ideas, concepts, and methods that sparked unprecedented change.

Implications for Purposeful Leadership

Paul's life teaches that leadership is not merely about authority but about influencing and inspiring others toward a higher purpose. Key leadership principles drawn from his example include:

1. **Embrace Disruption:** Like Paul, leaders should be willing to question the status quo and introduce innovative ideas that drive significant change.

2. **Inspiration and Influence:** Great leaders inspire others to pursue a shared purpose and motivate their teams to take transformative actions.

3. **Courage and Boldness:** Effective leadership demands the courage to confront opposition and adversity while steadfastly pursuing a meaningful mission.

4. **Overcoming Inertia:** Leaders must prioritize initiatives that produce lasting and meaningful societal impact.

5. **Commitment to Growth:** Just as Paul adapted and refined his methods, leaders should remain open to learning and continually improve their strategies.

By embodying these qualities, purposeful leaders can guide their teams and communities toward achieving substantial, positive change.

Cultivating Unyielding Resilience

Paul's Personal Testimony

In 2 Corinthians 11:22-32, Paul reflects on his sufferings, highlighting that his weaknesses are, in truth, a testament to his enduring faith. Similarly, in Romans 5:3-5, he explains that tribulations foster perseverance, reinforcing the idea that hardships can forge strength.

Even while imprisoned in Rome, Paul encouraged the Philippians to rejoice and express gratitude in all circumstances, setting a powerful example of unrelenting resilience.

Implications for Purposeful Leadership Through Resilience

Paul's teachings on resilience offer vital lessons for modern leaders:

1. **Embrace Vulnerability:** Acknowledging personal weaknesses can help leaders build authenticity and foster deeper team connections.

2. **Cultivate Perseverance:** Facing adversity with steadfast determination ultimately fosters growth and success.

3. **Foster a Positive Mindset:** Leaders who encourage gratitude and optimism can maintain high morale even in challenging times.

4. **Model Resilience:** Demonstrating calmness and steadfastness in the face of hardship sets a strong example and fosters a culture of resilience among team members.

5. **View Challenges as Opportunities:** By reframing setbacks as learning experiences, leaders can drive continuous growth and improvement.

These principles underscore the importance of cultivating a resilient, growth-oriented mindset that empowers teams and fosters long-term success.

Renewing the Mind: Meditation and Clarity

Paul's Call for Transformation

In Romans 12:2, Paul advises believers not to conform to the patterns of this world but to transform their lives through the renewal of their minds. This transformation process is crucial for discerning one's purpose and aligning one's actions with divine will. Moreover, Philippians 4:8-9 challenges believers to meditate on virtues such as truth, nobility, justice, purity, beauty, and praiseworthiness, thereby steering their focus toward positive, uplifting thoughts.

Implications for Purposeful Leadership in Mindset and Focus

Drawing from Paul's teachings, leaders can take the following steps to nurture a culture of positive transformation:

1. **Promote Personal Transformation:** Encourage team members to continually renew their thinking and align their personal growth with a shared vision.

2. **Foster Constructive Thought:** Cultivate an environment where positive and constructive ideas

are valued, thereby boosting morale and productivity.

3. **Model Clarity and Purpose:** Leaders who demonstrate clear, value-driven thinking inspire team confidence and commitment.

4. **Encourage Lifelong Learning:** A commitment to continuous learning enhances individual perspectives and fosters collective growth.

5. **Aligning Actions with Values:** Ensure that decisions and strategies align with the core values and virtues that drive your organization.

By prioritizing a renewed mindset, leaders can create purposeful and progressive environments.

Sharpening Focus to Attain Ultimate Goals

Paul's Guidance on Focus and Prioritization

In Philippians 3:13-14, Paul explains, "I have not yet attained it; I forget what lies behind and reach forward to what lies ahead, pressing toward the goal." He emphasizes the importance of focusing on future aspirations rather than being anchored by past experiences. Likewise, Philippians 3:7-8 reminds us that extraneous gains should be set aside to concentrate on what truly matters.

Furthermore, in Philippians 4:11-13, Paul teaches the importance of contentment in all circumstances, emphasizing that inner peace facilitates the effective pursuit of goals. His counsel in Titus 3:9-11 and 2 Timothy 2:4 also emphasizes the importance of constructive engagement, dedication, and the avoidance of distractions.

Implications for Purposeful Leadership in Goal Setting

From Paul's teachings, several actionable insights for leadership emerge:

1. **Maintain a Future-Focused Perspective:** Leaders must prioritize future goals and consistently inspire their teams to look beyond past setbacks.

2. **Prioritize What Matters:** The ability to identify and focus on key objectives is crucial for avoiding distractions and maintaining a strategic direction.

3. **Promote Contentment and Peace:** Cultivating balance and inner peace enables leaders and teams to navigate uncertainty with calm determination.

4. **Engage Constructively:** Preventing unnecessary conflicts fosters a harmonious and productive environment.

5. **Commit to Discipline and Improvement**: Stay dedicated to ongoing progress by consistently reviewing and refining strategies and integrating lessons learned. Following Paul's example, intentional, goal-oriented leadership inspires teams to pursue meaningful objectives with clarity, discipline, and unwavering commitment to growth.

Reference

Liberty University. The King James Study Bible (Second Edition). Thomas Nelson.

PART 4: UNRAVELING THE MINDSETS, EMOTIONS, AND MOTIVATIONS OF PURPOSEFUL LEADERSHIP

In this section, we examine the heart of purposeful leadership, drawing wisdom from historical biblical narratives to understand the mindsets, emotions, and motivations that propel leaders in today's rapidly changing environment. It is organized as follows:

- Mindset of purposeful leaders. It explores, "How did the leaders in the case studies exhibit those mindsets?" What lessons could contemporary leaders learn for effective leadership?"
- Navigating the emotional terrain of purposeful leadership. It probes the questions, "What emotions did the leaders in the case studies wrestle with? How did they respond to those emotions? What lessons could contemporary leaders learn to navigate the increasingly complex environment?"
- Motivation of purposeful leaders. It examines, "What motivated the leaders in the case studies to achieve historical success?"

Although the environment depicted in the historical biblical narratives profoundly differs from today's, the wisdom we glean from them is universal and timeless.

CHAPTER 15: THE MINDSET OF PURPOSEFUL LEADERS

This chapter explores how the leaders in the case studies demonstrated these mindsets. What lessons can contemporary leaders derive from effective leadership? Addressing these questions highlights the distinctive thought processes and beliefs of purpose-driven leaders, as well as their ability to inspire and influence their followers.

FORWARD-LOOKING MINDSET

A forward-looking mindset is essential for purposeful leadership. A forward-looking mindset is essential for effective leadership, enabling leaders to inspire and guide their teams purposefully. Several key components characterize this mindset:

- **Set a Clear Vision:** Purposeful leaders establish a crystal-clear vision that guides their actions and decisions.

- **Establish Realistic, Measurable Goals:** They set realistic and measurable goals, focusing on them while actively combating distractions and procrastination.

- **Prioritize Future Goals:** Leaders prioritize future objectives over past setbacks, ensuring they focus on what truly matters.

- **Cultivate Discipline and Commitment:** They nurture discipline and commitment, aligning their efforts with their core values and objectives.

- **Create a Monitoring System:** Purposeful leaders implement a system for monitoring and evaluating progress, enabling them to assess, reprioritize, and strategize effectively.

- **Foster a Culture of Growth and Continuous Improvement:** They cultivate a culture that values growth and continuous improvement.

- **Adaptability:** They demonstrate a strong capacity for adaptability, often undergoing significant transformations to meet evolving challenges.

- **Resilience:** Resilience is a critical trait characterized by perseverance, relentless determination, and the ability to adapt to change while maintaining a focus on the big picture.

How the Leaders in the Case Studies Demonstrated a Forward-Looking Mindset

The leaders in the case studies exemplified a forward-looking mindset through their unwavering faith. Abraham's faith stood out as he believed in God's promise to make him the father of nations despite the seemingly impossible odds. When God challenged him to count the stars and the sand, Abraham visualized this reality, demonstrating a mental vision akin to an architect's blueprint for a future project. This vision became the evidence of what was yet to come, even though it took twenty-five years for Abraham to have a son and hundreds of years after his death for the promise to be fully realized through Jesus Christ.

Similarly, Moses, David, Esther, and Daniel, as described in Hebrews 11:13, died still believing in God's promises, seeing them from a distance and welcoming them.

Contemporary Leaders Who Exemplify a Forward-Looking Mindset

Steve Jobs revolutionized technology with groundbreaking products—the Macintosh, iPhone, iPad, and iPod—which reset industry standards and transformed how people interact with technology (Runday.ai, 2024). His ability to foresee trends and challenge conventional thinking pushed his team to achieve what once seemed impossible.

Lessons Learned

Several insights emerge from these examples:

- **Visionaries Build Blueprints:** Leaders with a forward-looking mindset articulate a detailed vision of the future. Just as Moses detailed the ark's construction and David precisely outlined Solomon's temple, visionary leaders provide a clear plan for transforming ideas into reality.
- **Resilience and Inspiration:** A clear vision inspires resilience, enabling leaders to overcome formidable obstacles and mobilize followers toward collective action.
- **Foundational Leadership:** Visionary leaders lay the groundwork for a lasting legacy by uniting present and future generations around a shared goal, fostering an enduring impact.

Implications for Purposeful Leadership in a Fast-Changing, Complex Environment

The forward-looking mindset has profound implications for today's leaders:

- **Inspiration Through Vision:** By establishing clear visions and realistic goals, leaders create an environment that minimizes distractions and fosters excellence.

- **Building Trust and Credibility:** Discipline and commitment, firmly rooted in core values, build trust among team members.
- **Adaptive Growth:** Systematic monitoring of progress encourages continuous improvement, enabling leaders to adapt to changing environments swiftly.
- **Overcoming Adversity:** Adaptability and resilience equip leaders with the tools to face complexity and uncertainty head-on, driving sustainable success.

Conclusion

In conclusion, a forward-looking mindset is a cornerstone of purposeful leadership. Whether through the visionary faith of historical figures like Abraham, Moses, and David or the innovative drive of modern leaders like Steve Jobs and Elon Musk, this mindset transforms challenges into emerging opportunities.

Forward-looking leaders inspire collective progress and build enduring legacies by setting clear visions, maintaining discipline, and embracing adaptability and resilience.

CURIOUS MINDSET

A curious mindset is essential for purposeful leadership. It is characterized by a profound sense of wonder and an insatiable appetite for knowledge. Below are the key components of a curious mindset:

- **Sense of Wonder:** Leaders who cultivate curiosity question the status quo and explore why things are the way they are. This intrinsic drive fosters a culture of inquiry, motivating them to seek novel answers.
- **Questioning Nature:** Purposeful leaders consistently challenge existing paradigms and seek innovative solutions to complex problems. Their

habit of asking probing questions encourages critical thinking and sparks innovation.

- **Openness to Ideas:** Being receptive to new concepts, engaging in intentional learning, and staying aware of emerging trends enriches leaders' perspectives. Christensen et al. (2020) observed that this openness enhances decision-making capabilities.
- **Attentiveness to Surroundings:** Effective leaders are vigilant observers of their environments, noting events and trends that could impact their organizations. This attentiveness enables them to respond proactively to new challenges.
- **Boldness and Confidence:** A curious mindset empowers leaders to confront their fears and embrace new experiences. By stepping outside their comfort zones, they stimulate both personal and organizational growth.
- **Adventurous Spirit:** Purposeful leaders are willing to explore uncharted territories and seek innovative solutions. This adventurous spirit is critical for driving transformational change.
- **Focus on Passion:** Leaders benefit from concentrating on what they genuinely love. Their passion fuels motivation and inspires others to pursue excellence.
- **Embracing Uncertainty:** It is essential to accept ambiguity and navigate situations with limited information. Leaders who manage uncertainty foster resilience and adaptability.
- **Abandoning Familiarity:** Growth often requires leaving behind the comfort of the known. Purposeful leaders recognize that venturing into unfamiliar territory is where breakthrough innovation occurs.
- **Keen Observation:** Observing details and patterns enables leaders to gather valuable insights from their

experiences, ultimately leading to more informed decisions.

- **Anticipating Future Trends:** Leaders with a curious mindset continually look ahead, preparing for future shifts and adapting their strategies to maintain relevance and competitiveness.
- **Unyielding Expectations:** Leaders with a curious mindset foster a continuous drive for improvement and excellence by setting high standards for themselves and their teams.

How Leaders in the Case Studies Demonstrated a Curious Mindset

Historical and contemporary leaders illustrate the transformative power of curiosity:

- **Moses:** Although born a Hebrew and raised as an Egyptian, Moses chose his true identity and rejected the expectations imposed upon him (Hebrews 11:24-25). While tending sheep, his encounter with a burning bush that defied natural laws spurred his curiosity, leading him toward a life-changing mission.
- **Abraham:** Displaying profound inquisitiveness, Abraham asked God how he could have a son despite his advanced age (Genesis 15:2). His question not only reflected his curiosity but also paved the way for a covenant that would shape the course of history.
- **Paul:** In Athens, Paul observed widespread idolatry and engaged with philosophers and citizens on the topics of God and salvation (Acts 17:16). His willingness to question prevailing beliefs highlights how curiosity can drive meaningful dialogue and challenge cultural norms.
- **Jeff Bezos and Oprah Winfrey:** In the modern era, Bezos's relentless questioning of customer needs led

him to develop a customer-centric, innovative approach that transformed Amazon into a global powerhouse (Manoharan S.K., 2024). Similarly, Oprah Winfrey's empathetic curiosity in storytelling connects diverse perspectives and fosters a deeper collective understanding, making her a transformative influence in media (Manoharan S.K., 2024).

Lessons Learned

Curiosity reveals that leadership is not a fixed state but a dynamic journey of exploration and growth. Embracing a curious mindset allows leaders to:

- Break new ground by seeking and applying innovative solutions.
- Navigate complex challenges by remaining open and adaptive.
- Inspire transformation by continuously challenging the status quo.
- Create opportunities that arise from exploring the unfamiliar, ultimately driving both personal and organizational evolution.

Implications for Purposeful Leadership

A curious mindset is indispensable for purposeful leadership. It drives leaders to embrace continuous learning and innovation, challenge established norms, and harness the power of adaptability. By nurturing curiosity, leaders not only inspire their teams but also build resilient organizations capable of navigating today's rapidly evolving landscape. In essence, the lessons learned from both historical figures and modern exemplars remind us that curiosity is the engine of transformative leadership—fueling discovery, fostering growth, and ensuring sustained relevance in an ever-changing world.

ASSET-BASED THINKING MINDSET

Cramer et al. (2006) define an asset-based mindset as focusing on opportunities rather than problems, strengths rather than weaknesses, and controllable aspects of situations. This perspective encourages leaders to approach challenges proactively, fostering a culture of growth and resilience. Key principles of this mindset include:

- **Focus on Opportunities**: Leaders prioritize opportunities, leveraging strengths and capabilities to navigate challenges effectively.

- **Control What You Can**: By focusing on controllable aspects, leaders maintain urgency and direction, reducing feelings of helplessness during adversity.

- **Learning from Mistakes**: Mistakes are seen as learning experiences rather than failures, enabling continuous improvement and strategic adaptation.

- **Challenge Circumstances**: Leaders reframe challenges as opportunities, driving personal and organizational growth.

An asset-based mindset has a significant impact on leadership by enhancing individual performance, strengthening team dynamics, and boosting overall organizational effectiveness (Cramer et al., 2006). Passionate leaders can inspire their teams to adopt this perspective, fostering collaboration and innovation. By focusing on strengths, learning from experience, and challenging themselves to grow, leaders can cultivate a resilient, forward-thinking organizational culture.

How Leaders in the Case Studies Demonstrated This Mindset

Moses

Moses's introverted and independent leadership style often led to isolation. While this might have been perceived as a weakness, Moses transformed it into a strength. His followers admired his stamina, unwavering work ethic, and ability to set and achieve high goals. They regarded him as a tireless and resilient leader who excelled.

In today's demanding and high-pressure environments, leaders like Moses—high achievers who drive results—are crucial. However, overemphasizing performance can have negative consequences, such as burnout, stress, and strained relationships. For Moses, this imbalance led to emotional exhaustion, as reflected in his lament: "I cannot carry all these people by myself; the burden is too heavy for me" (Numbers 11:13-15, NKJV, Bible.com). He even wished for death to escape his feelings of despair.

This highlights the necessity for leaders to strike a balance between hard work and fostering relationships, as well as taking time to rejuvenate. Moses eventually adapted his approach by delegating responsibilities and transitioning from a solitary, strong leader to one characterized by empathy, connection, and understanding.

David

David also exemplified an asset-based mindset. In his lament over the deaths of Saul and Jonathan (2 Samuel 1:11-27), David highlighted Saul's strengths and virtues, despite their adversarial relationship. This ability to recognize and honor the positive qualities of others, even those of enemies, reflected a leadership culture that emphasized respect and strength-based thinking.

This mindset contrasts with modern leadership's often critical, divisive practices. David's reflective and respectful approach unified people and inspired societal transformation.

Moses and David faced challenges with confidence, calmness, and tact, demonstrating strengths that unified their communities and reshaped societal values.

Contemporary Leaders Demonstrating an Asset-Based Mindset

In today's world, several leaders exemplify an asset-based mindset:

- **Mary Barra, CEO of General Motors**: Barra focuses on building strong relationships with her teams and community, which has driven significant organizational success (Miller, 2023).

- **Southwest Airlines' Leadership**: Southwest Airlines emphasizes a strength-based leadership approach, focusing on employees' positive attributes and fostering a thriving organizational culture. This strategy has resulted in exceptional customer service, high employee engagement, and consistent profitability (Chancy, 2023).

Lessons Learned and Implications for Leaders in an Increasingly Complex World

1. **Balance Hard Work and Well-being:** Leaders must strive for excellence and high performance while maintaining a healthy balance. Safeguarding relationships and taking time to recharge are crucial for preventing burnout and fostering a sustainable leadership approach.

2. **Esteem Others, Especially in Disagreement**: Cultivating a culture that values diverse perspectives and respects differing opinions is critical. This inclusivity fosters collaboration, innovation, and stronger team dynamics.

By adopting an asset-based mindset, leaders can harness their strengths, learn from every experience, and adapt dynamically to an increasingly complex and fast-paced world. This approach equips leaders to inspire growth, resilience, and innovation within their teams and organizations.

GROWTH MINDSET

Carol S. Dweck defines a growth mindset as the ability to embrace challenges, strive for success, value effort, maintain focus, take risks, and foster innovation and creativity (Dweck, 2016). Christensen et al. (2020) describe this mindset as an organic process where individuals grow, evolve, and adapt. People with a growth mindset nurture their intelligence and capabilities, viewing mistakes and failures as opportunities for learning and progress.

How Leaders in the Case Studies Demonstrated a Growth Mindset

The case studies of Abraham, Moses, David, Esther, Daniel, and Paul illustrate a robust growth mindset in action. For instance, Abraham, Moses, and David left familiar surroundings to venture into uncharted territory. They unlearned outdated practices, relearned new approaches, and adapted to emerging challenges. By relinquishing long-held comforts and taking unprecedented risks, they forged new identities and embraced transformative change guided by their faith. Similarly, Esther, Daniel, and Paul underwent complete 360-degree transformations, demonstrating resilience, adaptability, and vision.

These leaders' journeys of continuous learning, adaptation, and foundation-building have had a lasting impact on generations past, present, and future. Despite their humble beginnings, they recognized their purpose, overcame obstacles, and created transformative pathways for their followers. Their enduring leadership continues to inspire and influence change across generations.

Lessons Learned

Contemporary leaders can draw several key lessons from the case study leaders regarding a growth mindset:

1. **Embrace Change and Step Out of Your Comfort Zone**
   Leaders like Abraham, Moses, and David demonstrated that transformative growth often begins when one leaves familiar territory. They willingly let go of long-held practices and beliefs, ventured into uncharted areas, and embraced new challenges. This highlights that authentic leadership requires taking risks and adapting to change.

2. **View Setbacks as Opportunities**

   These leaders treated mistakes and failures not as endpoints but as essential learning experiences. Their willingness to unlearn outdated approaches and relearn new methods underscores the importance of resilience and continuous improvement. Modern leaders can foster a culture in which failures yield valuable insights rather than discouragement.

3. **Pursue Continuous Personal and Professional Transformation**

The case leaders underwent profound transformations, reshaping not only their strategies but also their identities as leaders. This highlights the importance of ongoing self-reflection and personal growth. Today's leaders can benefit from continuously seeking personal development to ensure their leadership adapts to rapidly changing environments.

4. **Cultivate Innovation and Risk-Taking**

Innovation thrives on the ability to take risks and experiment. These historical figures' willingness to explore new ideas, even at significant personal risk, underscores that modern leadership involves balancing bold, innovative strategies with careful deliberation. This mindset promotes more effective decision-making and creative problem-solving in dynamic organizational settings.

5. **Build Enduring Foundations Through Vision and Adaptability**

The legacy of these leaders lies in their ability to lay enduring foundations—establishing principles and cultures that benefit generations. Contemporary leaders can learn to nurture their teams by instilling values of learning, flexibility, and forward thinking, ensuring their organizations are well-equipped to meet future challenges.

Contemporary Examples of a Growth Mindset in Leadership

In modern times, leaders such as Sheryl Sandberg and Satya Nadella exemplified the growth mindset. Sandberg, a prominent figure in the IT industry and advocate for women in the workplace, founded Lean In Circles to empower women to step into leadership roles and challenge gender norms (Risely, 2023). Similarly, Satya Nadella transformed Microsoft by promoting empathy, risk-taking, and continuous learning while emphasizing work-life balance to foster an inclusive and innovative environment (Risely, 2023; Zubair, 2023).

Implications for Purposeful Leadership

Research by Dweck (2016) underscores that leaders with a growth mindset are more likely to achieve their goals. Creating environments where challenges are welcomed, and failures are valuable lessons, leads to significant success (Armstrong, 2019). By adopting and nurturing a growth mindset, leaders can drive personal development while positively impacting their teams and organizations.

By internalizing these lessons, modern leaders can foster organizational transformation, much as the exemplary figures in case studies do.

BELIEVING MINDSET

A firm conviction in positive outcomes and endless possibilities characterizes a believing mindset. Faith gives rise to hope- a hope that satisfies, invigorates, and propels individuals forward. This resilient perspective inspires perseverance even in the face of severe tribulations. The joy and excitement that hope generates kindle passion, fueling the drive to overcome life's challenges and envision endless possibilities even in bleak situations.

A believing mindset is transformative and continually evolves through learning and application. It is adaptive, solution-oriented, and embraces change. Future-focused and open-minded, it encourages the acceptance of uncertainty and ambiguity while embracing new ideas and perspectives. Lessons from the past serve as corrective guides, and the vision of the future anchors our operational base.

How Leaders in the Case Studies Demonstrated a Believing Mindset

Abraham as a Model of Belief

Abraham, described in the Bible as the "father of all who believe" (Romans 4:16, NLT, 2014), exemplified a believing mindset through his faith in God's promises. His belief enabled him to overcome seemingly insurmountable challenges:

- **Faith Amidst Uncertainty:** Abraham left his homeland for an unfamiliar territory based on God's promise, despite not knowing it.

- **Hope Against the Odds:** At 75 years old, God promised Abraham a son. Even as he approached 100, with both he and his wife, Sarah, biologically incapable of bearing children, his belief remained steadfast. Eventually, his faith was rewarded with the birth of Isaac.

- **Unwavering Trust:** When instructed by God to sacrifice Isaac, Abraham obeyed without hesitation, demonstrating absolute trust. On the way to Mount Moriah, when Isaac inquired about the offering, Abraham replied, "God will provide," reflecting his unshakable confidence in God's omnipotence.

Key Lessons from Abraham's Story:

- **Trust and Integrity:** Belief is grounded in trust, credibility, honesty, and truth. It requires transparency, accountability, and responsibility. To demonstrate His commitment, God swore by His Own Name (Hebrews 6:13-18), ensuring that His promise was unbreakable. It is a common practice for contemporary leaders to take oaths upon assuming office, whether by election or appointment, and to make promises. Nevertheless, the challenge is that many of them fail to deliver.

- **Discerning truth from falsehood:** While belief should be rooted in reality, various factors can mislead us. Cognitive biases (Bishwarkarma, R., 2024), the spread of disinformation—especially in the digital age of artificial intelligence (Beauvais, C., 2022)—and the persistence of false beliefs (Ecker et al., 2022) all challenge our ability to tell truth from illusion.

- **Hope as a Driving Force:** Belief fosters hope for a yet-to-be-realized reality, motivating us to pursue future goals that are anchored in our convictions.

- **Transformative Nature of Belief:** Believing is an active process that evolves into a mindset, shaping our attitudes, customs, values, and worldview. Abraham's legacy as the "father of nations" reflects how a transformative belief can guide generations.

Implications for Leadership in an Increasingly Complex Environment

1. **Trust as the Foundation:** Effective leadership is built on a foundation of trust. Followers gravitate toward leaders who are honest, transparent, accountable, impartial, and respectful, qualities that become even more critical in a fluid environment.
2. **Transparency and Accountability:** To earn the trust of followers and establish yourself as a leader, you must act transparently, responsibly, and ethically. For instance, God's promise to Abraham was affirmed with an oath, underscoring His unchanging nature (Hebrews 6:13-18, NLT, 2014).

3. **Inspiration Through Hope:** In high-stress, volatile settings, leaders who project hope and resilience can galvanize their teams and inspire confidence.

4. **Ethical Integrity:** In an era marked by rapid technological advancements, including artificial intelligence, and widespread misinformation, leaders must adhere to robust ethical frameworks and insist on the responsible development and deployment of new technologies.

5. **Standards of Conduct:** Establishing clear behavioral standards enables leaders to act as stewards of responsible governance, shared values, and ethical decision-making.

Contemporary Leaders Demonstrating a Believing Mindset

In today's world, several leaders exemplify a strong believing mindset and have made transformative impacts across various sectors:

- **Malala Yousafzai:** The Pakistani activist for girls' education has demonstrated resilience and an unwavering belief in the power of education. Despite life-threatening opposition, her courage and resolve have inspired millions and made significant progress in girls' education (Bibliography.com, 2023).

- **Angela Merkel:** The former German Chancellor is renowned for her pragmatic, steady leadership. Her commitment to the stability of the European Union, especially during the Eurozone crisis, and her belief in the power of compromise earned her global respect (Petrikowski, 2024).

Conclusion: Fostering Meaningful Relationships

After analyzing the case studies, I concluded that a belief-based mindset nurtures meaningful relationships through deep bonds, empowering effective leadership.

Bonding is a recipe for strong relationships, as individuals come to know each other better over time. This involves acknowledging each other's strengths, weaknesses, opportunities, and the trials they face and overcome together. This process of growth and mutual understanding creates dynamic, vibrant, and long-lasting trusting relationships built on mutual respect.

In such a spirited and cordial environment, followers are often willing to go above and beyond for their leaders. For instance, Abraham immediately obeyed God's command, and God, in turn, faithfully fulfilled His promises, establishing a reciprocal relationship of friendship and trust (Isaiah 41:8; 2 Chronicles 20:7; James 2:2). This friendship was characterized by transparency and accountability, as evidenced by God's willingness to share His plans for Sodom and Gomorrah with Abraham (Genesis 18:19).

In such bonded relationships, followers support their leaders during challenging times. When Moses grew weary, his followers held up his hands to strengthen him and ensure they accomplished their goals together (Exodus 17:12). Similarly, King David's followers stood by him, protected him, and fought for him against Absalom's uprising (2 Samuel 15-18), demonstrating their commitment to their leader and their shared purpose. These examples showcase the sacrifice followers can make when they genuinely believe in their leaders.

Through these examples, strong bonds rooted in mutual trust and transparency empower leaders and followers to overcome challenges and achieve extraordinary outcomes together. By fostering these meaningful relationships, leaders can drive high engagement and commitment from their followers toward the shared cause and goals.

Bonding, as exemplified by Abraham, Moses, and David, is crucial for effective leadership, especially in environments characterized by uncertainty, ambiguity, and volatility. This timeless and universal principle is relevant and much needed today, helping leaders navigate the challenges they face with wisdom.

INTUITIVE MIND

Often described as a hunch or gut instinct, **intuitive thinking is an unconscious** process that provides clarity and solutions to complex issues. When thinking is involuntary, the conscious mind lays the groundwork, and natural inspiration strikes. This brilliant insight often resolves the issue at hand. Intuition involves contemplation, reflection, meditation, musing, and curiosity, which activate the intuitive mind.

The Bible provides several examples of intuitive thinking. Passages such as Romans 2:14-15, Proverbs 2:6-15, and Job 38:36-41 illustrate the wisdom and understanding that emanate from the heart and mind (BibleGateway, n.d.). In 1 Kings 4:29, it is noted that God gave Solomon "wisdom and very great insight and breadth of understanding as measureless as the sand on the seashore" (BibleGateway, n.d.).

How Leaders in Case Studies Demonstrate an Intuitive Mindset – Insights from Abraham

A key question arises: How did Abraham come to believe God's promise that he would have a son, given his struggle to understand it logically? Genesis 15:1–6 offers insight into this process. When God led Abraham outside, He showed him the stars in the sky and challenged him to count them.

To affirm His promise, God declared that Abraham's descendants would be as numerous as the stars. Witnessing this, Abraham believed. His response suggests that imagination played a central role; by visualizing the vast numbers in a clear mental vision, he was persuaded that the promise, though not yet fulfilled, was real.

Abraham's experience can be broken down into several key points:

- His initial questioning may have indicated either disbelief or curiosity; nonetheless, his transition to belief illustrates the power of imagination and visualization (Koenig, 2013).

- He demonstrated a willingness to listen to and be guided by divine counsel—a communication accessible only through an intuitive, spiritual mind.

- The stars served as a symbolic reminder of God's promise, continually reaffirming its future fulfillment; this symbolism bridged the gap between intuition and logic.

- Counting the stars engaged Abraham's mind to envision reality beyond his present circumstances and the fulfillment of the promise yet to come (Koenig, 2013).

- Ultimately, his leap of faith underscores how an intuitive mindset can resolve complex and seemingly insurmountable issues.

Implications for Leadership in an Environment of Uncertainty and Complexity

Abraham's experience parallels modern leadership practices in several significant ways:

1. **Vision Casting:** Just as Abraham visualized his future descendants through the stars, contemporary leaders use visualization techniques to create compelling visions and align their teams toward common goals (Adigwa, 2024).

2. **Navigating Uncertainty:** Abraham's ability to embrace a future he could not fully comprehend mirrors how modern leaders manage unpredictable and volatile environments (Hendrickson, 2024).

3. **Intuitive Decision-Making:** His decision to trust in God's promise—spurred by the visualization of the stars—reflects how leaders often integrate intuitive insights with analytical data when making critical decisions (Koenig, 2013).

4. **Symbolic Communication:** Abraham's narrative employs stars symbolically, much like contemporary leaders use metaphors and symbols to convey complex ideas effectively (Varghese, 2024).

Contemporary Leaders Demonstrating an Intuitive Mindset

Modern examples of intuitive leadership are evident across various sectors. **Steve Jobs**, co-founder of Apple Inc., was renowned for his unwavering, intuitive belief in his vision, even in the face of skepticism. His conviction in technology's transformative power fueled innovations that revolutionized multiple industries (Isaacson, 2011).

Similarly, **Nelson Mandela** maintained a steadfast intuitive belief in the power of reconciliation and unity—an outlook that was instrumental in ending apartheid in South Africa despite 27 years of incarceration (Mandela, 1994).

Conclusion

Abraham's response to God's promise in Genesis 15:1–6 exemplifies an intuitive leadership mindset. Through visualization, imagination, and faith, he transcended the limits of logic to embrace a divine promise. This biblical account resonates with contemporary leadership theories, which emphasize the importance of intuition, visualization, and symbolic communication in effective decision-making and vision casting.

References

Adigwa, C. (2024). Transformational leadership: A comparative exploration of the leadership prowess of Jeff Bezos and Steve Jobs. *Asian Journal of Economics, Business and Accounting, 24*(3), 68–89.

https://doi.org/10.9734/ajeba/2024/v24i31242

Armstrong, K. (2019). Carol Dweck on How Growth Mindsets Can Bear Fruits in the Classroom. Retrieved from

https://www.psychologicalscience.org/observer/dweck -growth-mindsets

Bible, Genesis 15:6. "Abraham believed the Lord, and he credited it to him as righteousness." Source: BibleGateway.com.

Bible.com. (2025). Numbers 11:13-15. Retrieved from

https://www.bible.com

BibleGateway. (n.d.-a). Romans 2:14 15; Proverbs 2:6 15; Job 38:36 41. Retrieved from https://www.biblegateway.com

BibleGateway. (n.d.-b). 1 Kings 4:29. "God gave Solomon wisdom and very great insight and breadth of understanding as measureless as the sand on the seashore." Retrieved from

https://www.biblegateway.com

Beauvais, C. (2022). Fake news: Why do we believe it? *Joint Bone Spine, 89*(4), 105371. doi: 10.1016/j.jbspin.2022.105371

Bishwarkarma, R. (2024). The Science of Formation. Retrieved from

https://medium.com/@rbishwak/the-science-of-belief-formation-5957748796e3

Chancy, S. (2023). The Power of Strength-Based Leadership. Retrieved from

https://ascenditur.no/blog/2023/03/04/the-power-of-strength-based-leadership/

Christensen, L., et al. (2020a). The Innovative Leader: How to Inspire and Drive Change.

Christensen, L., et al. (2020b). The most fundamental skill: Intentional learning and the career advantage. *McKinsey Quarterly.*

Cramer, K. C. (2006). Change the Way You See Everything Through Asset-Based Thinking. Running Press. Philadelphia.

Dweck, C. (2016). MINDSET: The New Psychology of Success. Ballantine Books.

Ecker, U.K.H., Lewandowsky, S., Cook, J., et al. (2022). The psychological drivers of misinformation belief and its resistance to correction. *Nature Reviews Psychology, 1*, 13–29.

https://doi.org/10.1038/s44159-021-00006-y

Hendrickson, J. (2024). Lerner's Dustin Sleesman's latest research explores when leaders use intuition. University of Delaware Lerner College of Business & Economics. Retrieved from

https://lerner.udel.edu/seeing-opportunity/lerners-dustin-sleesmans-latest-research-reveals-introverted-leaders-thrive-on-information

Isaacson, W. (2011). Steve Jobs. Simon & Schuster.

Koenig, S. M. (2013). Commentary on Genesis 15:1–6. Working Preacher. Retrieved from

https://www.workingpreacher.org/commentaries/revised-common-lectionary/ordinary-19-3/commentary-on-genesis-151-6-5#:~:text

Mandela, N. (1994). Long walk to freedom. Little, Brown and Company.

Manoharan, S.K. (2024). "Curiosity" _ A Crucial Quality of a Leader. Retrieved from

https://www.linkedin.com/pulse/curiosity-crucial-quality-leader-manoharan-mba-d-lit-#:

Miller, H. L. (2023). Strength-Based Leadership: How to Optimize Your Team's Abilities. Retrieved from

https://leaders.com/articles/leadership/strengths-based-leadership/

Petrikowski, N. P. (2024, August 19). Angela Merkel. Encyclopedia Britannica. Retrieved from Britannica

Risely. (2023). Unlocking Success: 5 Examples of Growth Mindset for Leaders. Retrieved from

https://www.risely.me/power-of-a-growth-mindset-for-leaders-unlocking/#:~:text=She%20encourages%20women

Runday.ai. (2024). The Legacy of Steve Jobs: Secrets to Success. Retrieved from

https://medium.com/@mediarunday.ai/the-legacy-of-steve-jobs-secrets-to-success-

Tyndale. (2014). New Living Translation Bible. Tyndale Publishing House.

Varghese, S. P. (2024). The power of visualization: How leaders and entrepreneurs use mental imagery for long-term success. LinkedIn Pulse. Retrieved from

https://www.linkedin.com/pulse/power-visualization-how-leaders-entrepreneurs-use-varghese-pudussery-bhfqc#:

Zubair, M. (2023). Inspiring examples of leadership in the workplace. Retrieved from

https://www.togetherplatform.com/blog/inspiring-leadership-examples#:~

CHAPTER 16: NAVIGATING THE MOTIVATIONAL LANDSCAPE OF LEADERSHIP

This chapter explores the questions: "What emotions did the leaders in the case studies struggle with?" How did they address those emotions? What lessons can contemporary leaders learn to navigate the increasingly complex environment?"

David, one of the leaders in the case studies, exemplifies the most effective way to tackle emotional challenges, serving as a compelling model for modern leadership.

David and Emotional Leadership

The biblical account of David's journey provides valuable insights into emotional leadership. His experiences with failure, betrayal, fear, and empathy are timeless lessons for leaders today.

Emotions: Confronting Failure with Humility

David's response to his moral lapse—his affair with Bathsheba and the subsequent confrontation by the prophet Nathan—demonstrates the importance of acknowledging mistakes and seeking renewal. In *Psalm 51*, David openly expresses remorse and asks for forgiveness.

Key Point: Leaders who engage in honest self-reflection, admit their mistakes, and accept corrective feedback foster personal growth, build character, and earn the trust of those they lead.

Betrayal: Navigating the Pain of Disloyalty

David faced betrayal on multiple fronts. The Ziphites disclosed his location to King Saul (1 Samuel 23), and later, betrayal by a close friend is mourned in *Psalm 55:12-14*. Despite the pain and indignation—including deep lament over human evil—David's experiences ultimately reinforced his trust in God.

Lesson: Although betrayal is a painful reality, processing such experiences constructively can build resilience and encourage reliance on core values or a higher purpose, even during challenging times.

Fear: Leading in the Face of Danger

While fleeing King Saul—a threat that led him to seek refuge in wilderness strongholds, hills, and caves—David experienced profound fear. Although he sometimes felt abandoned (as expressed in Psalms 13 and 55), he consistently sought strength and wisdom through his faith and in trusted relationships—most notably with his covenant friend Jonathan (1 Samuel 23).

In *Psalm 55:4–6* (King James Version, 2013), David poignantly states: "Fearfulness and trembling have come upon me, and horrors of death have fallen upon me... Oh, that I had wings like a dove! I would fly away and be at rest."

Key Takeaway: By confronting fear head-on, David built the resilience necessary to lead effectively, extending empathy and hope to his team during adverse times.

Empathy: Building Strong Communities

David's empathy is evident in his decisions, which focus on the well-being of his followers. Instead of punishing those who were too exhausted to fight, he ordered a fair distribution of resources between the combatants and those guarding the supplies (1 Samuel 30:23–25, New Living Translation). As Bondurant (n.d.) notes in his article, Walk Through 1 Samuel 30, David's leadership style fostered unity and reinforced the importance of each team member.

Lesson: Leaders who actively listen to and address their teams' needs foster inclusivity and build strong, supportive communities that can effectively navigate adversity.

Lessons from David's Emotional Leadership Journey for Contemporary Leaders

David's emotional journey offers several key takeaways that are highly relevant for modern leadership:

1. **Embracing Vulnerability and Accountability**

     o **Example:** David's honest confession and request for forgiveness in *Psalm 51.*

     o **Application:** Recognizing and owning mistakes builds trust and credibility, while vulnerability promotes authenticity in leadership.

2. **Building Emotional Resilience**

     o **Example:** David's perseverance in the face of King Saul's relentless pursuit (1 Samuel 23).

     o **Application:** In high-pressure environments, leaders must cultivate resilience through mindfulness, reflective journaling, and seeking counsel to remain calm and focused during times of crisis.

3. **Navigating Betrayal with Grace**

- o **Example:** David's composed response to betrayal, as reflected in the lamentations of *Psalm 55*.

- o **Application:** Leaders can transform the pain of betrayal into a reaffirmation of their core values and mission, sustaining organizational trust even in challenging times.

4. **Leading with Empathy and Compassion**

- o **Example:** David's equitable resource distribution, which recognized the contributions of all followers (1 Samuel 30:23–25, NLT).

- o **Application:** Empathetic leadership fosters loyalty, inclusivity, and strong team unity—qualities essential for navigating diverse and complex work environments.

5. **Balancing Reflection with Action**

- o **Example:** David's reflective practices that informed his decisions during moments of fear and uncertainty.

- o **Application:** Regular reflection—through methods such as coaching sessions, journaling, or soliciting feedback—ensures that leaders align their actions with their values and long-term vision.

6. **Fostering Team Unity and Shared Purpose**

- o **Example:** David's commitment to ensuring that every team member felt valued, even in the face of adversity (1 Samuel 30).

- o **Application:** Creating a shared sense of purpose and fostering equitable practices fosters cohesion, enabling teams to perform effectively under pressure.

7. **Relying on Trusted Relationships**

- o **Example:** David's deep bond with Jonathan encouraged him during his most challenging times (1 Samuel 23).

- o **Application:** Leaders should cultivate strong relationships with mentors, peers, or trusted advisors to gain perspective, receive honest feedback, and maintain emotional resilience.

Contemporary Leaders Who Exemplified Emotional Intelligence in Leadership

Howard Schultz, former CEO of Starbucks, faced significant challenges during the 2008 financial crisis. By prioritizing employee welfare and maintaining open communication, he transformed Starbucks into a globally recognized brand, demonstrating how emotional intelligence can lead to organizational success (Anonymous, n.d.).

Another example is Indra Nooyi, the former CEO of PepsiCo, who navigated the company through a significant transformation by embracing change and prioritizing sustainability. Her ability to connect emotionally with her team and stakeholders allowed her to turn challenges into opportunities, ultimately enhancing PepsiCo's performance (Shindler, 2021).

By understanding and effectively managing the emotional landscape, leaders can achieve greater resilience and effectiveness in navigating the path of purposeful leadership.

Conclusion

David's leadership journey underscores the importance of emotional intelligence, resilience, empathy, and reflection in navigating complex situations. As the examples of contemporary leaders illustrate, today's rapidly evolving world presents challenges that require not only technical skills but also emotional agility. By embracing vulnerability, practicing empathy, and cultivating resilience, leaders can effectively guide their teams and organizations through uncertainty, ensuring success both today and in the future.

References

Anonymous. (n.d.). Chapter 14: Management: A practical introduction. Retrieved from

https://www.studocu.com/en-us/document/university-of-florida/prins-of-management/chapter-14-management-a-practical-introduction/56037229

Bondurant, A. (n.d.). *Walk through 1 Samuel 30*. King James Version Study Bible (2013). Shindler, J. (2021). Leader personal reflection, vision creation, and growth pathway development: Chapter 14 from *Transformational leaders roadmap*. Retrieved from

https://www.academia.edu/10272206/Leader_Personal_Reflection_Vision_Creation_and_Growth_Pathway_Development_Ch_14_from_Transformative_Leaders_Roadmap

CHAPTER 17: NAVIGATING THE MOTIVATIONAL LANDSCAPE OF LEADERSHIP

This section examines the question, "What motivated the leaders in the case studies to achieve significant milestones in history?" By analyzing the driving forces behind leaders' actions in biblical narratives, we can uncover the universal and timeless motivations that fuel purposeful leadership across different eras and contexts. In essence, the discussion explores how motivation is modulated and how cultivating healthy motivational ecosystems can sustain our drive.

FAITH AND HOPE: CATALYSTS FOR LEADERSHIP

The Example of Abraham

What motivated Abraham to wait 25 years for the fulfillment of the promise? **Faith**, coupled with **hope**, was his driving force. His belief that he would indeed have a son fueled his hope—an expectation that served as a constant reminder to Abraham that the promise was forthcoming (Holy Bible, New International Version, 2011). This persistent hope encouraged him to "hang on" despite the long wait.

We can examine this from a broader perspective. Faith enables us to perceive an idea not as an abstract concept but as a tangible reality. The more one thinks, visualizes, or contemplates the desired outcome, the clearer and more concrete it becomes in the mind (Sinek, 2009). This mental clarity, in turn, inspires hope—an enduring expectation that bridges the gap between the present and the envisioned future. As long as hope endures, the envisioned goal becomes increasingly attainable. This process is analogous to an architectural drawing displayed on a billboard with the bold declaration, **"Coming Soon."** In this way, faith and hope work together to motivate both leaders and individuals.

Other Biblical Leaders: Faith and Hope in Action

The interplay of faith and hope is evident in the lives of several other biblical leaders:

- **Moses** led the Israelites through the wilderness for 40 years, driven by faith in God's promise of deliverance and hope for the Promised Land (Bible).

- **David**, although anointed as king, endured years as a fugitive fleeing for his life until King Saul's death. His faith in God's plan sustained him (Bible).

- **Daniel** defied the dangers of the lions' den, motivated by faith in God's protection and hope for justice (Bible).

- **Esther** risked her life to approach the king, driven by faith in her purpose and a hope for the salvation of her people (Bible).

- **Paul**, as an apostle, faced countless trials and upheavals, driven by faith in his mission and hope for spreading the Gospel (Bible).

The Role of Faith and Hope in Leadership

Faith and hope empower leaders to learn, adapt, and cultivate a forward-looking mindset. By steadfastly anticipating positive outcomes, leaders create an environment of resilience and growth—vital qualities in an ever-changing world.

The Role of Faith and Hope as Drivers for Purposeful Leadership in Today's Environments

In today's complex and dynamic landscape, faith and hope remain as relevant as ever. Like sailors navigating tumultuous seas, contemporary leaders require these qualities to steer their organizations toward success, adaptation, and growth. Faith and hope provide the motivational foundation that enables leaders to face challenges head-on and inspire their teams toward a shared vision of the future.

Conclusion

Faith and hope are timeless motivators of purposeful leadership. They offer clarity, endurance, and the strength to persevere through challenges. Biblical leaders like Abraham, Moses, David, Daniel, Esther, and Paul exemplify these qualities, demonstrating the ongoing importance of these principles in achieving significant milestones throughout history (Kouzes & Posner, 2017).

APPRECIATION AND THANKSGIVING: LEADERSHIP MOTIVATORS

Two prominent biblical leaders, **Paul** and **David**, exemplify leadership characterized by appreciation and gratitude.

- **Paul** customarily began his epistles with salutations, concluded them with affirmations, and consistently expressed heartfelt gratitude. He recognized individuals by name and acknowledged their specific contributions to the fellowship and ministry.

- **David** demonstrated gratitude by sending gifts to his followers and rewarding their contributions. In doing so, he built strong bonds within his community and motivated his followers to exceed their call of duty.

These practices illustrate that appreciation and thanksgiving are essential for:

- **Valuing others,**

- **Esteeming their unique contributions,** and

- **Believing in their ideas and efforts.**

Such recognition is critical to enhancing team performance and overall organizational success.

EMPATHY: A DRIVER OF LEADERSHIP

Every leader in the case studies exhibited empathy through their actions:

- **Abraham** interceded for Sodom and Gomorrah in the hope of protecting his nephew, Lot.

- **Moses** repeatedly interceded for the Israelites whenever they faced hardships.

- **Paul** advocated for his fellow Jews (see Romans 9).

- **Esther** intervened to save her people from Haman's genocidal plot.

- **Daniel** championed the interests of his people when they were on the verge of returning from captivity.

Empathy in leadership is crucial because it:

- **Helps leaders tune into their followers' emotions and challenges,**

- **Builds trust,** as followers recognize that their leader is aligned with their struggles.

- **Enhance self- and social awareness,** sharpening a leader's judgment and decision-making skills (McKee A. et al., 2008; Northouse, 2019).

PURPOSE: A LEADERSHIP CATALYST

A sense of purpose strongly drove the leaders in the case studies. **Purpose** serves as a significant motivator when leaders:

- **Discover, Embrace, and Internalize a Clear Sense of Purpose:** They transform this purpose into core values that shape their behavior and inform their decision-making.

- **Believe in a Higher Cause or Calling:** They are motivated by an idea or mission that is more significant than themselves.

A purposeful approach not only provides personal direction but also helps followers find meaning, satisfaction, and self-actualization in their work. Purpose-driven leaders weave these values into the fabric of their organizations by aligning systems, culture, and operations with a shared vision, reinforcing the organizational identity.

Purposeful leaders exhibit a deep commitment to their mission. They possess a clear understanding of why they do what they do, and this clarity of purpose drives every action they take. **Purpose** is a powerful source of motivation and a leading cause of perseverance (Kouzes & Posner, 2017). Individuals who excel in their work or personal lives and overcome formidable challenges are often internally motivated and intrinsically engaged. Kouzes and Posner (2017) note that passionate and purposeful leadership is especially vital during times of high uncertainty, as people seek direction and guidance amid risk and complexity.

CARROT AND STICK: LEADERSHIP MOTIVATORS

In The Carrot Principle, Gostick and Elton (2009) illustrate that effective managers use recognition—not merely extrinsic rewards, such as salary or bonuses—to engage their people, retain talent, and enhance performance. Their research underscores that praise and recognition are powerful motivators in modern organizations.

This insight can be paralleled with the biblical narrative of **Moses** and the journey to the Promised Land, which involved both reward and discipline:

- **Reward (Carrot):** The promise of a land "flowing with milk and honey" initially motivated the Israelites to leave Egypt with great enthusiasm.

- **Punishment (Stick):** As challenges arose—such as the Red Sea crossing, the threat of Pharaoh's army, water shortages, and the monotony of manna—motivation waned. In these instances, Moses continually reassured the people about the eventual rewards while mediating divine discipline.

Insights from Moses's experience include:

- **The accumulation of pressure:** Prolonged delays in realizing the promised reward can lead to mounting frustration and diminished hope.

- **Leadership challenges:** An overwhelming buildup of pressure may cause leaders to react impulsively rather than act proactively.

- **Transactional limitations:** A strict "carrot and stick" approach may encourage followers to view rewards as bargaining chips, complicating objective leadership.

- **Potential for victimization:** Followers might adopt a victim mentality to undermine leadership efforts.

- **The need for adaptive leadership:** Effective leaders, like Moses, evolve by delegating responsibilities and transforming from an authoritative figure to an empathetic, humble servant leader.

Implications for Purposeful Leadership in Complex Environments

In contemporary high-pressure, uncertain, and complex settings, leaders can draw valuable lessons from these biblical examples. Balancing rewards with constructive discipline, integrating empathy with purpose, and fostering a culture of recognition remain essential. Leaders who adopt these strategies are better equipped to inspire their followers, maintain morale during challenging times, and succeed in dynamic organizational environments.

PASSION: A DRIVING FORCE FOR LEADERSHIP

I explore passion as a leadership motivator last because it is a basket that carries the other motivators discussed earlier. Faith and hope, appreciation and thanksgiving, empathy, purpose, carrot-and-stick are catalysts for fully firing up motivation. Passion is a strong emotion that can be overpowering or compelling. It suggests a constant glow of feelings, such as excitement, enthusiasm, a restless, flame-like emotion, or an eagerness to pursue something (Webster's New World College Dictionary, 2008).

Passion, a restless, flame-like emotion, is a catalyst that ignites and drives faith, hope, appreciation, thanksgiving, empathy, purpose, and motivation. A passionate leader is relentless in pursuing their purpose and overflows with appreciation, thanksgiving, empathy, and a desire to reward others.

From the foregoing, I describe passion as a gauge of sentiment. Sentiment is a term extensively used by investors and traders. It refers to the overall attitude or sentiment market participants have toward a particular security, market, or economy—bullish (positive), bearish (negative), or neutral. Sentiment is critical because it influences market prices and trends, gauging the market's mood through indicators such as news articles, social media, trading volumes, and price movements (Microsoft Copilot, 2025). Likewise, passion can be a valuable indicator of leadership motivation at positive, negative, or neutral levels.

The leaders in the case studies—Abraham, Moses, David, Esther, Daniel, and Paul—demonstrated passionate leadership. They would not have relentlessly pursued their higher callings if they had not been passionate about them.

Below is a visual representation of passion as a tool to indicate positive, negative, or neutral levels of leadership motivation, drawing parallels with market sentiment indicators.

Passion as a Sentiment Gauge

```
+-------------------------------------------------+
|                  Passion Gauge                  |
+-------------------------------------------------+
|                                                 |
|          Positive Passion (Bullish)             |
|    High energy & enthusiasm                     |
|    Strong commitment                            |
|    Inspires and motivates teams                 |
|    → High Performance                           |
|                                                 |
+-------------------------------------------------+
|                                                 |
|              Neutral Passion                    |
|    Moderate engagement                          |
|    Steady performance                           |
|    Predictable results                          |
|    → Average Performance                        |
|                                                 |
+-------------------------------------------------+
|                                                 |
|          Negative Passion (Bearish)             |
|    Low energy & disengagement                   |
|    Passive behavior                             |
|    Decreased morale                             |
|    → Reduced Productivity                       |
|                                                 |
+-------------------------------------------------+
```

1. **Positive Passion (Highly Passionate):**

   o Represents high energy and enthusiasm in leadership.

   o Indicates strong commitment and the ability to inspire and motivate teams.

   o Leads to high performance in teams and organizations.

   o Positive passion in leadership is associated with transformational leadership styles. Leaders exhibiting positive passion are more likely to inspire and motivate their teams, resulting in higher employee engagement and overall organizational performance (Li, J. et al., 2017). This aligns with research showing that passionate leaders can create a favorable emotional climate that fosters enthusiasm and commitment among team members (Khan H. et al., 2020).

2. **Neutral Passion:**

   o Reflects moderate engagement and steady performance.

   o Characterized by predictable results, with neither significant highs nor lows.

   o Results in average performance among team members.

   o Neutral passion in leadership maintains a steady state within the organization. While these leaders may not inspire extraordinary outcomes, they provide consistency and reliability. This level of passion can lead to stable performance and moderate engagement among team members (Taggar S. et al., 2024).

3. **Negative Passion (Bearish)**:

- o Shows low energy and disengagement from leadership.

- o Leads to passive behavior and decreased morale within teams.

- o Generally, it results in reduced productivity and potential turnover.

- o Negative passion or a lack of enthusiasm in leadership can harm team motivation and organizational performance. Leaders displaying negative passion may create a toxic work environment, resulting in decreased employee engagement, lower job satisfaction, and reduced performance (Diao H. et al., 2019; Yin J. et al., 2022).

This graphic illustrates how passion can serve as a sentiment gauge in leadership, much like market sentiment influences investor behavior. This comparison highlights that leadership passion, like market sentiment, is a crucial indicator of an organization's overall emotional climate. Just as market sentiment influences prices and trends, leadership passion significantly impacts an organization's climate and performance.

By assessing passion levels, organizations can gain a deeper understanding of the emotional dynamics within their leadership and their impact on team motivation and performance.

Implications and Applications

1. **Leadership Development**: Organizations can use this framework to assess and develop leadership passion. By identifying leaders' current passion levels, targeted interventions can be designed to move towards more positive passion states.

2. **Organizational Climate Assessment**: The framework can be part of broader organizational climate assessments, helping to understand how leadership passion influences team dynamics and overall performance.

3. **Performance Prediction**: Like market sentiment indicators that predict market trends, leadership passion levels could be used to predict future organizational performance.

4. **Team Alignment**: Understanding leadership passion levels can help align team members with leaders who can best inspire and motivate them, potentially improving team performance.

5. **Intervention Strategies**: For leaders identified as having neutral or negative passion, specific intervention strategies can be developed to help shift towards more positive passion states, potentially including emotional intelligence training, coaching, or leadership development programs (Psico-smart Editorial Team, 2024).

In conclusion, this comprehensive framework provides a structured approach to understanding and evaluating leadership passion levels and their impact on organizational effectiveness. Drawing parallels with market sentiment indicators provides a fresh perspective on how leadership passion can be viewed as a crucial indicator of organizational health and future performance potential. This framework serves as a valuable tool for leadership development, organizational assessment, and strategic human resource management.

MODERATING MOTIVATION AND NURTURING HEALTHY ECOSYSTEMS

Emotions as Catalysts for Leadership Motivation

Emotions serve as internal sources of motivation, driving individuals to achieve their goals and inspiring others. In Chapter 4, which addresses the heart dimensions of leadership, we learned that emotions significantly influence the physiological processes involved in energy regulation. Specific chemical substances and hormones play a moderating role in shaping these emotional and motivational behaviors.

Adenosine Triphosphate (ATP)

ATP, often referred to as the "energy currency" of the cell, is produced and distributed throughout the body by the heart (Dunn et al., 2023). Although the processes governing ATP production, distribution, and maintenance are complex, the mitochondrial membrane in the heart functions as an autoregulator, balancing ATP supply and demand (Xinhua et al., 2017). Research suggests that each cardiac cell contains between 5,000 and 8,000 mitochondria, collectively producing approximately 6 kg of ATP per day in the human heart (Xinhua et al., 2017).

Key factors affecting ATP synthesis in cardiac cells include:

- **Substrate Availability:** Fatty acids, glucose, lactate, and ketone bodies serve as primary substrates. In the adult human heart, fatty acids contribute 70–90% of ATP synthesis, while the oxidation of glucose, lactate, ketone bodies, and amino acids accounts for the remaining 10–30% (Doenst et al., 2013).

- **Other Influences:** Hormonal regulation, cardiac workload, oxygen availability, and overall mitochondrial function also play crucial roles.

Hormonal Regulation of Emotions and Motivational Behavior

Atrial natriuretic peptide (ANP) hormones trigger emotions that influence our motivation and behavior. Elevated levels of ANP can reduce anxiety and prevent panic attacks by inhibiting the release of stress hormones, thereby promoting a calmer emotional state (HeartMath Institute, 2024; Wiedemann et al., 2000; Hodes & Lichtstein, 2014).

Oxytocin, a hormone integral to social bonding, emotional regulation, and stress response, interacts with the brain's reward system. By modulating dopamine release, oxytocin enhances the perceived reward of social interactions, suggesting a significant role in motivational processes (Hanson et al., 2021). Additionally, oxytocin influences neural regions such as the amygdala and prefrontal cortex to reduce stress and foster positive social interactions, further reinforcing social cohesion and trust (Zhylin et al., 2024; Quintana et al., 2013).

Cultivating Healthy Motivational Ecosystems

Maintaining adequate ATP levels—and, by extension, a vibrant motivational state—requires a multifaceted approach. Essential strategies include:

Lifestyle Factors
Sleep Optimization

Research has demonstrated that healthy sleep is crucial for ATP production and maintenance. For example, Hu et al. (2024) found that sleep deprivation triggers mitochondrial dysfunction and neural inflammation, leading to cognitive impairments. Similar conclusions are suggested by Mauri et al. (2022). Ensuring 7–9 hours of quality sleep per night is therefore essential.

Stress Management

Chronic stress can diminish cellular energy production and alter mitochondrial structure (Picard & McEwen, 2018). Techniques such as meditation, deep breathing exercises, yoga, regular physical activity, and professional support can help mitigate these adverse effects.

Dietary Strategies

A balanced diet that meets individual nutritional needs, including adequate carbohydrates, proper hydration, and essential nutrients, supports robust ATP production and overall cellular health.

Medical and Supplementation Considerations

Personalized medical advice and supplementation tailored to an individual's health status can further support maintaining healthy energy levels.

Spiritual Dimension

Exploring the modulation of motivation and cultivating healthy motivational ecosystems reveals a profound spiritual dimension. This perspective emphasizes:

Biblical Teachings

Principles of love, forgiveness, rejoicing, thanksgiving, faith, hope, and acknowledging worry and anxiety underscore the spiritual foundation of a healthy motivational ecosystem.

Purposeful Leadership Insights

The case studies presented in Part 4 of the book highlight how spiritual values underpin purposeful leadership.

Inner Source of Leadership

Ultimately, purposeful leadership originates from the depths of the heart. Embracing this inner source allows leadership to radiate outward, fostering a culture rich in love and compassion.

Implications for Purposeful Leadership in High-Pressure Settings

In today's high-pressure, uncertain, and complex environments, leaders must regulate their emotions to stay aligned with their personal purpose and organizational goals. By managing their emotional states effectively and fostering robust motivational ecosystems, leaders can maintain clarity and resilience and inspire confidence even under challenging conditions. This holistic approach enables leaders to navigate uncertainty through empathy and strategic foresight, promoting a culture of sustained energy and positive behavior.

<h1 style="text-align:center">References</h1>

Diao, H., Song, L. J., Wang, Y., & Zhong, J. (2019). Being passionate to perform: The joint effect of leader humility and follower humility. *Frontiers in Psychology, 10*, 1059.

https://doi.org/10.3389/fpsyg.2019.01059

Doenst, T., Nguyen, T. D., & Abel, E. D. (2013). Cardiac metabolism in heart failure: Implications beyond ATP production. *Circulation Research, 113*(6), 709–724.

Dunn, J., & Grider, M. H. (2023). Physiology, adenosine triphosphate. In *StatPearls [Internet]*. Treasure Island, FL: StatPearls Publishing.

Gostick, A., & Elton, C. (2009). The Carrot Principle: How the best managers use recognition to engage their people, retain talent, and accelerate performance. McGraw-Hill.

Hanson, J. L., Williams, A. V., Bangasser, D. A., & Peña, C. J. (2021). Impact of early life stress on reward circuit function and regulation. *Frontiers in Psychiatry, 12*, 744690.

HeartMath Institute. (2024). Chapter 01: Heart-brain communication. Retrieved from

https://www.heartmath.org/research/science-of-the-heart/heart-brain-communication/#:~

Hodes, A., & Lichtstein, D. (2014). Natriuretic hormones in brain function. *Frontiers in Endocrinology, 5*, 118213.

Holy Bible, New International Version. (2011). Zondervan.

Hu, Y., et al. (2024). Sleep deprivation triggers mitochondrial DNA release in microglia to induce neural inflammation: Preventative effect of hydroxytyrosol butyrate. *Antioxidants, 13*(7), 833.

Khan, H., Rehmat, M., Butt, T. H., et al. (2020). Impact of transformational leadership on work performance, burnout and social loafing: A mediation model. *Futur Bus J, 6*, 40.

https://doi.org/10.1186/s43093-020-00043-8

Kouzes, J. M., & Posner, B. Z. (2017). The leadership challenge: How to make extraordinary things happen in organizations (6th ed.). Jossey-Bass.

Li, J., Zhang, J., & Yang, Z. (2017). Associations between a leader's work passion and an employee's work passion: A moderated mediation model. *Frontiers in Psychology, 8*, 1447.

https://doi.org/10.3389/fpsyg.2017.01447

Mauri, S., et al. (2022). Mitochondrial autophagy in the sleeping brain. *Frontiers in Cell and Developmental Biology, 10*, 956394.

McKee, A., et al. (2008). Becoming a RESONANT LEADER. Harvard Business Press.

Northouse, P. G. (2019). Leadership: Theory and practice (8th ed.). Sage.

Picard, M., & McEwen, B. S. (2018). Psychological stress and mitochondria: A systematic review. *Psychosomatic Medicine, 80*(2), 141–153.

Psico-smart Editorial Team. (2024). What are the most effective psychometric tools for measuring emotional intelligence in the workplace? Retrieved from https://psico-smart.com/en/blogs/blog-what-are-the-most-effective-psychometric-tools-for-measuring-emotional-intelligence-in-the-workplace-104134#:~:text

Quintana, D. S., Kemp, A. H., Alvares, G. A., & Guastella, A. J. (2013). A role for autonomic cardiac control in the effects of oxytocin on social behavior and psychiatric illness. *Journal of Neuroendocrine Science, 7.*

https://doi.org/10.3389/fnins.2013.00048

Simon Taggar, A., Domurath, A., & Coviello, N. (2024). Peer effects on passion levels, passion trajectories, and outcomes for individuals and teams. *Journal of Business Venturing, 39*(4), 106405.

https://doi.org/10.1016/j.jbusvent.2024.106405

Sinek, S. (2009). Start with why: How great leaders inspire everyone to take action. Portfolio.

Tahir, S. (2020). Organizational performance: What it is and how to measure and improve it. Retrieved from

https://www.ckju.net/en/organizational-performance-what-it-is-how-to-measure-and-improve-it#:~:text

Wang, X., Zhang, X., Wu, D., Huang, Z., Hou, T., Jian, C., Yu, P., Lu, F., Zhang, R., & Cheng, H. (2017). Mitochondrial flashes regulate ATP homeostasis in the heart. *eLife, 6,* e23908.

Webster's New World. (2008). Webster's New World College Dictionary (4th ed.). Wiley Publishing, Inc.

Wiedemann, K., Jahn, H., & Kellner, M. (2000). Effects of natriuretic peptides upon hypothalamo-pituitary-adrenocortical system activity and anxiety behavior. *Experimental and Clinical Endocrinology & Diabetes, 108*(1), 5–13.

https://doi.org/10.1055/s-0032-1329209

Yin, J., Qu, M., Liao, G., Jia, M., & Li, M. (2022). Exploring the relationships between team leader's conflict management styles and team passion: From the emotional perspective. *Frontiers in Psychology, 13*, 921300.

Zhylin, M., et al. (2024). Genetic basis of emotional regulation: Integrative analysis of behavioral and neurobiological data. *OBM Neurobiology, 8*(4).

PART 5: UNRAVELING THE PRINCIPLES OF PURPOSEFUL LEADERSHIP

In Part 5, we explore the principles of purposeful leadership by drawing from the rich biblical narratives highlighted in our case studies. We shed light on these timeless principles and their practical applications, empowering leaders to build profound connections with their teams and inspire meaningful change. This journey leads to self-discovery, learning, growth, and transformation.

We focus on the following in each chapter of the leadership principles:

- **Core Principles of Purposeful Leadership**

We define the foundational principles of purposeful leadership, exploring their transformative impact on leaders and organizations. In today's evolving leadership landscape, the traditional model of the all-knowing hero leader is no longer sufficient (Joly H., 2022).

- **Actionable Leadership Framework**: We present an actionable leadership framework that practically applies these principles, detailing the transformational journey of leaders who adopt them. This framework provides step-by-step guidance on integrating core principles into daily leadership practices, from defining personal and organizational purpose to implementing human-centric leadership strategies. This path enables leaders to achieve profound personal and organizational growth while leading with purpose and impact.

- **Practical Tools and Techniques**: We introduce tools and practices that leaders can use to embody these principles and enhance their capabilities. This includes strategies for developing self-awareness, such as engaging in reflective exercises and seeking constructive feedback, as well as methods for building authentic relationships and valuing team contributions. By applying these tools, leaders can foster a thriving organizational culture that aligns with purposeful leadership.

The core principles I gleaned from the biblical case studies are: understanding the times and knowing what to do; communication; envisioning; serving; learning, adapting, and improving; skillful hands and integrity of the heart; faith and hope; appreciation and thanksgiving; and accountability.

CHAPTER 18: THE LEADERSHIP PRINCIPLE OF UNDERSTANDING THE TIMES AND KNOWING WHAT TO DO: ITS TRANSFORMATIVE IMPACT ON LEADERS AND ORGANIZATIONS

Biblical Foundations and Timely Leadership

The chapter grounds its leadership concept in rich biblical imagery. It cites verses such as Ecclesiastes 3:1—reminding us that there is "a time for everything"—and highlights examples from 1 Chronicles 12:32 and Esther 4:14. These scriptures illustrate that leaders with a deep awareness of the times are uniquely positioned to act decisively during pivotal change. The biblical narrative of Esther, for example, emphasizes that individuals may be strategically placed for critical moments, urging leaders to remain alert to opportunities and challenges.

The Value of Time in Leadership

Leaders today recognize that time is an invaluable asset. Prioritizing tasks, planning strategically, adapting swiftly, and aligning resources with core organizational goals are central behaviors emphasized in the chapter. These practices align with broader ideas in transformational leadership research, where leaders motivate teams to excel by making proactive decisions that drive high performance (Northouse,

2019). In rapidly changing environments, effective time management intertwines with the ability to read the context and respond in ways that position the entire organization for success.

Understanding the Times and Making Informed Decisions

At the heart of this leadership model is a deep contextual awareness. It is not simply about managing time but about grasping the essence of changing socio-cultural, economic, political, and technological dynamics. Leaders who "understand the times" are likened to those who can discern subtle trends and anticipate future needs—actions that differentiate reactive management from proactive leadership. This is similar to how transformational leaders inspire and guide their teams by setting clear visions that align with external realities, as evidenced by research on leadership dynamics (Northouse, 2019).

Transformative Impact on Leaders and Organizations

When leaders master this principle, the ripple effects throughout their organizations can be profound. By interpreting environmental shifts and mobilizing teams around a clear, future-oriented vision, leaders can foster creativity, enhance collaboration, and drive strategic change.

This transformative impact parallels findings from studies on transformational leadership, which show that leaders who communicate a compelling vision often inspire exceptional performance and innovation within their teams (Northouse, 2019). Like farmers who understand the seasons to yield a bountiful harvest, the principle of understanding times and knowing what to do illustrates how timely decision-making can lead to sustained organizational success.

Actionable Framework for Leaders: Practicing the Principle of Understanding Times and Knowing What to Do

Drawing inspiration from biblical figures such as the sons of Issachar and Esther, this model underscores the importance of understanding historical contexts and contemporary dynamics. Such understanding allows leaders to make decisions that resonate with their followers and align with societal needs.

Environmental Awareness

- **Stay Informed:** Monitor news outlets, industry reports, and social media to stay up to date on current events and emerging trends.
- **Build Expert Networks:** Build a network of trusted advisors and experts who can offer insights into potential risks and opportunities.
- **Conduct Environmental Scans:** Periodically evaluate the external environment to identify unusual events related to developments and potential threats.

Intelligence Gathering

- **Systematic Data Collection:** Develop a structured approach to gathering and analyzing data from internal reports, customer feedback, and market research.
- **Data Visualization:** Use visualization tools to highlight patterns and correlations among data points.
- **Foster Information Sharing:** Foster a culture of collaboration within the organization, ensuring that insights and information circulate freely among team members.

Seasonal Understanding

- **Studying Historical Patterns:** Examine past trends and cycles in your industry or sector to identify recurring themes and anticipate future shifts.
- **Expert Engagement:** Collaborate with specialists in economics, politics, and technology to gain deeper insights into the broader forces shaping the current landscape.
- **Ongoing Assessment:** Regularly assess your organization's standing in the current season and adjust strategies as needed.

Recognizing Contextual Shifts

- *Monitor Early Indicators:* Keep an eye on leading indicators and early warning signs—such as changes in consumer behavior or emerging technologies—that may indicate upcoming shifts.
- *Scenario Planning:* Engage in scenario planning exercises to envision and prepare for various potential futures.
- *Collect Diverse Perspectives:* Involve a diverse group of stakeholders to gain comprehensive insights into the trends shaping the environment.

Assessing Implications

- *SWOT Analysis:* Use SWOT analysis to evaluate strengths, weaknesses, opportunities, and threats. This tool enables leaders to make informed decisions by identifying areas for improvement and potential opportunities (Wood C., 2024).
- *Risk Assessments:* Conduct regular risk assessments to identify vulnerabilities and develop appropriate mitigation strategies.

- *Strategic Foresight:* Engage in exercises that examine the long-term implications of current developments for more comprehensive decision-making.

Crafting a Response

- ***Develop a Clear Vision:*** Create a compelling vision for the organization's future that aligns with current context and seasonal trends.
- ***Stakeholder Engagement:*** Involve relevant stakeholders in developing the response to ensure the final strategy has broad buy-in and alignment.
- ***Roadmap for Implementation:*** Create a detailed roadmap that addresses both immediate concerns and long-term goals, guiding the organization through each phase of transformation.

Continuous Learning

- **Cultivate a Learning Culture:** Establish an organizational culture that encourages learning and experimentation, with insights consistently shared.
- **After-Action Reviews:** Conduct systematic reviews following key initiatives to determine what worked well and what can be improved.
- **Invest in Professional Development:** Provide ongoing training and development opportunities to enhance the organization's ability to adapt to changing times (Future Learn, 2023).

Practical Tools and Techniques

- **SWOT Analysis:** This tool provides a clear overview of internal and external factors by evaluating organizational Strengths, Weaknesses, Opportunities, and Threats, thus supporting informed decision-making (Wood C., 2024).
- **PEST Analysis:** Analyze Political, Economic, Social, and Technological factors to foresee external changes and modify strategies accordingly.

- **Develop a Comprehensive Leadership Toolbox:** Build a collection of leadership tools that empower you to navigate various situations and achieve desired results in stable and turbulent times (Level Five Associates, 2022).
- **Data-Driven Decision Making:** Depend on regular analyses and up-to-date data to ensure decisions are grounded in solid evidence rather than intuition (Wood C., 2024).
- **Commit to Continuous Learning:** Prioritize your personal growth and leadership abilities through training programs, workshops, or reading—this dedication to learning fosters effective leadership (Barbosa, 2021).

Overarching Actionable Framework

• **Interpreting Context:** Cultivate the ability to analyze current trends, societal shifts, and historical patterns to anticipate upcoming challenges and opportunities.

• **Vision Crafting:** Transform contextual insights into a compelling narrative that inspires teams to pursue a shared purpose.

• **Adaptability and Resource Alignment:** Turn timely insights into strategic initiatives, ensuring that organizational resources and processes can pivot as necessary.

• **Proactive Decision Making:** Approach transitions confidently instead of merely reacting to unforeseen issues, similar to transformational leaders who encourage proactive behaviors and job satisfaction.

Conclusion

The principle of "understanding the times and knowing what to do" goes beyond simple time management. It encompasses an integrated approach involving environmental awareness, systematic intelligence gathering, and strategic responsiveness. Leaders who embrace this principle can become transformative agents, guiding their organizations through change with vision, deliberate planning, and purpose.

This approach, supported by biblical wisdom (Bible Hub, 2024) and contemporary leadership research (Barbosa, 2021; Wood, 2024), guarantees that decisions are timely, informed, and aligned with both immediate needs and long-term objectives in today's dynamic global landscape.

References

Barbosa, G. (2021). *Create clarity: Why leaders must be focused on collaborative coherence.* Retrieved from LinkedIn

Bible Hub. (2024). Ecclesiastes 3:1. Retrieved from https://biblehub.com

Wood C. (2024). 26 essential recommendation books by and for IT leaders. Retrieved from https://www.cio.com/article/479905/essential-book-recommendations-by-and-for-it-leaders.html

Level Five Associates. (2022). Practical Leadership Tools. Retrieved from

https://www.levelfiveassociates.com/practical-leadership-tools/

Future Learn. (2023). How to improve leadership skills and demonstrate leadership. Retrieved from https://www.futurelearn.com/info/blog/how-to-improve-leadership-skills

CHAPTER 19: THE LEADERSHIP PRINCIPLE OF ENVISIONING: ITS TRANSFORMATIVE IMPACT ON LEADERS AND ORGANIZATIONS

Defining the Leadership Principle of Envisioning

The envisioning leadership principle refers to a leader's capacity to develop and communicate a compelling future vision that guides an organization's trajectory. This vision not only sets a direction for strategic action but also aligns individual goals with broader organizational objectives.

The Impact of Vision on Leaders and Organizations

Vision is fundamental in leadership for several reasons:

- **Alignment of Purpose:** Vision delineates the purpose of leaders, aligning individual goals with organizational objectives, and directs steps, intentions, resources, and aspirations.
- **Inspiration and Resilience:** Vision inspires determination to develop character and endure complex challenges, building resilience for future journeys in demanding environments.
- **Trust and Collaboration:** A clear vision is crucial in inspiring trust, unwavering loyalty, and confidence while fostering effective team collaboration.
- **Motivation and Commitment:** Vision is a source of resolve, courage, and commitment.

- **Attracting Support:** A clear vision attracts support, help, and resources from unexpected sources.

Envisioning can profoundly transform leaders and organizations by crafting an inspiring future vision complemented by a clear long-term plan with well-defined goals and strategies. **Effective communication of this vision to followers is crucial for success** (Akhigbe A., 2024; GGI Insights, 2024).

How Purposeful Leaders Envision

From the case studies, we learn that purposeful leaders demonstrate envisioning through:

- **Allowing Vision to Evolve Organically:** They allow the vision to develop naturally without manipulating or enforcing the process.
- **Openness to Input and Collective Effort:** Visionary leaders are open to feedback and input from others. For example, in 1 Samuel 25:23-35, Abigail persuades David not to take revenge against her household. David listens empathetically, accepts his mistake, and changes course. This illustrates that visionary leaders listen empathetically, accept their mistakes, and incorporate others' ideas into their **decision-making.**
- **Embracing a Higher Purpose:** They embrace divine involvement, allowing for enlightenment, direction, empowerment, and support for the vision before them, and remain committed to fulfilling their calling.
- **Empowering and Developing Others:** Visionary leaders develop and empower their followers, creating a supportive environment that enables them to excel. In 2 Samuel 23, David's mightiest warriors perform great exploits, demonstrating how

leaders seek out talented individuals, draft them into their **vision, and achieve exemplary results.**

- **Accountability and Innovation:** They take responsibility for their actions, own up to mistakes, welcome constructive criticism, and foster an environment that encourages creativity and innovation.

Additionally, visionary leaders exhibit a forward-thinking mindset, emphasizing the importance of future focus and encouraging active participation from followers (Liu et al., 2022). This approach fosters curiosity, continuous learning, adaptability, and resilience, transforming leaders into agents of change and showcasing their strategic thinking prowess.

Relevance in Today's Complex Environment

In today's fast-paced and complex world, envisioning is highly relevant. Organizations face rapid changes that require leaders to:

- **Adapt Quickly:** Leaders can anticipate changes and prepare accordingly by envisioning the future.
- **Foster Innovation:** Encouraging innovative thinking helps organizations remain competitive.
- **Promote Collaboration:** Envisioning a common goal unites individuals with diverse backgrounds, perspectives, and values.
- **Build Resilience:** A strong vision empowers teams to withstand challenges and maintain their focus on long-term objectives.

Conclusion

Envisioning leadership principle is essential for leaders who aspire to inspire and guide their organizations toward a prosperous future. By fostering a culture of **innovation, collaboration, and accountability**, leaders can effectively navigate the complexities of modern organizational challenges and drive their teams toward success. **Visionary leaders must consistently communicate their vision until followers understand, internalize, and act upon it, thereby achieving their goals.**

Actionable Framework for Leaders: Practicing the Principle of Envisioning

Three-Step Framework for Envisioning

This framework draws on the insights of Prophet Habakkuk and blends with contemporary perspectives.

1. **Questioning and Lamenting: Arouse an unquenchable desire for change and visualize the possibilities for the future you want.**

   - **Action Steps:**
     - Conduct a thorough analysis of the organization's current state, identifying areas that require change and improvement.
     - Engage in open discussions with team members to gather their insights and concerns.
   - **Understand the Vision**: Scan the environment to grasp the needs of the people and consult with stakeholders.
     Action Steps:
     - Conduct surveys, interviews, and focus groups with stakeholders to gain a deeper understanding of their needs, expectations, and aspirations.

- o Analyze market trends, competitor strategies, and industry developments to gain a comprehensive understanding of the external environment.
- **Identify Resources**: Determine the necessary resources for implementing the vision and strategize how to secure them.
  - **Action Steps:**
    - o Develop a comprehensive resource plan that outlines the necessary human, financial, and technological resources required to achieve the vision.
    - o Identify potential funding sources, partnerships, and collaborations to secure the necessary resources.

Identify Risks: Recognize potential risks and challenges and develop mitigation strategies.

  - **Action Steps:**
    - o Conduct a risk assessment to identify potential obstacles and challenges that may hinder the realization of the vision.
    - o Develop contingency plans and mitigation strategies to address these risks proactively.
- **Enhance Stakeholder Engagement**: Maintain regular consultations and provide timely updates to keep stakeholders informed and engaged.
  - **Action Steps:**
    - o Establish a stakeholder engagement plan, outlining the frequency and methods of communication with different stakeholder groups.
    - o Regularly update stakeholders on the progress of the vision and seek their feedback and input.

Step 2: Writing

- **Break Down the Vision**: Analyze and structure the vision for clarity and ease of implementation.

  Action Steps:
  - Decompose the vision into specific, measurable, achievable, relevant, and time-bound (SMART) goals and objectives.
  - Create a roadmap that outlines the key milestones and deliverables required to achieve the vision.
- **Train Stakeholders**: Conduct workshops, seminars, or online training to educate stakeholders on the vision and its execution.

  Action Steps:
  - Develop a comprehensive training program that covers the key aspects of the vision, its rationale, and the roles and responsibilities of different stakeholders.
  - Deliver training through various channels, including in-person workshops, webinars, and e-learning modules.
- **Communicate the Vision**: Effectively convey the vision to stakeholders, gather feedback, and make necessary adjustments.

  Action Steps:
  - Develop a communication plan that outlines the key messages, target audiences, and communication channels for sharing the vision.
  - Regularly communicate the vision through various media, such as town hall meetings, newsletters, and social media.

o Encourage stakeholder feedback and input and adjust the vision based on their insights.

Step 3: Waiting

- **Wait for the Appointed Time**: Utilize this period for preparation activities, stakeholder engagement, or further training.
    Action Steps:
    o Use the waiting period to refine the implementation plan, secure necessary resources, and build stakeholder support.
    o Continue to engage with stakeholders, providing updates on the progress and addressing any concerns or questions they may have.
- **Assess Effectiveness**: Evaluate the implementation's effectiveness and impact through surveys, interviews, or data analysis.
    Action Steps:
    o Develop a monitoring and evaluation framework to assess the progress and impact of the vision.
    o Collect data through various methods, such as surveys, interviews, and performance metrics.
    o Analyze the data to identify areas of success and areas that require further improvement.
- **Regularly Review the Vision**: Conduct annual reviews and stakeholder consultations to ensure the vision remains relevant and practical.
    Action Steps:
    o Schedule regular reviews of the vision involving key stakeholders.

- o Evaluate the relevance and practicality of the vision, considering the shifting internal and external factors.
- o Adjust the vision as necessary based on the review's findings.

This framework guides leaders through envisioning by encouraging thorough understanding, effective communication, and continuous evaluation. By following these steps, leaders can transform their visions into relevant, impactful, and actionable plans.

Embedding Envisioning in an Organization: Practical Tools and Techniques

Insights from Prophet Habakkuk

In ancient times, the Prophet Habakkuk emphasized the importance of confronting injustice and acknowledging violence within Israel's leadership (Habakkuk 1:2–4). His heartfelt appeal for divine intervention, along with God's command to document a prophetic vision on a tablet, shows that questioning and lamenting are vital starting points in the quest for transformative solutions. Vision, in essence, arises from a deep, sometimes desperate, desire for change—a concept that remains timeless and universal.

Tool: Tablet – Technique & Writing Action Step
Leaders are encouraged to participate in reflective practices, such as journaling or meditation, to identify pain points within the organization. By capturing these insights, they can develop a compelling vision that addresses these issues and inspires meaningful change.

Evolution of Envisioning Tools and Techniques

Over time, the methods for envisioning have evolved from simple tools, such as writing on tablets, to sophisticated strategies utilized by contemporary leaders. Today's leaders draw on a variety of tools and techniques to envision and prepare for the future:

• **SWOT Analysis:** This method identifies both internal strengths and weaknesses, as well as external opportunities and threats, which shape an organization's strategic objectives (Kenton, 2024).

• **Scenario Planning:** Involves crafting detailed and plausible future scenarios to prepare organizations for uncertain times.

• **Design Thinking:** Integrates people's needs, technological capabilities, and business objectives through empathy, problem definition, ideation, prototyping, and testing (Schwartz et al., 2023).

• **Future Mapping:** Future thinking involves creating a range of possible scenarios by exploring trends and drivers, highlighting adaptability and flexibility (Arruda, 2021).

• **Environmental Scanning:** Utilizing surveys and data analysis to identify external opportunities and threats that may impact strategic decisions.

• **Strategic Foresight:** Applies various methodologies to anticipate and prepare for future challenges and opportunities (Gorbis, 2024).

• **Benchmarking:** Involves comparing an organization's processes and performance metrics against the industry's best practices.

• **Data Analytics and AI-Assisted Forecasting:** Utilizes big data and artificial intelligence to predict future trends and inform decision-making (Nonprofit Megaphone, 2024).

Conclusion

By harnessing these practical tools and techniques, leaders can effectively embed the principle of envisioning within their organizations. This integrated approach enables the development of compelling visions that not only inspire change but also provide strategic guidance for decision-making and long-term success.

References

Akhigbe, A. (2024). The impact, vision, and transformation that truly matters in leadership. Retrieved from

https://www.linkedin.com/pulse/impact-vision-transformation-truly-matters-leaadership..

Arruda, A. P. (2021). Future scenarios: Clarifying the possible. Retrieved from

https://schoolofdesignthinking.echos.cc/blog/2021/03/future-scenarios-clarifying-the-possible/#:~:

Dowse, A. (2021). Scenario planning methodology for future conflict. Retrieved from

https://www.airuniversity.af.edu/JIPA/Display/Article/2527810/scenario-planning-methodology-for-future-conflict/#:~

GGI Insights. (2024). Visionary leadership: Steering transformation in the modern era. Retrieved from

https://www.graygroupintl.com/blog/visionary-leadership...

Gorbis, M. (2024). Using strategic foresight to create the future we want. Retrieved from

https://ssir.org/articles/entry/futures-thinking-nonprofit-strategy#:~

Kenton, W. (2024). How to perform SWOT analysis. Retrieved from

https://www.investopedia.com/terms/s/swot.asp#:~:

Liu, M., et al. (2022). How and when does visionary leadership promote followers' taking charge? The roles of inclusion of leader in self and future orientation. *Psychology Research and Behavior Management Journal*, 15, 1917-1929. doi: 10.2147/PRBM.S366939

Nonprofit Megaphone. (2024). Measuring nonprofit impact: 25 metrics and tools for success. Retrieved from

https://nonprofitmegaphone.com/measuring-nonprofit-impact-25-key-metrics-other-tools-for-success/#:~

Schwartz, J. O., et al. (2023). How to anchor design thinking in the future: Empirical evidence on the usage of strategic foresight in design thinking projects. *Futures*, 149. Retrieved from

https://www.sciencedirect.com/science/article/pii/S0016328723000411 doi.org/10.1016/j.futures.2023.103137

CHAPTER 20: THE LEADERSHIP PRINCIPLE OF COMMUNICATION: ITS TRANSFORMATIVE IMPACT ON LEADERS AND ORGANIZATIONS

Effective communication is vital for transformational leadership. It allows leaders to inspire, guide, and unite their teams. In today's complex environment, purposeful communication not only conveys information but also embodies an organization's ethos, values, and vision.

Definition of the Communication Leadership Principle

The communication leadership principle refers to a leader's ability to convey information, expectations, feedback, and vision effectively. This process is bidirectional, involving both the sender and the receiver through verbal and nonverbal cues and a feedback loop that facilitates continuous improvement. Essentially, intentional, strategic, and timely communication is an organization's lifeblood, reflecting its core beliefs and purpose.

Transformative Impact of Communication

Communication is a powerful tool that builds trust, fosters collaboration, and aligns teams with shared goals. By clearly communicating goals and expectations, leaders create an environment of transparency and inclusivity that enhances employee engagement, job satisfaction, and overall performance (Lazono et al., 2023).

To be impactful, communication must:

• Clearly articulate its purpose.

• Address issues in simple and accessible language.

• Persuasively inspire action among followers.

When executed effectively, communication not only shapes organizational culture but also drives high engagement and aligns individual values with the organization's mission (Nallalingham, 2023; Kirwan, 2023).

Lessons from Biblical Figures

The Bible offers timeless lessons on effective communication. Several examples illustrate how leaders can harness dialogue to drive transformation:

- **Abraham's Negotiation (Genesis 18:17–33):** Abraham's respectful and persistent dialogue with God over the fate of Sodom and Gomorrah demonstrates the power of thoughtful negotiation.
- **Moses and Aaron (Exodus 4:10–17):** Moses' acknowledgment of his limitations and reliance on Aaron as a spokesperson highlights the value of leveraging individual strengths.
- **Nathan's Confrontation (2 Samuel 12:1–14):** Using a parable to address King David's misstep, Nathan shows how storytelling can gently confront complex issues and encourage personal growth.
- **Esther's Dispatch (Esther 8:9–14):** The swift, clear communication of a life-saving decree in a crisis underscores the necessity for timely and unambiguous messaging.
- **Daniel's Interpretation (Daniel 2:1–49):** Daniel's confident interpretation of Nebuchadnezzar's dream reinforces the importance of clarity and assertiveness in building trust and credibility.

- **Paul's Address at the Areopagus (Acts 17:16–34):** Paul's adaptable communication style, tailored to his diverse audience, illustrates the need to find common ground across cultures.

These examples reinforce several key lessons:

- **Purposeful Communication:** Every message should reflect an organization's mission and vision.
- **Organizational Lifeblood:** Communication must flow through all levels, defining identity and guiding future direction.
- **Accuracy and Record-Keeping:** Maintaining clear, concise, and secure records supports collective knowledge and prevents misinformation.
- **Resolving Disputes:** Effective communication grounds discussions in facts and truth, helping resolve conflicts.
- **Cultural Unity:** Communication that transcends cultural and racial differences can rally diverse groups toward common goals.
- Educational Leadership: Leaders must continuously teach and communicate to ensure alignment and progress.

A biblical reminder comes from Numbers 20:11, where Moses' emotional outburst while striking the rock illustrates that leaders must manage their emotions to avoid undermining their message.

Communication of Purposeful Leaders

Purposeful leaders exemplify effective communication through:

- **Authenticity and Integrity:** Communicating with genuine humility and unwavering integrity.
- **Objectivity:** Avoiding personal bias to unify individuals while fostering diversity and inclusivity.

- **Vision-Driven Messaging:** Grounding their communication in a higher purpose and clear, collective goals.
- **Adaptability:** Modifying messages to reflect changing circumstances and inspire hope and transformation.

Practical Strategies for Effective Communication

Leaders can adopt several strategies to institutionalize effective communication:

- **Establish Clear Channels:** Set up organized communication channels and protocols to ensure timely and accurate information flow.
- **Foster a Feedback Culture:** Encourage open, honest dialogue to build trust and support continuous improvement.
- **Leverage Storytelling:** Use stories and analogies to clarify complex concepts and make them memorable.
- **Tailor to the Audience:** Adjust communication styles to accommodate the varied backgrounds, preferences, and needs of the audience.
- **Invest in Training:** Promote ongoing training and development to improve communication skills throughout the organization.

Conclusion

In conclusion, effective communication is crucial for leaders who seek to inspire and drive organizational success. By fostering a culture of trust, transparency, and collaboration, leaders can navigate contemporary challenges and guide their teams toward achieving shared goals. As illustrated by biblical narratives and reinforced through practical strategies, the transformative power of communication lies in its ability to align, educate, and motivate. Leaders must continuously refine their communication to ensure that every message is clearly understood, internalized, and acted upon in pursuit of a collective vision.

Actionable Framework for Leaders: Practicing and Measuring Communication Effectiveness

To ensure organizational communication is practical and transformative, leaders can implement a structured framework based on clearly defined metrics and best practices drawn from modern insights (Snapcomms, 2022) and timeless biblical examples.

I. Communication Effectiveness Metrics

Measurement Method :

Include all communication channels in your metrics (Snapcomms, 2022)—not just face-to-face interactions but digital channels such as emails and intranet posts.

Benchmark Criteria:

- **Communication Frequency:** Ensure that weekly communications are both practical and meaningful.
- **Message Clarity Score:** Use tools like comprehension quizzes or quick polls to measure how clearly messages are understood.
- **Feedback Loop Efficiency:** Set expected response times (for example, responses within 24 hours on business days) to sustain a dynamic and responsive communication process.

II. Enhancing Effective Listening Practices

Leaders should prioritize several key listening principles to improve interactions with team members (Cormier S. et al., 2003):

- **Active Listening:** Stay fully present during conversations and reduce distractions.
- **Listening for Understanding:** Paraphrase, reflect, and empathize—address the content of messages and acknowledge their emotional nuances.
- **Listening for Accuracy:** Encourage clear understanding by seeking clarification when messages are unclear.
- **Listening for Themes:** Summarize and distill discussions to extract key messages and underlying themes, which can provide a foundation for informed feedback.

III. Benchmark Criteria for Effective Listening

Measuring effective listening can be accomplished through specific criteria and tools tailored to each listening practice:

1. Active Listening

  ○ Benchmark Criteria:

- Engagement Level: Leaders should remain fully present during at least 90% of conversation time, avoiding interruptions.
- Distraction-Free Interactions: Strive to conduct meetings free from digital distractions (e.g., phones, emails).

Measurement Tools:

- Observation checklists to monitor attentiveness during meetings.
- Employee feedback surveys to gather team perceptions of the leader's listening habits.

2. Listening for Understanding
  o **Benchmark Criteria:**

- Paraphrasing Frequency: Leaders should paraphrase key points at least once during significant conversations.
- Empathy Ratings: Aim for an average empathy rating of 4 or higher on a 1–5 scale, as reported by team members.
- Resolution Effectiveness: Achieve a satisfactory resolution rate of 85% or greater for issues resolved through practical understanding.

Measurement Tools:

- Communication assessments that review the frequency of paraphrasing and empathetic responses.
- Emotional intelligence surveys to evaluate the leader's ability to connect with team members.

3. Listening for Accuracy
  o **Benchmark Criteria:**

- Clarification Requests: When necessary, leaders should ask at least two clarifying questions per meeting to ensure mutual understanding.
- Understanding Accuracy: Strive for at least 90% accuracy in interpreting messages.
- Feedback Implementation: Ensure that 80% of clarified information results in actionable outcomes.

Measurement Tools:

- Interaction analyses to examine instances of clarification.
- Team feedback on the leader's ability to understand and act on messages accurately.

4. Listening for Themes
- **Benchmark Criteria:**
    - Summary Provision: Leaders should provide summaries during all significant discussions.
    - Theme Identification: Achieve at least an 85% success rate in recognizing the core themes or concerns of discussions.
    - Strategic Alignment: Integrate identified themes into 75% of relevant organizational strategies and decisions.

Measurement Tools:

- Analysis of meeting recaps or follow-up communications.
- Understanding surveys to assess team perceptions regarding the leader's comprehension of key themes.

Practical Tools and Techniques

Measurement Methods Inspired by Biblical Examples:

Biblical figures illustrate principles that remain relevant today:

- **Abraham's Negotiation (Genesis 18:17–33):** Demonstrates the value of clear, persistent communication. Leaders can measure the frequency and clarity of their messages.
- **Moses' Reliance on Aaron (Exodus 4:10–17):** Highlights the importance of recognizing personal communication strengths and knowing when to seek support.
- **David's Confrontation with Nathan (2 Samuel 12:1–14):** Illustrates how indirect communication

and storytelling can effectively address sensitive issues.

- **Esther's Crisis Communication (Esther 8:9–14):** Emphasizes the necessity for timely and unambiguous messaging during emergencies.
- **Daniel's Interpretation and Promotion (Daniel 2:1–49):** Underscores the role of confident, clear communication in building trust and credibility.
- **Paul's Areopagus Address (Acts 17:16–34):** Reflects the importance of adapting messages to various audiences.

Use these examples as benchmarks for developing metrics that assess the frequency, clarity, and timeliness of communication.

Assessment Tools:

- **Communication Effectiveness Audits:** Regular audits help identify bottlenecks in the communication process, similar to how Moses recognized his limitations (Exodus 4:10–17).
- **Feedback Surveys:** Frequent, short surveys capture immediate, actionable feedback—mirroring the feedback loop seen in David's encounter with Nathan (2 Samuel 12:1–14).
- **Two-Way Communication Metrics:** Incorporate metrics that evaluate how effectively leadership listens to employees, as exemplified by Abraham's negotiation (Genesis 18:17–33).

Conclusion

The leadership principle of communication is essential for driving organizational success. By adopting a framework that evaluates communication effectiveness and improves listening practices, leaders cultivate a culture of trust, transparency, and collaboration. Consistent, clear, and empathetic communication ensures that team members not only comprehend the messages conveyed but also internalize and act upon them. Integrating insights from biblical figures with modern assessment tools empowers leaders to leverage the full transformative potential of effective communication.

References

Lazono, J. R. et al. (2023). Leadership, Communication, and Job Satisfaction for Employee Engagement and Sustainability of Family Businesses in Latin America. Adm. Sci. 2023, 13, 137.

https://doi.org/10.3390/admsci13060137
Kirwan, C. (2023). How Company Culture Impacts Organizational Performance. Retrieved from

https://workvivo.com
Nallalingham, L. (2023). The Impact of Communication on Organizational Transformation. Retrieved from

https://www.linkedin.com/pulse/impact-commuication-organizational-transformaton-lee-nallalignham

Cormier, S. et al. (2003). Interviewing and Change Strategies for Helpers: Fundamental Skills and Cognitive Behavioral Interviews. Brooks/Cole, a division of Thomson Learning, Inc.

Snapcomms. (2022). How to Measure Communication Effectiveness with the Right Matrix. Retrieved from

https://www.snapcomms.com/blog/measuring-communication-effectivenes

CHAPTER 21. THE LEADERSHIP PRINCIPLE OF SERVING AND ITS TRANSFORMATIVE IMPACT ON LEADERS AND ORGANIZATIONS

Acts 13:36 emphasizes that David served God's purpose in his generation, underscoring the fundamental importance of serving in leadership. This principle is crucial for modern leaders facing complex challenges today and in the future.

Key Elements Leadership Principle of Serving

- **Purposeful Service**: Serving is intentional and lies at the core of effective leadership. It involves prioritizing the needs of others, the community, and future generations over personal gain.
- **Values-Based Leadership**: Serving is built on virtues and ethical morals that guide the leadership process, ensuring decisions are made with integrity.
- **Empowerment of Others**: Effective leaders inspire, motivate, and develop others to reach their full potential and become better than they were before.
- **Collaborative Approach**: Being open to others' ideas, delegating responsibilities, and involving team members in decision-making fosters a sense of ownership and unity (Towler, A. 2019).
- **Stewardship**: Leaders responsibly manage resources to meet today's needs while ensuring sustainability for the future.

- **Higher Purpose Alignment**: Inspired by a higher purpose aligned with a guiding "North Star," serving leaders navigate with clarity and purpose.
- **Community Building**: They focus on building strong communities, fostering unity, and creating a sense of belonging among team members.
- **Leading by Example**: Serving leaders embody integrity, authenticity, and honesty, inspiring trust and commitment in their followers.
- **Humility and Compassion**: Leading with humility, temperance, and loving compassion creates an environment where team members feel valued and respected.
- **Visionary Communication**: They possess a long-term vision and communicate effectively to mobilize and align team members toward common goals.

Serving: Its Transformative Impact on Leaders and Organizations

Prioritizing people's needs and interests is essential to transforming leaders and organizations. This includes caring for and supporting the most vulnerable, pursuing common goals, and demonstrating responsible stewardship of resources.

Leading by Example: It is not what leaders say that matters most; what they do matters. Jesus challenged His followers to emulate His actions. In **John 13:4-13**, Jesus washed His disciples' feet, setting a profound example of servant leadership. Before this act, the disciples had been disputing who among them was the greatest (**Luke 22:24-27**), equating greatness with traditional notions of leadership. Jesus used this moment to teach them the leadership they overlooked and often despised – leadership that centers on serving.

Highlighting Flaws in Traditional Leadership:

Jesus pointed out the flaws in the disciples' desired leadership style, characterized by authority over others, desire for reverence, and dominance. These traits are often associated with the "dark side of leadership" (Northouse, p. 2019). By washing their feet, Jesus challenged their assumptions and demonstrated that authentic leadership is about serving others.

This act required a complete transformation from a mindset focused on personal greatness to one centered on servant leadership.

The Transformational Journey

- **Adopting New Values and Mindset**: Transforming into a serving leader involves embracing humility and changing one's values, priorities, and mindset.
- **Developing New Competencies**: This requires developing new knowledge, skills, and competencies centered on serving others (Towler, 2019).
- **Pursuing Common Goals**: Such transformation leads leaders to prioritize common goals over personal gains, putting others' needs above their own. Inspiring His disciples to improve and serve others, Jesus illustrated how serving can profoundly transform leadership, benefiting both leaders and their organizations.

The Transformative Impact in Today's Context

Considering the challenges facing leaders today and, in the future - such as globalization, technological change, and social complexities, the principle of serving has a transformative impact:

- **Enhancing Organizational Performance**: Serving leaders fosters environments where employees feel valued, increasing motivation and performance.
- **Building Resilient Organizations**: Serving leaders foster resilience against external challenges by cultivating strong relationships and communities within their organizations.
- **Innovative Problem-Solving**: Collaborative and empowering approaches encourage diverse ideas and innovative solutions (Towler, A. 2019).
- **Ethical Leadership**: Values-based serving leadership ensures ethical decision-making, which is crucial in a rapidly changing world.
- **Sustainable Growth**: Responsible stewardship and a focus on long-term vision contribute to sustainable organizational growth.

Conclusion

The principle of serving transforms leadership by shifting the focus from self-interest to collective well-being. This approach addresses current and future challenges by promoting ethical practices, empowering others, and fostering unity within organizations. Leaders who embrace serving enhance their effectiveness and contribute to their organization's long-term success and resilience.

Actionable Framework for Leaders: Practicing the Principle of Serving

Servant leadership is a timeless principle exemplified by some of history's most influential leaders. Moses, Paul, and David serve as inspiring models who embedded service into their leadership, transforming themselves and the people they led. This framework distills their experiences into practical steps that modern leaders can follow to embark on a transformational journey toward servant leadership.

Framework Overview

The leadership principle of serving is rooted in personal transformation, an inclination to serve others, empathy, empowerment, and stewardship. By applying these principles, leaders can foster environments that promote growth, collaboration, and lasting positive impact.

1. Personal Transformation

Example Leaders:

- **Moses:** Transformed from an Egyptian prince to a humble shepherd and ultimately a servant leader of the Israelites.

- **Paul:** Shifted from persecuting Christians to becoming a devoted apostle who spread the Gospel.

- **David:** Evolved from a shepherd boy to the king of Israel, maintaining humility throughout his reign.

Key Elements:

- **Mindset Shift:** Embracing humility over pride.

- **Value Realignment:** Prioritizing compassion, patience, and dedication.

- **Self-Sacrifice:** Letting go of personal ambition to serve a greater good.

Action Steps for Leaders:

- **Self-Reflection:** Regularly assess your motives and goals. Are they self-serving or geared toward the greater good?

- **Embrace Humility:** Recognize and acknowledge personal weaknesses and shortcomings.

- **Commit to Growth:** Seek experiences that challenge and refine your character and values.

2.Overarching Inclination to Serve Others

Example Leaders:

- **Moses:** Consistently prioritized the needs of the Israelites over his own.

- **Paul:** Traveled extensively to minister to various communities, often at personal risk.

- **David:** Served his people by uniting the tribes of Israel and establishing Jerusalem.

Key Elements:

- **Inner Drive:** A genuine desire to meet others' needs.

- **Selflessness:** Prioritizing others' interests over personal gain.

- **Ministering Mindset:** Actively seeking ways to uplift and support others.

Action Steps for Leaders:

1. **Cultivate Empathy:** Practice active listening to understand the needs of others.

2. **Serve Actively:** Identify and address gaps within the team or community.

3. **Promote Others' Success:** Create opportunities for others to succeed and grow.

3. Identifying with People's Sufferings

Example Leaders:

- **Moses:** Chose to share in the hardships of his people rather than enjoy the privileges of Egyptian royalty.

- **Paul:** Empathized with both Jews and Gentiles, thereby bridging cultural divides.

- **David:** Led his men into battle and shared in their struggles.

Key Elements:

- **Empathy:** The ability to understand and share the feelings of others.

- **Potential Focus:** Seeing beyond faults to the inherent potential in every person.

- **Sacrificial Leadership:** The willingness to endure hardship for the benefit of others.

Action Steps for Leaders:

1. **Engage Directly:** Spend time with team members in their work environments to better understand their challenges.

2. **Affirm Potential:** Encourage and acknowledge the strengths and capabilities of others.

3. **Support Actively:** Be present and available during challenging times, offering assistance and guidance.

4. Developing and Empowering Others

Example Leaders:

- **Moses:** Delegated authority to capable leaders, including Joshua and the elders of Israel.

- **Paul:** Mentored Timothy and Titus, entrusting them with leadership responsibilities.

- **David:** Assembled a team of mighty men, developing their skills and leadership abilities.

Key Elements:

- **Delegation:** Assigning responsibilities to others to promote growth.

- **Teamwork:** Promoting collaboration and shared decision-making.

- **Mentorship:** Guiding others through personal and professional growth and development.

Action Steps for Leaders:

1. **Identify Leaders:** Recognize and invest in individuals with leadership potential.

2. **Provide Opportunities:** Allow others to take on meaningful tasks and projects.

3. **Encourage Input:** Foster an environment where team members feel comfortable sharing their ideas.

5.Stewardship and Succession Planning

Example Leaders:

- **Moses:** Prepared Joshua to succeed him in leading the Israelites.

- **Paul:** Entrusted the continuation of his missionary work to his protégés.

- **David:** Laid the groundwork for Solomon to build the temple and lead Israel.

Key Elements:

- **Long-Term Vision:** Focusing on the community's or organization's enduring well-being.

- **Resource Investment:** Contributing time, knowledge, and resources to ensure future success.

- **Generational Impact:** Planning for the prosperity of future generations.

Action Steps for Leaders:

1. **Develop Successors:** Actively mentor individuals who can carry on the organization's mission.

2. **Document Knowledge:** Create resources and guidelines to preserve institutional knowledge.

3. **Plan Strategically:** Establish long-term goals and vision beyond personal tenure.

Additional Tips for Implementation

- **Consistency:** Apply these principles consistently, not just in significant moments.

- **Feedback Loop:** Encourage and be receptive to feedback to continue growing as a servant leader.

- **Community Building:** Foster a culture that values service, empathy, and mutual support among all members.

Integrating these principles into your leadership approach enhances your effectiveness and contributes to the development and well-being of those you lead. The journey of servant leadership is ongoing and requires dedication, yet its transformative impact on individuals and communities is profound and lasting.

Embedding the Leadership Principle of Serving in an Organization

Embedding the leadership principle of serving within an organization can significantly enhance its culture and effectiveness. Here are the key steps to achieve this:

- **Articulate and Communicate the Vision**
  - Clearly define the organization's vision aligned with its purpose.
  - Communicate the vision effectively to all team members.
  - Encourage everyone to take ownership of the vision.
- **Empower Team Members**
  - **Teach, train, develop, coach,** and **mentor** team members.
  - Enable them to pursue the vision with confidence and competence.
- **Set Strategic Objectives and Goals**
  - Craft strategic objectives aligned with the vision.
  - Clearly delineate tasks and responsibilities.
- **Define Ethical Values and Principles**
  - Establish core values and principles to guide ethical decision-making.
  - Ensure these are communicated and embraced throughout the organization.
- **Implement Effective Structures and Processes**
  - Establish structures, processes, and procedures to ensure efficient operations.
  - Monitor performance regularly to ensure alignment with goals.

- **Facilitate Open Communication**
  - Establish vibrant reporting and communication channels.
  - Track and address trouble spots promptly.
  - Explore underlying issues to craft effective responses.
- **Lead by Example**
  - **Model the way** by demonstrating the expected behaviors and attitudes.
  - Uphold the organization's values in all actions.
- **Prioritize Collective Interests**
  - Put the interests of followers, stakeholders, and shared interests above personal gains.
  - Foster a culture of collaboration and mutual support.
- **Demand Accountability**
  - Hold team members accountable for their responsibilities.
  - Encourage ownership and responsibility at all levels.

Leaders can effectively embed a serving mindset by following these steps, fostering a supportive, productive organizational environment.

References

Liberty University. (2013). The King James Study Bible (Second Edition). Thomas Nelson.

Gilbert A. (2024). The Servant Leadership of Moses. Retrieved from

https:// www.bridgesforpeace.com/letter/the-servant-leadership-of-moses/#:~:

Northouse, P. G. (2019). Leadership: Theory and Practice (8th ed.). Sage Publications.

Towler, A. (2019). The qualities of transformational leaders and what distinguishes them from transactional leaders. Retrieved from

https://www.ckju.net/en/dossier/qualities-transformational-leaders-and-what=distinguishes them…

CHAPTER 22: THE LEADERSHIP PRINCIPLE OF SKILLFUL HANDS AND INTEGRITY OF HEART: ITS TRANSFORMATIVE IMPACT ON LEADERS AND ORGANIZATIONS

Definition

The principle of skillful hands in leadership refers to a leader's ability to apply technical proficiency, problem-solving skills, and operational expertise to navigate complex challenges effectively. In contrast, integrity of heart represents the ethical and moral foundation that guides decisions and actions, emphasizing honesty, fairness, and genuine concern for others. This ethical integrity not only enhances social judgment but also fosters effective collaboration and trust among team members. For example, the biblical figure David exemplifies these qualities, as in Psalm 78:72, which states, "So David shepherded them with integrity of heart and guided them with skillful hands." Together, these attributes enable leaders to achieve their goals ethically, benefiting all stakeholders.

Impact on Leaders

Leaders who embody both skillful hands and an integrity of heart excel at motivating their teams and cultivating a secure, supportive work environment. Their authenticity and honesty foster loyalty and commitment, which strengthen team cohesion. Furthermore, by consistently making ethical decisions aligned with core organizational values, these leaders exhibit resilience and adaptability, which are essential for managing change and uncertainty.

Impact on Organizations

Organizations led by individuals with these qualities often cultivate a culture that values and supports employees while remaining closely aligned with their mission. This positive atmosphere enhances the organization's reputation and appeals to top talent (Khan et al., 2020). Furthermore, by establishing credibility with customers, partners, and investors, these organizations are more likely to achieve long-term success. Their active engagement in social causes also elevates their reputation within the community.

Actionable Framework for Leaders: Practicing the Principle of Skillful Hands and Integrity of Heart

To effectively apply these leadership principles, leaders can adopt a framework that details the key components necessary for transformational growth. This framework is organized into two main sections:

Skillful Hands

- **Wisdom:** Cultivate a deep understanding and discernment in decision-making. Historical leaders—such as Abraham, who balanced faith with insightful judgment—exemplify how wisdom can navigate complex social dynamics (Rozenberg, 2023).

- **Skills:**

- **Technical Skills:** Develop specialized knowledge to manage tasks effectively and guide teams toward achieving organizational goals.

- - **Human Skills:** Improve interpersonal abilities to connect with team members and foster strong relationships. The Apostle Paul, for instance, demonstrated these skills by effectively bridging cross-cultural gaps with humility and adaptability.

- **Conceptual Skills:** Enhance your capacity to analyze complex situations and think strategically. As noted by Northouse (2019), this competence is essential for navigating challenges and is exemplified by leaders such as Moses, who guided his people through difficult times while upholding ethical standards.
- **Competencies:**
  - **Problem-solving skills**: Tackle challenges creatively and efficiently using innovative solutions. David's decisive actions exemplify courageous and effective problem-solving.

  - - **Social Judgment Skills:** Cultivate the ability to understand and manage social dynamics within the organization, promoting a harmonious work environment. A leader's integrity is crucial for honing this skill.

  - - **Knowledge:** Commit to ongoing learning to stay informed and adaptable. Embracing new ideas and technologies is essential for transformational leaders who aim to enhance their technical competencies and remain current with industry developments.

Integrity of Heart

- **Pure Intentions and Righteous Actions:** Act genuinely and ensure that every action aligns with your core values and ethical standards. Daniel's unwavering integrity under pressure serves as a notable example of upholding excellence through sincere intentions.

- **Authenticity and Humility:** Lead with genuine humility by acknowledging personal limitations and demonstrating a willingness to learn. Apostle Paul's leadership style, characterized by humility and adaptability, underscores the importance of these qualities.

- **Ethical and Moral Principles:** Base each decision on solid moral foundations. Leaders such as Moses, who upheld ethical values and laws, remind us that fairness and justice should guide leadership practices.

- **Conviction and Emotional Awareness:** Listen to your inner voice and lead with passion and determination. Transformational leaders inspire others by demonstrating unwavering conviction and emotional intelligence.

- **Repentant Heart:** Embrace the willingness to acknowledge mistakes and pursue continuous personal growth. David's readiness to repent serves as a lasting reminder of the importance of humility and ongoing self-improvement.

- **Receptiveness to Advice:** Welcome input from others and promote a collaborative atmosphere that encourages diverse perspectives. Being open to feedback builds trust and nurtures cohesive team dynamics.

- **Accountability:** Take responsibility for your decisions and actions and learn from past experiences. Transformational leaders consistently hold themselves accountable, creating opportunities for personal and organizational growth.

Tools and Techniques to Embed the Leadership Principles in an Organization

Leaders can use various tools and techniques to instill the principles of skillful hands and integrity of heart within their organizations:

- **Role Modeling:** Demonstrate desired behaviors and values to serve as a model for others. Transformational leaders inspire their followers through their actions and behaviors.

- **Mentorship Programs:** Encourage experienced leaders to mentor others, promoting skill development and ethical practices. Mentorship programs can nurture the skills and competencies needed for effective leadership.

- **Training and Development:** Provide ongoing education in technical skills, ethical decision-making, and emotional intelligence. Continuous learning is crucial for leaders to refine their technical competencies and develop their ethical decision-making skills.

- **Feedback Mechanisms:** Establish systems to receive and act on feedback that promotes accountability and continuous improvement. Feedback mechanisms can help leaders learn from their experiences and grow.

- **Recognition Systems:** Acknowledge and reward behaviors demonstrating expertise and integrity, emphasizing their importance. Recognizing and rewarding positive behaviors can help embed the leadership principle within the organization.

- **Cultural Initiatives:** Foster a culture within the organization that emphasizes alignment of values, open communication, and a shared purpose. A strong organizational culture can nurture the development of skilled hands and integrity of heart in leaders.

Application Utilizing Historical Leaders as Examples

The transformational journeys of historical figures offer valuable insights into embodying these leadership principles:

• **Abraham:** Demonstrated faith and wisdom while navigating complex social dynamics with integrity of heart.

• **Moses:** Displayed leadership by guiding people through challenges, upholding ethical laws, and showcasing conceptual skills.

• **David:** Exhibited courageous problem-solving and demonstrated repentance when he erred, aligning with the principle of integrity.

• **Daniel:** Maintained his integrity under pressure, serving with excellence and pure intentions despite external challenges.

• **Paul:** Connected across diverse cultures using interpersonal skills, leading with conviction, adaptability, and humility.

By reflecting on these examples, modern leaders can draw inspiration for their transformational journeys, integrating skillful hands and integrity of heart into their leadership practices.

Application in Today's Leadership Context

In the contemporary organizational landscape, integrating skillful hands and integrity of heart is vital for effective leadership:

• **Embrace Continuous Learning:** Stay informed about industry advancements and improve technical skills. Transformational leaders emphasize ongoing learning to stay knowledgeable and flexible (Baker, C., 2023).

• **Prioritize Ethical Decision-Making**: Make decisions rooted in ethical principles to cultivate trust and credibility within the organization. A leader's integrity guides them in making ethical choices that benefit all stakeholders.

• **Develop Emotional Intelligence:** Enhance self-awareness and empathy to foster effective connections with team members. Emotional intelligence is a crucial component of transformational leadership, allowing leaders to inspire and motivate their followers.

• **Foster a Collaborative Culture:** Encourage input and collaboration by leveraging diverse perspectives to foster innovation. Transformational leaders foster trust and promote collaboration by remaining open to feedback and embracing diverse viewpoints.

• **Lead by Example:** Demonstrate behaviors and values that reflect skillfulness and integrity, inspiring others to do the same. Purposeful leaders motivate their followers through their actions and behaviors, serving as role models for others to emulate.

By adopting these strategies, leaders can navigate the complexities of today's business environment, inspire their teams, and drive organizational success.

Conclusion

The leadership principle of skillful hands and integrity of heart provides a strong framework for guiding leaders on their transformational journey. By developing the skills, competencies, and attributes outlined in this chapter, leaders can effectively navigate challenges, build trust and collaboration, and drive positive organizational change. Historical figures such as Abraham, Moses, David, Daniel, and Paul serve as inspiration for modern leaders seeking to embody these principles in their leadership practices. In today's complex and ever-changing business landscape, integrating skillful hands and integrity of heart is more crucial than ever for effective leadership and organizational success.

References

Baker, C. (2023). What is transformational leadership? Retrieved from

https://leaders.com/articles/leadership/transformational-leadership/

Biblehub.com. (2024). Psalm 72:78 So David shepherded them with integrity of heart and guided them with skillful hands. Retrieved from

https://biblehub.com/psalms/78-72.htm

Birt, J. (2024). 11 Leadership Principles to Implement in the Workplace. Retrieved from

https://www.indeed.com/career-advice/career-development/leadership-principles

Northouse, P. G. (2019). *Leadership: Theory and Practice* (8th ed.). London: Sage.

Khan, H., Rehmat, M., Butt, T.H. *et al.* (2020). Impact of transformational leadership on work performance, burnout and social loafing: a mediation model. *Futur Bus J* 6, 40.

https://doi.org/10.1186/s43093-020-00043-8

Rozenberg, T. (2023). The Art of Leadership: A Journey Through History's Inspirational Leaders. Retrieved from

https://www.linkedin.com/pulse/art-leadership-journey-through-

historys-most-leaders-tomer-rozenberg/

CHAPTER 23. LEADERSHIP PRINCIPLE OF ACCOUNTABILITY: ITS TRANSFORMATIVE IMPACT ON LEADERS AND ORGANIZATIONS

Accountability requires leaders to take responsibility for their behaviors and actions, ensuring they align with the organization's policies, vision, and the broader community's goals and values, including those of employees and stakeholders. It promotes purposeful leadership, in which leaders recognize the impact of their actions on others and exemplify shared goals, empowerment, and the advancement of all.

Key Points on Accountability

- Accountability fosters trust and respect within teams, creating a sense of fairness (Brogan, J. 2022)
- Strong leadership connects strategy, people, and results through accountability (Gouldsberry, M., 2023).
- Accountable leaders set clear goals, honor their promises, and cultivate a culture of responsibility (Helbig, B., 2023).
- Promoting a culture of accountability leads to high-performing teams and organizational success (Amin, H., 2024).

Feedback, whether solicited or unsolicited, forms the foundation of accountability. It involves gathering and sharing information about a leader's feelings, attitudes, thoughts, motives, intentions, and convictions. This openness allows leaders to reflect on their actions, align their behaviors with organizational values, and accept responsibility for their impact on others.

- **Resolving Difficult Issues:** In Genesis 21:9-11, when Sarah tells Abraham to send Hagar and her son Ishmael away, Abraham is distraught. This highlights that accountability is essential in addressing painful issues and relationships.
- **Making Timely Decisions:** In Esther 3-4, Haman conspires to annihilate the Jews, and Mordecai turns to Queen Esther for assistance. Though initially reluctant, Esther is convinced to act. This illustrates how accountability illuminates problems, enabling leaders to make informed and timely decisions.
- **Learning from Unsolicited Feedback:** In Exodus 2:11-14, Moses kills an Egyptian who was beating a Hebrew and hides the body, believing no one saw him. When confronted by another Hebrew, he realizes his actions are known and flees. This example shows that unsolicited feedback, like accountability, can provide valuable insights crucial for a leader's success.
- **Responding to Challenges:** In Numbers 16:1-13, Korah and a group of influential leaders rebelled against Moses's authority. Moses tries to engage in constructive dialogue, but they escalate the conflict. This highlights the importance of accountability in recognizing and correcting judgment errors and nurturing critical thinking to tackle personal and leadership challenges effectively.
- **Self-Reflection and Growth**: In 2 Samuel 11-12, after King David commits adultery and orchestrates Uriah's

death, the prophet Nathan confronts him. David responds with genuine remorse, as expressed in Psalm 51. This highlights that leaders must recognize their humanity, reflect on their hearts, learn from their mistakes, and develop into authentic leaders who lead with compassion.

- **Building a Lasting Legacy:** In 1 Chronicles 22-29, David meticulously plans the temple's construction, detailing resources and coordinating strategically. This illustrates how accountability enables leaders to pursue long-term visions, establish achievable goals, mobilize resources, and gather support to realize their vision, thus leaving a lasting legacy for future generations.

- **Measuring Leadership Effectiveness:** Moses faces numerous challenges while leading the Israelites (Exodus 14:10-12; 16; 17; Numbers 14:1-4). The people's ongoing complaints illustrate how accountability can expose gaps between leaders and followers. A wider gap signifies greater discontent, mistrust, dissatisfaction, suspicion, and disengagement, whereas a narrower gap indicates higher satisfaction and engagement. Accountability is a benchmark for leaders to learn, improve, adapt, and transform.

Diagram: Measuring the Leader-Follower Gap with Benchmarks and Criteria for Measurement

The following diagram illustrates the relationship between leaders and followers, emphasizing the gap that accountability seeks to bridge. Benchmarks and criteria are included to assess and enhance leadership effectiveness.

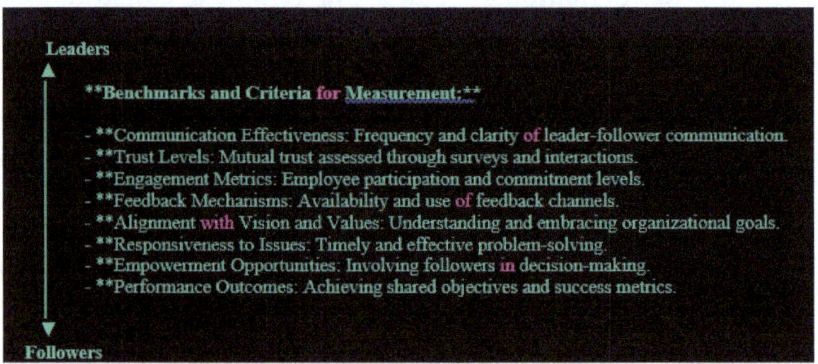

By assessing these criteria, leaders can recognize the degree of the gap between themselves and their followers. Implementing strategies to improve these areas fosters a culture of accountability, leading to stronger relationships, greater satisfaction, and organizational success.

Spiritual Accountability

These examples illustrate the importance of spiritual accountability: the ability of leaders to connect with their hearts and seek divine guidance, direction, inspiration, renewal, and strength. Spiritual accountability involves self-reflection and helps build resilience to tackle complex challenges in a rapidly changing environment.

Conclusion

Accountability is transformative for leaders and organizations. It builds trust, empowers teams, and encourages intentional leadership. By embracing accountability, leaders can tackle challenges, make informed decisions, and create a lasting positive impact.

Framework for Leaders to Foster a Culture of Accountability in Organizations: Its Impact on Purposeful Leadership

The Accountability Framework is a structured approach for organizations to maintain compliance, governance, and ethical standards (Captain Compliance, 2024). It provides a roadmap for turning values and decisions into measurable actions that promote continuous improvement. Additionally, it ensures ethical practices are enacted today while establishing a foundation for sustainability that benefits future generations.

Key Elements and Steps for Implementation

The following action steps offer a comprehensive framework for leaders to apply the principle of accountability within their organizations. Each step promotes a culture of accountability, aligns actions with the organization's mission and values, and drives continuous improvement.

1. **Define Policies and Objectives:** Align policies with the organization's values, mission, and stakeholders' needs while setting clear objectives to guide actions. Use SMART and OKR tools to establish effective goals (Amin H., 2024). This step lays a foundation for accountability by clarifying expectations and offering a roadmap for success.

2. **Measure Results:** Establish key performance indicators (KPIs) and benchmarks to assess progress and outcomes, facilitating data-driven decision-making. By measuring performance, leaders can

objectively evaluate their responsibility and identify areas for improvement.

3. **Continuous Monitoring:** Establish tracking systems to meet targets and ensure adherence to policies, procedures, and standards. Report any deficiencies (Captain Compliance, 2024). Continuous monitoring maintains accountability and allows for timely adjustments.

4. **Transparent Reporting**: Document and communicate outcomes and challenges with stakeholders to ensure accountability. Effective communication builds trust and demonstrates a commitment to accountability at all levels of the organization.

5. **Feedback Channels:** Encourage open communication to gather and incorporate feedback into decision-making processes. Leverage feedback loops to provide timely and constructive responses. Actively seeking and responding to feedback demonstrates a commitment to learning and growth, fostering a culture of accountability.

6. **Learning:** Use insights from monitoring, measurement, and feedback to foster learning, adaptation, change, and innovation. By adopting a growth mindset, leaders can consistently enhance their accountability and propel organizational progress.

7. **Implement Improvements**: Implement the insights gained to make necessary adjustments and promote continuous improvement. Acting on data and feedback is a vital part of accountability, as it showcases a commitment to ongoing enhancement.

8. **Drive Transformation:** Utilize accumulated knowledge and enhancements to transform the organization, aligning it more closely with its mission and stakeholders' expectations. By consistently applying the principles of accountability, leaders can create a lasting impact on their organization's culture and performance.

Impact of the Accountability Framework on Purposeful Leadership

Implementing an Accountability Framework greatly influences intentional leadership within an organization. It enables leaders to cultivate a culture of accountability that aligns with the organization's mission and values, ultimately boosting performance and sustainability.

- **Guides Individuals and Organizations Toward Meaningful Goals:** By clarifying roles, responsibilities, and expectations, the framework enhances flexibility and alignment within the organization, leading to improved performance and high-performing teams (Theseira D., 2022). For instance, a non-profit organization utilized the framework to align its programs with its mission of empowering underserved communities, which resulted in a 30% increase in program effectiveness.

- **Embodying Stewardship:** Embedding accountability into the organizational culture ensures that decisions made today do not compromise the ability of future generations to meet their own needs. For instance, the Accountability Framework Initiative aims to make ethical supply chains the new standard, promoting long-term sustainability (Accountability Framework Initiative, 2024). By prioritizing accountability, leaders can make decisions that balance short-term gains with long-term effects.

- **Exemplifies Authenticity and Value-Driven Decision-Making:** Accountable leaders inspire trust and set an example for their teams by upholding values and fostering ethical practices of integrity, fairness, compassion, and inclusivity (Join The Collective, 2024). When leaders consistently show accountability, they create a culture where employees feel empowered to follow suit.

- **Aligning Vision and Actions with a Higher Purpose:** Leaders utilize the accountability framework to pursue long-term goals that align with the organization's vision and strategic activities, connecting actions to a higher purpose. By consistently evaluating progress against the organization's mission, leaders can ensure their actions serve the greater good.

- **Drawing from Inner Wisdom to Inspire Care, Creativity, and Resilience:** Through self-reflection and introspection, leaders can access their reservoir of strength, inspiring and guiding others through challenging times (Aaron, 2024). By holding themselves accountable, leaders can demonstrate the resilience and adaptability necessary to navigate uncertainty and change.

- **Promoting Organizational Change and Innovation:** Feedback, accountability, and learning are crucial for organizational change and innovation. These elements enable leaders to evaluate and adjust strategies, ensuring the organization stays competitive and responsive to external changes (Acker W.V. et al.; G., 2015). When leaders prioritize accountability, they foster an environment encouraging experimentation and learning, fueling innovation and growth.

- **Empowers Others to Seek Collective Betterment:** Leaders prioritize the needs of others and foster community growth, placing shared goals above personal gains (Greenleaf, R.K., 1977). By demonstrating accountability, leaders empower their teams to take ownership of their work and contribute to the organization's success.

In conclusion, implementing an Accountability Framework is crucial for fostering a culture of accountability within organizations. It facilitates purposeful leadership that boosts organizational performance and promotes ethical practices and sustainability. By adopting this framework, leaders can motivate their teams towards shared goals, drive ongoing improvement, and create a positive impact on current and future generations.

Actionable Tools and Techniques to Embed Accountability in an Organization

The tools and techniques described below offer a structured outline for embedding and measuring accountability through specific organizational metrics, benchmarks, and criteria. By concentrating on trust levels, employee engagement, communication effectiveness, and performance outcomes, leaders can evaluate and enhance their impact on the organization and promote purposeful leadership.

1. Trust Levels Metrics

- **Measurement Method**: Specifying the frequency of surveys (e.g., quarterly or bi-annually) can ensure consistent data collection.

- **Benchmark Criteria**:
  - **Trust Index Score**: A target of **>80%** is ambitious and reflects a strong organizational trust environment.
  - **Feedback Responsiveness**: Clarify whether the response time of **<48 hours** includes weekends and holidays.
- **Assessment Tools**:
  - **Stakeholder Engagement Surveys**: Ensure anonymity to encourage honest feedback.
  - **One-on-One Meetings and Interactions**: Regular scheduling (e.g., monthly) can strengthen relationships.
  - **Peer reviews**: Measure trust levels between team members, not just leadership.

2. Employee Engagement Metrics

- **Measurement Method**: Diversify methods by including focus groups or suggestion boxes for more insights.
- **Benchmark Criteria**:
  - **Engagement Rate**: Aiming for **>75%** aligns with industry best practices.
  - **Turnover Rate**: Consider segmenting turnover rates by departments for targeted interventions.
  - **Absenteeism Rate**: Tracking patterns can help address underlying issues.

- **Assessment Tools**:

  - **Employee Engagement Surveys**: Update the reference to reflect current sources.

o **Participation Metrics and Commitment Assessments**: Utilize real-time analytics tools for up-to-date information.
o **Implement stay interviews** to understand why employees remain with the organization, enhancing retention strategies.

3. Communication Effectiveness Metrics

- **Measurement Method**: Include digital communication channels (e.g., emails, intranet posts) in your metrics.
- **Benchmark Criteria**:
  o **Communication Frequency**: Weekly communications are effective; ensure they're meaningful.
  o **Message Clarity Score**: Tools like comprehension quizzes can quantify understanding.
  o **Feedback Loop Efficiency**: Define the expected timeframe clearly (e.g., 24 hours during business days).
- **Assessment Tools**:
  o **Communication Effectiveness Audits**: Regular audits can identify bottlenecks.
  o **Feedback Surveys**: Short, frequent surveys can capture immediate feedback.
  o **Incorporate two-way communication metrics** to assess how well leadership listens to employees.

4. Performance Outcomes Metrics

- **Measurement Method**: Align performance metrics with the organization's strategic goals.

- **Benchmark Criteria**:
  - **Goal Achievement Rate**: >90% is aspirational; ensure goals are realistic and attainable.
  - **Project Completion Rate**: On-time completion of >85% reflects good project management.
  - **Quality Performance Indicators**: Regular quality reviews can maintain high standards.
- **Assessment Tools**:
  - **Performance Dashboards and KPIs Tracking**: Make these accessible to all team members for transparency.
  - **Success Metrics Analysis**: Use data analytics to identify trends and inform decision-making.
  - **Incorporate customer satisfaction metrics** if applicable, linking leadership accountability to customers.

Conclusion

Focusing on measurable and actionable metrics will help embed accountability within the organization and foster purposeful leadership.

References

Aaron. (2024). Lead with Purpose: Strategies for Purposeful Leadership. Leader Navigation. Retrieved from https://www.leadernavigation.com/lead-with-purpose-2/#...

Acker W.V., et al. (2015). The Role of Feedback, Accountability and Learning in Organizational Change and Innovation: A Theoretical Framework. Retrieved from https:// www.researchgate.net/publication/311007402_The_role_of_Feedback_Accountability_a nd_Learning_in_Organizational_Change_and_Inno vation_A_theoretical_framework

Join The Collective. (2024). The Crucial Role of Accountability in Leadership Ethics. Retrieved from https://www.jointhecollective.com/article/leadership-accountability-in-ethical-   practices/

Greenleaf, R. K. (1977). Servant leadership: A journey into the nature of legitimate power and greatness. Paulist Press.

Accountability Framework Initiative. (2024). Together Making Ethical Supply Chain the New Norm. Retrieved from https://accountability-framework.org

Theseira, D. (2022). How to Effectively Empower Teams With an Accountability Framework. Retrieved from   https://www.ardoq.com/blog/accountability-framework

Amin, H. (2024). 7-Steps to make accountability a core part of your culture. Retrieved from https://hypercontext.com/blog/management-skills/create-culture-accountability- workplace

Brogan, J. (2022). What is leadership accountability and why is it so important? Retrieved from https://www.peptalk.com/post/leadership-accountability

Gouldsberry, M. (2023). Leadership Accountability: Why It Matters and How to Fuel It. Retrieved from https://www.betterworks.com/magazine/accountability-in-leadership/

Helbig, B. (2023). Leadership Accountability: What It Looks Like, Why It Matters. Retrieved from

https:// jobs.washingtonpost.com/article/leadership-accountability-what-it-looks- like-why-it-matters/

CHATER 24: LEADERSHIP PRINCIPLE OF LEARNING, ADAPTABILITY, AND IMPROVEMENT

In today's volatile and rapidly changing environment, the leadership principles of adaptability and continuous learning are more essential than ever. Historical figures such as Abraham, Moses, David, Esther, Daniel, and Paul exemplify this principle. Drawing insights from their experiences, we can grasp how adaptability influences purposeful leadership and remains significant in our modern context.

Morphed into a New Identity

Adapting to new challenges often requires leaders to embrace a new identity, reshaping their personality and approach. For instance, Moses transitioned from a prince of Egypt to the leader of the Israelites, adopting a new identity essential for his role as a liberator and lawgiver. Similarly, Paul experienced a profound transformation from Saul, a persecutor of Christians, to one of Christianity's most influential apostles. This underscores the importance of personal transformation for effective leadership.

Developing a New Culture, Practice, and Values

Influential leaders frequently cultivate new values that inspire and align with their purpose and vision. David united the tribes of Israel, creating a new culture and practices that promoted unity and strength. He established a solid and enduring kingdom by instilling values that resonated with his people.

Transitioning to a New Role

Adaptability involves transitioning into roles that align with one's purpose. Esther, originally a Jewish exile who later became queen, embraced her position to advocate for her people. By leveraging her influence, she prevented a genocide, demonstrating the significance of aligning one's role with a greater purpose.

Transforming Mindset

A transformed mindset—embracing new perspectives and philosophies—is crucial for leaders confronting fresh challenges. Daniel upheld his faith and integrity while serving in the courts of foreign kings. His ability to harmonize his beliefs with his duties underscores the importance of a flexible, resilient mindset.

Adapting to New Socio-Economic, Scientific, and Governance Systems

Leaders who adapt to new systems become catalysts for change and innovation. Abraham left his homeland to create a new nation, navigating unfamiliar socio-economic structures and establishing the foundations for future governance systems. His journey illustrates how adaptability can drive significant societal transformations.

Adapting to a New Cross-Cultural Environment

Promoting diversity, inclusiveness, tolerance, and integration is essential for modern leadership. Paul traveled extensively, sharing his message across various cultures and adapting his communication to engage diverse audiences. His efforts highlight the importance of cross-cultural adaptability in effective leadership.

Learning from Mistakes and Embracing Vulnerability

Great leaders make mistakes, experience failure, and show vulnerability, but they learn from these experiences to become better role models. David, for example, faced personal failures but acknowledged his mistakes and sought improvement. This humility and willingness to learn enhanced his leadership qualities.

Becoming Teachers and Pushing Knowledge Frontiers

These leaders became educators, expanding the frontiers of knowledge and fostering a culture of continuous learning. Moses provided laws and teachings that formed the moral foundation for his people. Paul's epistles have enlightened and inspired generations. Their commitment to sharing knowledge ignited unprecedented change and innovation.

Fostering Innovation through Adaptability and Continuous Learning

Adaptability and continuous learning are essential for personal growth and innovation within organizations. Leaders who embrace these principles cultivate a culture encouraging experimentation, risk-taking, and learning from failures. This creates an environment where new ideas can flourish, leading to breakthrough innovations and competitive advantage.

Impact on Purposeful Leadership and Its Relevance in Today's Dynamic Environment

In today's rapidly changing world, the principles demonstrated by these historical figures remain highly relevant. Adaptable leaders inspire others to thrive under pressure and collaborate effectively to solve complex issues (Miles M., 2023). By cultivating a culture of continuous learning, leaders can navigate uncertainty and propel their organizations forward.

A recent study indicates, "Just when leaders need fresh thinking and decisiveness, they tend to revert to tried-and-true methods (Brassey J. et al., 2021). This emphasizes the need for leaders to overcome the adaptability paradox by embracing change and fostering innovation.

Contemporary Examples of Adaptability and Continuous Learning

To illustrate the relevance of these principles in modern leadership, consider the following examples:

- Satya Nadella's leadership at Microsoft has been defined by a commitment to continuous learning and adaptability, leading to the company's successful transformation and growth in the cloud computing and AI markets.

- Angela Merkel's leadership during the European migrant crisis showcased her ability to navigate complex and rapidly changing situations while balancing the needs of her country with humanitarian concerns.

Strategies for Implementing Adaptability and Continuous Learning

To embrace the principles of adaptability and continuous learning, contemporary leaders can take the following steps:

1. Cultivate a growth mindset: Foster a culture that values learning from failures and embraces challenges.

2. Foster a learning organization: Invest in employee development, encourage knowledge sharing, and create opportunities for ongoing learning.

3. Embrace diversity and inclusion: Seek diverse perspectives and cultivate an environment where different viewpoints are valued and respected.

4. Encourage experimentation and risk-taking: Establish a safe space for employees to test new ideas and learn from their results.

5. Lead by example: Show a commitment to personal growth and adaptability through your actions and behaviors.

Conclusion

The experiences of Abraham, Moses, David, Esther, Daniel, and Paul illustrate that adaptability and continuous learning are essential to purposeful leadership. These leaders brought about profound societal transformation by embracing new identities, developing inspiring values, transitioning into roles aligned with their purpose, transforming their mindsets, and adapting to new environments. Leaders who embrace these principles in our dynamic modern landscape are better prepared to navigate challenges and drive meaningful change. This underscores the need for contemporary leaders to adopt these timeless principles and actively work to incorporate them into their leadership practice. By doing so, they can inspire their teams, promote innovation, and lead their organizations to success in an ever-changing world.

Actionable Framework for Leaders: Practicing the Principle of Adaptability, Continuous Learning, and Improvement

Applying Leadership Principles Practically

We present a framework for applying these leadership principles, outlining the transformational journey of leaders who embrace them. This framework is grounded in the principles of adaptive leadership, which emphasize the ability to anticipate future needs, articulate them to foster collective support and understanding, adjust responses through continuous learning, and demonstrate accountability through transparency (Ramalingam B. et al., 2020).

By integrating these principles, leaders can enhance their followers' job attitudes and proactive behaviors, ultimately improving organizational adaptability and success.

1. **Embrace Feedback for Continuous Improvement**
   - **Keep Accountability:** Regularly seek out and act on feedback to enhance leadership skills, promoting a culture of accountability and transparency.
   - **Encourage Open Communication:** Establish a culture that values constructive criticism, fostering continuous learning and improvement (Agility at Scale, 2024).
2. **Practice Regular Reflection**
   - **Meditate and Reflect:** Set aside time for self-examination to improve decision-making in line with the principles of adaptive leadership.
   - **Document Insights:** Maintain a journal to record growth and lessons learned, fostering continuous learning and improvement (Agility at Scale, 2024).

3. **Empower Through Delegation**
   - o **Develop Teams:** Assign responsibilities to cultivate leadership in others, fostering adaptability and resilience within the organization.
   - o **Provide Resources:** Ensure teams have the necessary tools to succeed, empowering them to adapt to changing circumstances.
4. **Collaborate and Seek Counsel**
   - o Engage with Peers: Consult other leaders and stakeholders for diverse perspectives to foster adaptability and continuous learning.
   - o ∘ **Adapt to Change:** Be open to modifying strategies based on collective wisdom, showing flexibility and resilience (Center for Creative Leadership, 2021).
5. **Adapt in Diverse Environments**
   - o **Cultural Competence:** Understand and appreciate diverse cultures to lead effectively, improving adaptability in various environments.
   - o **Maintain Identity:** Stay true to your core values while adapting, ensuring consistency and authenticity in leadership.
6. **Monitor Progress and Encourage Growth**
   - o **Track Achievements:** Regularly evaluate goals and milestones, aligning with the principles of continuous improvement (Agility at Scale, 2024).
   - o **Build Communities:** Enhance relationships and cultivate a supportive network that promotes adaptability and resilience within the organization.

Conclusion

By integrating adaptability and continuous learning, leaders and organizations can achieve transformative growth. Embracing feedback, reflecting, empowering teams, seeking counsel, and adapting to diverse environments enhance leadership effectiveness and foster innovation and engagement within organizations. This framework, rooted in the principles of adaptive leadership, provides a practical approach for leaders to navigate the complexities of today's world and position their organizations for long-term success (Mary Uhl-Bien & Michael Arena, 2018).

Methods and Strategies for Integrating Learning, Adaptation, and Improvement within an Organization

Drawing inspiration from leaders like Abraham, Moses, David, Daniel, and Paul, we can discover practical tools and techniques to cultivate a culture of continuous learning and adaptability. By integrating these principles with modern examples, organizations can effectively navigate the complexities of today's dynamic environment and drive innovation and growth.

By integrating these principles with contemporary examples, organizations can navigate the complexities of today's fluid environment and drive innovation and growth.

1. Seeking Feedback and Embracing Improvement

- o **Moses:** Accepted counsel from Jethro, learning to delegate tasks and responsibilities, which helped build strong teams and increase accountability (Schulze J.H. et al., 2020; Crans, S. et al., 2022).
- o **Paul:** Received guidance from the Elders' Council in Jerusalem to address contentious issues, demonstrating openness to new ideas and adaptability.

2. Encourage feedback about leadership practices

- o Conduct anonymous surveys or hold regular one-on-one meetings with team members.

3. Implement improvements to advance organizational goals

- o Utilize insights gained from feedback to promote ongoing learning and adaptation. Contemporary Example: Google's "Googlegeist" survey enables employees to submit anonymous feedback on different facets of the company, cultivating a culture of continuous improvement and flexibility.

4. Practicing Meditation and Reflection

- o **David, Daniel, and Paul:** Regularly engaged in meditation and reflection, which enhanced their decision-making and leadership effectiveness (Ramalingam B. et al. (2020).

Action Steps:

- o Incorporate regular periods of reflection to assess actions and strategies, such as weekly or monthly review sessions.
- o Use insights gained to inform future decisions and adaptations, ensuring the organization remains agile and responsive to change. Contemporary Example: Salesforce's "V2MOM" (Vision, Values, Methods, Obstacles, and Measures) process encourages employees to reflect on their goals and progress regularly, fostering a culture of continuous learning and adaptation (Ramalingam B. et al. (2020).

5. Deploying Leadership Teams for Growth

- o **Paul and Barnabas:** Tracked and monitored progress by revisiting cities where they preached, fostering accountability and strengthening communities.

Action Steps:

- o Send teams to gather intelligence and provide training while ensuring the organization stays connected to its stakeholders and responsive to their needs.
- o ◦ Resolve conflicts and encourage continuous development among followers, fostering a culture of learning and growth.
- o ◦ Contemporary Example: Amazon's "Two-Pizza Teams" concept promotes small, agile teams working together to solve problems and drive innovation, nurturing a culture of continuous learning and adaptation.

6. Engaging in Input from Others

- o **Moses:** Embraced Jethro's advice to delegate, enhancing team strength and accountability adaptation (Mary Uhl-Bien, Michael Arena. (2018).
- o **Paul:** Collaborated with the Elders' Council, showing the importance of collective wisdom.

Action Steps:

- o Engage with stakeholders, including customers, employees, and industry experts, to seek advice and gather diverse perspectives.
- o Be open to new ideas and the critical changes necessary for growth, nurturing a culture of continuous learning and adaptation.

- o ◦ Contemporary Example: IBM's "Innovation Jams" bring together employees, customers, and partners to collaborate on fresh ideas and solutions, promoting a culture of ongoing learning and adaptation (Mary Uhl-Bien, Michael Arena. (2018).

7. Learning and Adapting in Cross-Cultural Environments

- o **Daniel:** Trained in the language and literature of the Chaldeans, he adeptly navigated a foreign culture while maintaining his identity.
- o **Moses:** Educated in Egyptian wisdom, he remained true to his roots and became a great leader.
- o **Abraham:** Left his homeland to venture into the unknown, learning and adapting to become a renowned leader.

Action Steps:

- o Embrace learning opportunities in new environments by sending employees on international assignments or collaborating with diverse suppliers.
- o ◦ Adapt while upholding core values and cultural identity to ensure the organization remains true to its mission and purpose.
- o ◦ Contemporary Example: Unilever's "Diversity and Inclusion" initiatives encourage cross-cultural learning and adaptation, fostering a culture of continuous learning and growth.

Organizations can foster a culture of continuous learning, adaptation, and improvement by integrating these tools and techniques with contemporary examples. This approach enables leaders to anticipate future needs, articulate them to build collective support and understanding, adapt responses through continuous learning, and demonstrate accountability through transparency (Ramalingam B. et al., 2020). In today's rapidly changing world, embracing these principles is essential for organizations to navigate uncertainty and drive innovation and growth.

References

Crans, S., Aksentieva, P., Beausaert, S., & Segers, M. (2022). Learning leadership and feedback seeking behavior: Leadership that spurs feedback seeking. *Frontiers in psychology, 13,* 890861. https://doi.org/10.3389/fpsyg.2022.890861

Agility at Scale. (2024). Adaptability and Continuous Improvement: The Agile and Lean Path to Sustained Success. Retrieved from https"//agility-at-scale.com/principles/continuous- improvement/

Brassey J.et al. (2021). Future proof: Solving the 'adaptability paradox' for the long-term. Retrieved from

https://www.mckinsey.com/capabilities/people-and-organizational- performance/our-insights/future-proof-solving-the-adaptability-paradox-for-the-long- term

Center for Creative Leadership. (2021). Adapting to change requires flexible leadership. Retrieved from https://www.ccl.org/articles/leading-effectively-articles/adaptability-1-idea-3-facts-5-tips/

Miles M. (2023). 7 Types of adaptability skills that'll help you grow professionally. Retrieved from https://www.betterup.com/blog/types-of-adaptability-skills

Ramalingam B. et al. (2020). 5 Principles to Guide Adaptative Leadership. Retrieved from https://hbr.org/2020/09/5-principles-to-guide-adaptive-leadership hbr.org/2020/09/5-principles-to-guide-adaptive-leadership

Uhl-Bien, M., Michael Arena. (2018). Leadership for organizational adaptability: A theoretical synthesis and integrative framework, The Leadership Quarterly, Volume 29, Issue 1, Pages 89-104, ISSN 1048-9843, https://doi.org/10.1016/j.leaqua.2017.12.009.

CHAPTER 25: THE LEADERSHIP PRINCIPLE OF FAITH AND HOPE: ITS TRANSFORMATIVE IMPACT ON LEADERS AND ORGANIZATIONS

Faith and hope are powerful forces that can profoundly impact leaders and organizations. Grounded in biblical teachings, these principles provide a framework for ethical leadership and organizational resilience in today's fast-paced environment.

Biblical Foundation

Faith is defined as a cognitive conviction—confidence in the unseen and the belief that what we hope for will materialize —as expressed in Hebrews 11:1. Hebrews 11 describes the essence of faith, highlighting its foundational role. Romans 4:18 illustrates the power of hope: "Against all hope, Abraham in hope believed and thus became the father of many nations." This underscores how faith guides individuals toward their destiny. Galatians 3:6 refers to Abraham as "our father of faith," emphasizing that his faith enabled God to impute his righteousness to him, allowing him to understand and fulfill his purpose.

Defining Faith and Hope

While hope reflects our desires and attitudes—a longing for something yet to be achieved, characterized by steadfast expectation—faith is a guiding principle that shapes our actions and choices. These concepts are interconnected, both rooted in the foundation of belief

Impact on Leaders and Organizations

Faith as a Moral Compass

Faith offers leaders a foundation of values that directs ethical behavior and decision-making. It fosters resilience and determination, encouraging leaders to strive for a higher purpose focused on societal improvement.

Fostering Empathy and Compassion

Faith fosters a supportive atmosphere, strengthens community ties among members, and encourages transparency and ethical behavior. It promotes inclusivity and collaboration within teams, nurturing a servant leadership style that prioritizes serving and uplifting others (Mujuru F., 2023). Leaders can nurture this environment by actively listening to their team members, demonstrating vulnerability, and creating opportunities for personal and professional development.

Hope as an Antidote to Adversity

Hope empowers leaders to tackle challenges with perseverance. It weaves purpose into the organization, fosters trust and credibility among stakeholders, and sparks curiosity, which drives innovation and creativity (Mark C., 2017). By nurturing a hopeful perspective, leaders can inspire their teams to embrace change and perceive setbacks as chances for growth and learning.

Enhancing Work Ethics and Productivity

Hope fosters a positive work ethic, leading to enhanced performance and productivity. It cultivates a forward-thinking mindset that propels organizational success.

Driving Innovation and Creativity

Faith and hope play a crucial role in driving innovation and creativity within organizations. By fostering a culture of trust and psychological safety, leaders can create an environment where team members feel empowered to take risks and share their ideas. For instance, Google's "20% time" policy, which allows employees to dedicate a portion of their workweek to personal projects, has led to innovative products such as Gmail and Google Maps. Likewise, leaders who embody faith and hope can inspire their teams to think creatively and push the boundaries of what is possible.

Contemporary Relevance

In today's rapidly changing environment, the principles of faith and hope are more relevant than ever. Leaders who exemplify these principles can guide their organizations through uncertainty, inspire their teams, and drive meaningful change. For instance, during the COVID-19 pandemic, leaders like New Zealand's Prime Minister Jacinda Ardern showed faith in their nation's ability to overcome the crisis and hope for a better future, leading their countries through challenging times with compassion and resilience.

Implications for Purposeful Leadership

- Embracing faith and hope empowers leaders to:
- Cultivate a resilient and ethical organizational culture by establishing clear values and expectations and consistently demonstrating those behaviors.
- Encourage innovation through a hopeful perspective by celebrating successes, learning from failures, and providing resources and support for experimentation.
- Build strong, compassionate communities within their organizations by fostering a sense of belonging, promoting work-life balance, and offering opportunities for social impact and giving back.

- Lead with purpose toward societal betterment by aligning organizational goals with a greater mission and engaging stakeholders in pursuing a more just and sustainable world.

Conclusion

In summary, faith and hope profoundly influence leaders and organizations, cultivating a culture of resilience, ethical behavior, and community engagement. By incorporating these principles, leaders can navigate challenges and steer their organizations toward a purposeful and prosperous future. To integrate faith and hope into their leadership practices, contemporary leaders should:

1. Reflect on their values and beliefs and how these align with the organization's mission and vision.

2. Communicate openly and honestly with their teams, sharing their vision for the future and the role of faith and hope in achieving it.

3. Foster a culture of trust and psychological safety, where team members feel empowered to take risks and share new ideas.

4. Celebrate successes and learn from failures, using them as opportunities for growth and improvement.

5. Engage with stakeholders, including employees, customers, and the broader community, to understand their needs and aspirations and co-create a more hopeful and purposeful future.

By embracing the transformative power of faith and hope, leaders can inspire their organizations to achieve greatness and make a positive impact on the world.

Framework for Practicing the Leadership Principle of Faith and Hope

Inspired by Abraham, leaders can cultivate a culture of faith and hope to reach the goals they aspire to for their teams and organizations.

Awareness of Purpose:

- Understand your purpose or your organization's purpose by reflecting on your core values and mission.
- Clarify the desired future state and goals, aligning them with your purpose.

Action Steps:

   o Conduct a personal or organizational values assessment to identify your core beliefs and mission.
   o Develop a clear, compelling purpose statement guiding your decision-making and actions.

Contemporary Example: Patagonia's founder, Yvon Chouinard, has centered his company on the mission of "using business to inspire and implement solutions to the environmental crisis," which guides the organization's goals and strategies.

Vision:

- Envision the end state from the beginning, creating a clear image of what success looks like.
- Build confidence and assurance (faith) in your ability to achieve unseen, aspirational goals.
- Maintain a consistent expectation and anticipation (hope) that you will reach your desired future state.

Action Steps:

- o Formulate a vivid vision statement that encapsulates your desired future and the impact you wish to achieve.
- o Consistently visualize your vision, strengthening your faith and hope in its realization.

Contemporary Example: Martin Luther King Jr.'s "I Have a Dream" speech powerfully expressed his vision for racial equality, inspiring hope and faith in millions of people.

Journey:

- Identify your North Star: the values and beliefs that guide your leadership journey, shaped by life's narratives and challenges.
- Embrace adversity as an opportunity for personal growth, fostering perseverance, resilience, and the right mindset.

Action Steps:

- o Reflect on your life experiences to identify the core values and beliefs that have shaped your leadership style.
- o When facing adversity, view it as an opportunity for growth and learning while maintaining hope and confidence in your ability to overcome.

Contemporary Example: Oprah Winfrey's journey from a challenging childhood to becoming a media mogul illustrates the power of perseverance and resilience in the face of difficulties.

Diagram Below: Illustrates the transformative journey of faith and hope

Diagram below: Illustrates the transformative journey of faith and hope.

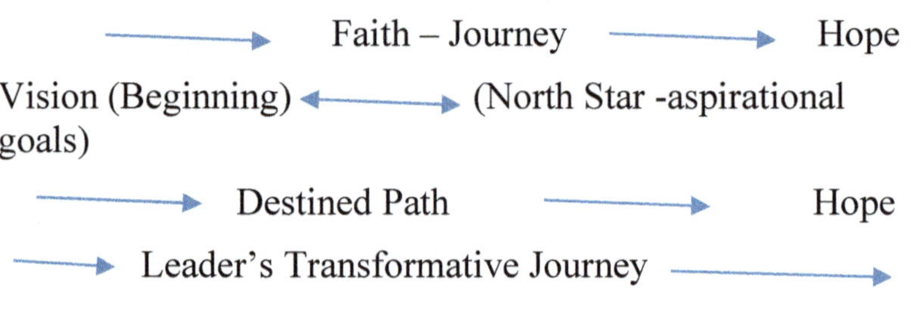

Faith – Journey Hope Vision (Beginning) (North Star - aspirational goals)

Destined Path Hope – A Leader's Transformative Journey

Cultivating a Culture of Confidence: To Sustain Faith and Hope

- Develop perseverance by setting and achieving small, incremental goals toward larger aspirations, recovering from setbacks and difficult times.
- Foster accountability, collaboration, and initiative within teams, establishing a foundation of resilience.
- Cultivate mental and emotional toughness to excel under pressure, remaining focused on your purpose and vision.
- Embrace reinvention by staying at the cutting edge of innovative thinking, seeking feedback, and celebrating accomplishments.

- Engage in regular reflection and learning to derive lessons from experience and promote continuous improvement.

Action Steps:

- o Break down your vision into smaller, achievable goals, celebrate progress, and learn from setbacks.
- o Foster a culture of psychological safety within your team to encourage open communication, collaboration, and accountability.
- o Practice mindfulness and self-care to maintain mental and spiritual resilience when facing challenges.
- o Regularly seek stakeholder feedback and adapt your approach based on their input, remaining open to new ideas and perspectives.
- o Conduct regular retrospectives with your team to identify lessons learned and areas for improvement.

Contemporary Example: Satya Nadella's leadership at Microsoft focuses on fostering a culture of growth mindset, resilience, and innovation, driving the company's success in cloud computing and AI.

Conclusion

This journey highlights the interplay between a leader's values, the challenges they face, and the resilience they build. By concentrating on these elements and taking action to implement this framework, leaders can inspire hope and cultivate a culture of confidence that drives themselves and their teams toward success. Embrace the transformative power of faith and hope in your leadership practice, and watch your vision come to life.

Embedding Faith and Hope in an Organization: Practical Tools and Techniques

Embedding faith and hope within an organization can cultivate a supportive and inclusive workplace culture. Here are some practical tools and techniques to achieve this, along with modern examples for each practice:

Creating an Open Environment for Faith Discussions

It involves:

- Encouraging employees to share their beliefs and practices without fear of retaliation.
- Promoting interfaith dialogue and respect for diverse perspectives.

Contemporary examples include Intel hosting several faith-based employee groups, such as Christian, Jewish, and Muslim communities, which create an environment where employees can openly express their beliefs. The company also organizes interfaith events that promote understanding and respect among people of different faiths.

Establish Care Centers for Nursing Mothers

- Provide dedicated spaces where nursing mothers can attend to their babies during specific times during work.
- Support work-life balance and the well-being of working parents.

Contemporary Example: Google provides on-site lactation rooms and a Mother's Room program. It offers private spaces for nursing mothers to express milk or care for their infants during work hours, supporting work-life balance and well-being.

Offer Counseling Services

- Set up counseling centers to help employees with mental health issues and those who are bereaved.
- Ensure access to professional resources for personal support.

Contemporary Example: Johnson & Johnson offers an Employee Assistance Program (EAP) that provides free, confidential counseling services to employees and their families. The program addresses mental health issues and supports bereaved individuals.

Communicate Positive and Inspiring Messages

Share uplifting messages during times of stress or uncertainty.

- Reinforce hope and resilience within the organization.

Contemporary Example: During the COVID-19 pandemic, Salesforce CEO Marc Benioff sent regular emails to employees, sharing positive messages and reinforcing hope and resilience in uncertainty.

Foster Appreciation and Gratitude Practices

- Implement initiatives that make employees feel valued and appreciated.
- Regularly recognize individual and team achievements.

Contemporary Example: At Zappos, employees are encouraged to send "thank you" notes to colleagues who have helped them, fostering a culture of appreciation and gratitude. The company also holds regular recognition events to celebrate individual and team achievements.

Promote a Culture of Diversity and Inclusivity

- Cultivate an environment where all employees feel a sense of belonging.
- Embrace diversity and ensure inclusivity in all organizational practices.

Contemporary Example: Accenture is firmly committed to diversity and inclusion. Its employee resource groups support various communities, including those based on race, ethnicity, gender, sexual orientation, and disability. The company also ensures inclusivity in its hiring practices and career development opportunities.

By integrating these practices, organizations can build a stronger, more cohesive workforce anchored in faith and hope.

References

Mujuru, F. (2023). Christian's Faith Transformative Influence in Leadership. Medium. Link

Mark, C. (2017). The importance of hope – a key principle of leadership and life. LinkedIn. Link

CHAPTER 26: THE LEADERSHIP PRINCIPLE OF APPRECIATION AND THANKSGIVING: ITS TRANSFORMATIVE IMPACT ON LEADERS AND ORGANIZATIONS

Appreciation and thanksgiving are powerful leadership principles that involve expressing gratitude and recognizing others' contributions. This practice enriches personal relationships and has a profound, transformative impact on leaders and organizations.

Definition

The leadership principle of appreciation and thanksgiving entails acknowledging and valuing the efforts and achievements of others. Michael G. Rogers (2020) states that it embodies "having a heart of thankfulness." Effective appreciation should be specific, authentic, genuine, and personal (Lisa T., 2022; McCann R., 2023).

Biblical Foundation of Appreciation and Thanksgiving

The biblical foundation for appreciation and thanksgiving is extensive:

• Leviticus 23:1-44: God ordained festivals and holidays for worship and joyful celebration, where people expressed gratitude, offered sacrifices, and exchanged gifts. These practices emphasize God's expectation that we be appreciative and thankful for what we have received and that we bless others in return.

• The Sabbath: Designated as a day of rest and worship, the Sabbath underscores the importance of taking time to reflect, appreciate, and give thanks. It liberates individuals from daily pressures, promoting peace of mind and alleviating stress.

• The Psalms: Teach us to live a life of daily thanksgiving, expressing gratitude first to God for His blessings and then to others.

• Philippians 4:4-6 & 1 Thessalonians 5:15: The Apostle Paul exhorts believers to rejoice always and give thanks in all circumstances, highlighting the significance of gratitude regardless of life's situations.

The biblical principles of appreciation and thanksgiving provide a strong foundation for their application in leadership and organizational contexts.

Importance of Appreciation and Thanksgiving

As highlighted by Arianna Huffington in her article "The Small Miracle of Gratitude" (2024): Antidote to Stress and Anxiety: Gratitude lowers stress and depression levels, improves sleep, helps us reset, and provides perspective.

- Fosters Optimism and Happiness: Regularly expressing gratitude increases overall well-being and a positive outlook on life.
- Improves Physical Health: Gratitude lowers inflammation levels and enhances heart health.
- Encourages Generosity and Healthier Behaviors: It reduces materialism, increases generosity, and leads to healthier lifestyle choices.

- Reduces Loneliness: Particularly among the elderly, gratitude decreases feelings of isolation.

Transformative Impact on Leaders and Organization

Impact on Leaders

Expressing appreciation can significantly reduce stress and enhance a leader's well-being. Gratitude fosters empathy and understanding, allowing leaders to connect more deeply with team members. This connection builds stronger relationships based on trust and loyalty. Practicing gratitude empowers leaders to combat negativity, shifting their mindset from defensiveness to acceptance and appreciation (McCann R., 2023).

Additionally, it promotes healthier behaviors and improves overall quality of life (By The A Group, 2020). For instance, Google has a program called "gThanks" that allows employees to publicly thank colleagues for their contributions. This initiative fosters a culture of appreciation and recognition, increasing employee morale and creating a more positive work environment.

Impact on Organizations

A culture of appreciation enhances employee engagement, motivation, and retention, thereby increasing productivity and performance (Rogers, M. G., 2020; McCann, R., 2023). It nurtures an environment that promotes creativity and innovation, inspiring personal and professional growth for leaders and employees (Lisa T., 2022; McCann R., 2023). Building trust and respect through appreciation strengthens employee loyalty and reduces turnover rates (Threlfall D., 2016; Perry E., 2023).

Organizations foster a more positive and productive workplace culture by integrating appreciation and gratitude into leadership practices. A study by a leading HR firm found that companies with a robust culture of appreciation enjoyed 50% higher employee retention rates than those without (BambooHR, 2023).

Relevance in Today's Stressful and Demanding Environment

In today's fast-paced and demanding world, the principles of appreciation and gratitude are more relevant than ever. High levels of stress and burnout are prevalent in many workplaces. Incorporating gratitude into leadership and organizational culture serves as a counterbalance, promoting mental well-being and fostering a supportive work environment.

For instance, the Cleveland Clinic: The healthcare system has a "Caregiver Appreciation Program" that encourages employees to recognize and thank their colleagues for their dedication and compassion in patient care. The program includes a platform for sending appreciation messages and a monthly recognition event.

Practical Strategies for Leaders

- To incorporate appreciation and thanksgiving into daily practices, leaders can:
- Regularly express gratitude to team members through verbal or written acknowledgments.
- Initiate gratitude rituals, such as starting meetings with a round of thanks.
- Foster a culture of peer-to-peer recognition and appreciation.
- Lead by example, demonstrating gratitude in both actions and words.

Implications for Purposeful Leadership

Embracing appreciation and thanksgiving empowers leaders to:

- Enhance personal well-being: Reduce stress and promote healthier behaviors.
- Build stronger relationships: Foster trust, loyalty, and open communication with team members.
- Improve organizational culture: Create a positive environment encouraging engagement, innovation, and retention.
- Promote societal betterment: Lead by example, inspiring others to practice gratitude and contribute positively.

Conclusion

Appreciation and gratitude are transformative principles that greatly influence leaders and organizations. By embracing thankfulness, leaders improve their well-being, build stronger relationships, and foster a positive organizational culture that encourages engagement, innovation, and growth. In a world full of challenges and stress, appreciation and gratitude provide a pathway to resilience, happiness, and collective success.

Actionable Framework for Leaders: Practicing Appreciation and Gratitude Overview

Drawing on the Apostle Paul's example, leaders can cultivate a culture of appreciation and gratitude by prioritizing positive reinforcement and supportive communication. This strategy not only boosts team morale but also encourages resilience and growth. To put this into practice, leaders can adopt a framework that emphasizes positive reinforcement and supportive communication.

Emphasize Strengths Over Weaknesses

- Concentrate on individuals' strengths to foster confidence.

Spotlight Opportunities Rather Than Threats

- Foster a growth-oriented mindset.

Recognize Assets Instead of Faults

- Recognize the unique contributions of each team member. A healthcare organization hosts quarterly appreciation events to honor staff members for their dedication and the value they add to the organization.

Acknowledge Good Deeds

- Treat mistakes as gentle teaching opportunities to encourage learning. When an employee makes an error, a leader can discuss what occurred, what was learned, and how to avoid similar mistakes in the future without focusing on the negative aspects.

Empower Individuals

- Inspire confidence and independence in team members. A sales manager motivates her team to set goals and develop strategies to achieve them, offering guidance and support.

Underscore Adaptability and Resilience

Promote a culture of learning and development. A manufacturing company provides regular training sessions and encourages employees to attend industry conferences to stay current with the latest technologies and best practices.

Apostle Paul's approach to appreciating his followers is a practical example for leaders to practice gratitude.

Effective Practices:

Comment Faithfulness

- Acknowledge and celebrate followers' dedication. For instance, a leader can send personalized thank-you notes to employees who consistently commit to the organization's mission and values.

Acknowledge Mutual Support

- Foster a sense of community through shared love and care. A team leader can arrange regular team-building activities to strengthen relationships and promote collaboration among team members.

Praise Resilience

- Emphasize perseverance during difficult times. When a project encounters setbacks, a leader should recognize the team's hard work and determination in overcoming challenges, reinforcing their capacity to adapt and grow.

Seek Opportunities to Praise

- Focus on positive feedback instead of criticism. A manager can consistently offer regular, specific praise for employees' achievements and contributions, both privately and publicly, before their peers.

Maintain a Positive Attitude

- Encourage followers to stay hopeful during tough times. In uncertain situations, a leader can share stories of resilience and success, reminding the team of their capacity to overcome challenges.

Provide Clarity on Unsettling Issues

- Communicate openly to reduce uncertainty and ambiguity. When encountering difficult decisions or changes, a leader can hold town hall meetings to ensure transparency and address employees' concerns.

Lead by Example

- Build trust and loyalty through consistent actions. Leaders can show appreciation and gratitude by regularly thanking their team members and recognizing their efforts.

Encourage Effective Communication

- Encourage followers to grow and seize opportunities. A leader can promote open communication by having regular one-on-one meetings with employees, actively listening to their ideas and concerns, and offering personalized feedback and coaching.

Promote Gratitude

- Cultivate a habit of gratitude regardless of the circumstances. A leader can encourage employees to maintain gratitude journals, share their thankfulness during team meetings, and engage in community service projects to give back to others.

Benefits of Fostering a Culture of Appreciation and Gratitude

By applying these principles, leaders can experience several benefits, including:

- Increased employee engagement and motivation.
- Higher retention rates and reduced turnover.
- Improved team performance and collaboration.
- Enhanced resilience and adaptability in the face of challenges.
- A more positive and supportive work environment.

Conclusion

Appreciation and gratitude are powerful tools for leaders. They foster an atmosphere of calm and focus, particularly during uncertain and challenging times. By adopting these principles, leaders can motivate their teams to excel in the face of adversity, promoting a culture that values growth, resilience, and mutual support. Through consistent practice and sincere appreciation, leaders can create a workplace where employees feel valued, inspired, and empowered to give their best effort.

Tools and Techniques for Embedding Appreciation and Thanksgiving in an Organization

Embedding appreciation and gratitude in an organization is essential for fostering a positive work culture, boosting employee morale, and enhancing overall well-being. By utilizing the following tools and techniques, leaders can cultivate an environment where gratitude becomes a fundamental part of the organizational fabric.

Implement Employee Recognition Programs

- Develop formal recognition systems to acknowledge employee achievements and contributions. For instance, a points-based system where employees earn points for their accomplishments can be redeemed for rewards.
- Leverage peer-to-peer appreciation platforms that allow employees to recognize each other's efforts. A study by Globoforce found that peer-to-peer recognition is 35.7% more likely to positively impact financial results than manager-only recognition (Schneider L., 2023).
- Organize award ceremonies or appreciation events to celebrate successes. For example, a quarterly "Gratitude Gala" where employees are honored for their contributions in front of their peers.

Provide Tools for Expressing Appreciation

- Provide thank-you cards or digital platforms for employees to send notes of appreciation. For instance, a company like Salesforce uses a "Thanks" tool within its internal communication platform, allowing employees to express gratitude.
- Implement employee recognition software that tracks and rewards acts of gratitude. This software can generate reports on recognition trends, helping leaders identify areas for improvement.
- Facilitate anonymous compliments to ensure even the most introverted employees can participate. For example, the "Kudos" feature on the Microsoft.com platform allows employees to give and receive anonymous praise (Learn.microsoft.com, 2024).
- Feature stories of teamwork and support in internal newsletters or communications. For instance, a monthly "Gratitude Spotlight" section in the company newsletter highlights employees who go above and beyond for their colleagues.

Encourage Gratitude Exercises

- **Gratitude Journals:** Encourage employees to keep journals emphasizing what they appreciate at work. A study by the University of California, Davis, found that participants who maintained a gratitude journal for just three weeks saw a 25% increase in their happiness levels (Emmons R.A., et al., 2003).
- **Gratitude Boards:** Create a shared space where employees can post notes of appreciation. For example, a physical or digital board in the break room where employees can write thank-you notes to their colleagues.

- **Mindful Appreciation Moments:** Include brief sessions for teams to share gratitude for recent achievements. This could be a 5-minute gratitude check-in at the beginning of team meetings.
- **Gratitude Walks:** Organize group walks where employees can express appreciation for their surroundings and each other while enjoying some exercise and fresh air.
- **Gratitude Circles:** Hold regular gratitude circle sessions, during which employees sit in a circle and take turns sharing something they are grateful for.

Conduct Training and Workshops

- Organize workshops focusing on the benefits of gratitude and how to practice it effectively. For example, host a workshop titled "The Science of Gratitude" that explores the psychological and physiological advantages of gratitude.
- Provide training in emotional intelligence and effective communication, including courses on active listening, empathy, and the ability to give and receive feedback.
- Invite guest speakers to shed light on the importance of appreciation in the workplace. For instance, consider inviting a well-known author or researcher in gratitude to share their insights and experiences with employees.

By using these practical tools and techniques, organizations can foster a culture of appreciation and gratitude that reaches every level of the company. This enhances employee well-being and engagement while fostering a more positive, productive work environment.

References

BambooHR. (2023). "The Impact of Appreciation on Employee Retention." BambooHR   Research Institute.

Emmons R.A., et al. (2003). Count Blessings Versus Burdens: An Experimental Investigation of Gratitude and Subjective Well-being in Daily Lives. *Journal of Personality and Social*   *Psychology.* Vol. 84, No. 2, 377–389. Retrieved from

https://emmons.faculty.ucdavis.edu/wp-content/uploads/sites/90/2015/08/2003_2-
          Emmons_McCullough_2003_JPSP.pdf   DOI: 10.1037/0022-3514.84.2.377

Learn.microsoft.com. (2024). Employee Kudos for Power Platform. Retrieved from

https://   learn.microsoft.com/en-us/power-platform/enterprise-templates/hr/employe kudos/overview

Rogers M. G. (2020). The Simple Leadership Principle of   Gratitude.   Retrieved   from https://www.teamworkandleadership.com/the-simple-leadership-principle-of-gratitude/..

Lisa, T. (2022). Lessons in Leadership from the Thanksgiving Table – Thank Up, Thank Together and Thank All Around. Retrieved from

https://pathwayhealth.com/lessons-in-   leadership-from-the-thanksgiving-table-thank-up-thank-together-and-thank-all-around/#:

Threlfall D. (2016). Gratitude: The Leader's Most Underused   but   Powerful   Tool.   Retrieved   from https://www.teamgantt.com/blog/gratitude-the-leaders-most-underused-but-powerful-tools#:

McCann R. (2023). The Intersection of Gratitude and Leadership: Cultivating a Culture of Appreciation for Empowered Teams and Effective Leaders. Retrieved from https://www.stopatnothing.com/the-intersection-of-gratitude-and-leadership/#....

By The A Group. (2020). How Gratitude Impacts Your Leadership and Teams. Retrieved from

https:// www.agroup.com/blog/how-gratitude-impacts-your-leadership-and-teams/#...

Perry E. (2023). Show Gratitude with "Thank you for your leadership and vision." Retrieved from htttps://www.betterup.com/blog/thank-you-for-your-leadership-and-vision#:~

Huffington, A. (2024). The Small Miracles of Gratitude: On My Mind. Retrieved from

https://www.linkedin

Schneider L. (2023). Peer-to-Peer Recognition: 8 Best Practices. Retrieved from https:// compt.io/blog/peer-to-peer-recognition-best-practices/#:~:text

PART 6: CULTIVATING THE TRAITS OF PURPOSEFUL LEADERSHIP

In Part 6, we examine the essential traits of purposeful leadership, using biblical case studies to demonstrate how these qualities influence a leader's actions and promote organizational success. These traits are driven not by the desire for power, fame, glory, or financial gain, but by a profound commitment to serving and cultivating positive change. The trait approach, a fundamental theory in leadership studies, posits that leaders possess specific qualities that others may lack, which can be either innate or developed (Northouse, 2019).

We examine how leaders who embody these traits can transform teams and organizations, presenting real-life examples to illustrate the profound impact of purposeful leadership. By studying the lives of godly, courageous biblical leaders, we gain valuable insights into maintaining respect for authority while standing firm in one's convictions. Throughout this section, we emphasize that a leader's heart requires a love that actively engages with the struggles and challenges faced by their followers, addressing issues with a sense of security derived from knowing God and His purposes (Joly H., 2022).

By understanding and embracing these foundational traits, leaders can develop a leadership style that prioritizes the well-being and growth of their team members, ultimately resulting in a healthier and more effective organization.

Examining temperament, attitude, mindset, ego, and worldview provides insight into a leader's character and informs their behavior and approach. Purposeful leaders exhibit traits that enable them to excel, be effective, and positively influence the lives of others. The characteristics identified from the case studies include humility, integrity, courage, empathy, and intelligence.

Outline:

1. **Defining Core Traits of Purposeful Leadership**

   - Introduce the foundational traits derived from the biblical case studies and explain how they influence a leader's actions and affect organizational success in each chapter.
   - Provide contemporary examples of leaders who effectively embody these traits.
   - Emphasize the transformative effect of these traits on teams and organizations.
   - Outline strategies for fostering these traits within an organization.

2. **Crafting a Personal Leadership Development Plan**

   - Help readers craft a personalized plan to enhance their leadership skills.

CHAPTER 27: THE TRAIT OF HUMILITY IN LEADERSHIP

Defining Humility

Humility, often misconstrued as self-deprecation or low self-esteem, is a positive trait that directs a person toward others. It is demonstrated through gentleness, kindness, generosity, and a willingness to prioritize others. John Baldoni highlights the significance of humility, pointing out that it validates a person's humanity (2009).

Insights from Biblical Case Studies

- **Abraham:** In Genesis 21:10, Sarah tells Abraham to send away Hagar and her son Ishmael. Although this grieves him, Abraham follows God's counsel on the issue. Even though one might view Sarah's request as insulting or domineering, Abraham shows humility by listening to his wife and obeying her.
- **Moses:** In Numbers 10:31, Moses requests Hobab to accompany the Israelites since Hobab knows the wilderness better than anyone else and can guide them. Despite his leadership role, Moses recognizes his limitations and seeks help, demonstrating remarkable humility.
- **David:** In 2 Samuel 16:13, as David flees from an uprising led by his son Absalom, Shimei curses him, throws stones, and kicks up dust. Although David could have ordered his men to kill Shimei—just as his armorbearer Abishai suggested—he exercises restraint, demonstrating humility and controlled power.
- **Esther:** In Esther chapters 5 and 7, Esther hosts banquets for the king and Haman but waits to reveal

her true request until the perfect moment when the king is most eager to hear it. Her patience shows humility, prioritizing the right timing over personal urgency.

- **Daniel:** In Daniel 1:8, Daniel resolves not to defile himself with the king's delicacies. By renouncing his desire to honor God, he demonstrates humility through self-discipline and commitment to higher principles.

- **Apostle Paul:** In Philippians 3:8-12, Paul considers everything a loss when weighed against the value of knowing Christ. In Romans 12:3, he warns against thinking too highly of oneself. Similarly, Proverbs 3:5 and 3:7 caution against self-reliance. Paul's humility is evident as he sets aside personal accolades to pursue a greater purpose.

Humility is a cornerstone trait of purposeful leadership, profoundly influencing a leader's actions and the success of their organization. Through the lens of biblical figures, we observe humility expressed through listening to others, acknowledging personal limitations, exercising restraint, exhibiting patience, surrendering personal desires, and demonstrating modesty. These examples illustrate that humility is not a sign of weakness but a source of strength that validates a leader's humanity and fosters genuine connections with others.

By embracing humility, purposeful leaders cultivate a supportive and empowering environment that drives organizational success and positively impacts the lives of those they lead. By prioritizing the collective over the individual and exemplifying servant leadership, they leave a legacy of integrity, resilience, courage, and empathy.

Humility in a Complex and Fast-Changing Environment

In the modern context, humility involves recognizing that no single leader has all the answers, and that success often requires input from diverse perspectives. This acknowledgment enables leaders to be open to new ideas and innovations, which is crucial in a dynamic environment. Understanding various contexts and viewpoints can significantly impact outcomes, as a shift in perspective can change everything (Blum, F., 2022).

Moreover, humility helps leaders effectively contextualize their strategies and approaches. It allows them to balance core values with the necessity to adapt to cultural and market changes without compromising integrity.

Leaders in an increasingly interconnected world must navigate unfamiliar territories, both literally and figuratively. Humility equips leaders to listen and learn from others, fostering an environment where team members feel valued and empowered. This collaborative atmosphere enhances problem-solving and drives innovation.

Furthermore, embracing humility can lead to transformative personal and organizational growth. Understanding how our worldview shapes our thinking can lead to significant paradigm shifts (Sang, R. 2018). Applying this to leadership, humility enables reassessment of preconceived notions and the adoption of new strategies better suited to current challenges.

Contemporary Examples of Leaders Who Embody Humility

- ***Nelson Mandela:*** Despite decades of imprisonment, Mandela emerged without bitterness and worked toward reconciliation in South Africa, demonstrating profound humility.

- ***Satya Nadella:*** As the CEO of Microsoft, Nadella is recognized for his empathetic leadership style, willingness to listen, and capacity to cultivate a culture of humility and collaboration within the organization.

The Transformative Impact of Humility on Teams and Organizations

- **Listening to Followers:** Leaders who appreciate and consider their team's input create goodwill, enhance relationships, and cultivate trust and loyalty.

- **Acknowledging Limitations:** When leaders acknowledge their limitations, it fosters goodwill among followers, enhances mutual understanding, and encourages lively engagement among team members.

- **Exercising Restraint:** Leaders who exhibit restraint in challenging situations can ease tensions, prevent conflicts from escalating, and unify teams around shared goals.

- **Exhibiting Patience:** Patience enables leaders to wait for the best moment to take action or make decisions, fostering team cohesion and leading to improved outcomes.

- **Surrendering Personal Desires:** Leaders who prioritize the organization's purpose above personal ambitions inspire followers to come together to pursue a shared vision.

- **Demonstrating Modesty:** Modest leaders encourage team members to embrace a cause, foster strong support, enhance engagement, and promote a healthy, supportive work environment.

In conclusion, the importance of humility in contemporary leadership is increasingly evident as we move beyond biblical insights. In a landscape where change is the only constant, humble leaders who listen, learn, and adapt are better equipped to guide their organizations effectively. Embracing humility enhances leadership effectiveness and fosters a more collaborative, innovative, and resilient organizational culture.

Strategies for Cultivating the Trait of Humility

Role Modeling the Trait of Humility

Humility is a mindset (Philippians 2:5-8). Its characteristics include not seeking reputation or accolades, serving others, being selfless, humbling oneself, and being obedient. Leaders must embody these traits in their lives and workplaces, becoming role models.

Build and nurture a culture of collaboration

Recognizing that no one has all the answers to a problem and advising against excessive self-reliance, leaders should take the lead in developing, encouraging, and supporting collaboration among followers, fostering teamwork and team spirit, while warning against over-dependence and excessive independence.

Reflection, meditation, and journaling

Leaders guide their followers in practicing reflection, meditation, and journaling, using the lessons learned to foster improvement.

Appreciation and gratitude

Foster and promote a culture of appreciation, gratitude, and recognition for the efforts and commitment of employees in the workplace.

References

Baldoni, J. (2009). *Humility as a Leadership Trait*. Harvard Business Review. Retrieved from https://hbr.org/2009/09/humility-as-a-leadership-trait

Blum, F. (2022). Biblical Context Matters. Retrieved from https:// intentionalfilling.com/biblical-context-matters/

Sang, R. (2018). Paradigm Shifts and Gestalt Switches: How Our Worldview Affects Our Thinking About God. Retrieved from https://drawingontheword.com/paradigm-shift-worldview-thinking-of-god/

CHAPTER 28: THE TRAIT OF COURAGE IN LEADERSHIP

Courage is a vital leadership trait that empowers individuals and leaders to face the most daunting challenges many would shy away from (Northouse, 2019). It is a quality that sets leaders apart, making them perceived as heroes or prominent figures in their fields. In today's fast-paced and increasingly complex world, courage is more crucial than ever, as leaders must navigate uncertainty, make difficult decisions, and adapt to shifting circumstances (Yukl, 2013).

Components of Courage

Courageous leaders display several key characteristics that shape their approach to leadership:

Facing and overcoming formidable challenges: Courageous leaders are undeterred by the scale of their obstacles. They confront challenges directly, leveraging their knowledge, skills, and determination to find solutions and reach their goals (Covey, 2004).

Taking calculated risks: These leaders are willing to step beyond their comfort zones and embrace risks to achieve their objectives. They recognize that substantial rewards often come with significant risks and are eager to explore uncharted territory (George, 2007).

Asset-based thinking: Courageous leaders tackle challenges by focusing on their strengths, opportunities, and aspects within their control. They learn from their mistakes, maintain resilience in the face of setbacks, and harness their experiences to devise innovative solutions (Kouzes & Posner, 2017).

Perseverance and learning from setbacks: These leaders are not deterred by repeated failures; instead, they see mistakes as valuable learning opportunities that inform their strategies and approaches (Covey, 2004).

Attention to detail: Courageous leaders leave nothing to chance and possess a keen eye for detail. They understand that success often hinges on small, seemingly insignificant elements of their work (Yukl, 2013).

Thinking outside the box: These leaders often face misunderstanding because their thinking and actions differ from the norm. They generate novel ideas that others might regard as unconventional or peculiar, yet these ideas frequently lead to breakthroughs and innovation (George, 2007).

Determination and commitment: Courageous leaders are deeply determined and committed to their goals. They possess an unwavering resolve to bring their vision to fruition, regardless of the obstacles they encounter (Kouzes & Posner, 2017).

Adventurous long-term vision: These leaders maintain a bold long-term vision and a clear roadmap. They are unafraid to undertake ambitious journeys that may span years or even decades (Northouse, 2019).

Courage as a Trait of Purposeful Leadership

Courage is not just a trait that enables leaders to undertake challenging tasks; it is a deliberate leadership quality that compels them to pursue a higher calling and meet the needs of their followers (Covey, 2004). Courageous leaders are driven by a profound sense of purpose and a wish to make a positive impact on the world around them. They give up their comfort and security to promote the greater good and encourage others to do the same (George, 2007).

Insights from Case Studies

Throughout history, significant biblical figures have demonstrated the trait of courage in their leadership:

1. **Abraham:** Left his home country to venture into the unknown, demonstrating faith and courage in the face of uncertainty (Genesis 12:1-9).
2. **Moses:** Confronted Pharaoh with military might and guided the Israelites through a hostile environment, facing increasing pressure, criticism, and rebellion (Exodus 5-14).
3. **David:** He killed a lion and a bear, dared to confront and slay the fearsome giant Goliath, and fled from the furious King Saul into the wilderness, highlighting his courage and resilience. (1 Samuel 17, 1 Samuel 21-22).
4. **Esther:** Unafraid of death, approached the king in defiance of the law to save her people from imminent genocide, demonstrating extraordinary bravery and selflessness (Esther 4-5).
5. **Daniel:** He continued his prayer schedule and rituals after learning about the possibility of being thrown into the lions' den, demonstrating unwavering faith and courage in the face of danger (Daniel 6).
6. **Paul:** He endured shipwrecks, stoning, beatings, imprisonment, and many hardships, including sleeplessness, thirst, and hunger, yet he remained undeterred in his cause, exemplifying the utmost perseverance and courage. (2 Corinthians 11:23-27).

The Role of Courage in Today's Leadership Landscape

In today's rapidly changing and increasingly complex world, courage is a crucial leadership trait. The business environment is marked by turbulence, volatility, ambiguity, and uncertainty, making it vital for leaders to have the courage to navigate these challenges effectively (Yukl, 2013). Courageous leaders can adapt to changing circumstances, make tough decisions, and inspire their teams to persevere in difficult times (Northouse, 2019).

Examples of Contemporary Leaders Embodying this Trait

These contemporary leaders have exemplified courage in their leadership:

Malala Yousafzai, Nobel Peace Prize Laureate: Malala has displayed incredible bravery in her advocacy for girls' education, even after surviving an assassination attempt by the Taliban. She continues to speak out and fight for the rights of girls and women worldwide, inspiring others to join her cause (Yousafzai, 2013).

Greta Thunberg, Climate Activist: Thunberg has shown remarkable bravery in her fight against climate change. Despite facing criticism and personal attacks, she has challenged powerful corporations and governments, demanding action and accountability (Thunberg, 2019).

Strategies for Cultivating the Trait of Courage in an Organization

To foster a culture of courage within an organization, leaders can implement the following strategies:

1. **Encourage experimentation with ideas:** Create a safe environment that allows employees to test new ideas and learn from failures, thereby fostering a culture of innovation and risk-taking (Kouzes & Posner, 2017).
2. **Set realistic, achievable goals:** Break down larger objectives into smaller, manageable tasks, building on small wins to develop confidence and momentum (Covey, 2004).

3. **Promote open communication and transparency:** Encourage honest dialogue and the sharing of diverse perspectives, creating an atmosphere where employees feel comfortable expressing their thoughts and ideas (George, 2007).
4. **Lead by example:** Demonstrate courageous leadership by tackling challenging tasks, making difficult decisions, and admitting to and learning from mistakes (Northouse, 2019).
5. **Provide support and resources:** Offer training, mentorship, and resources to empower employees to develop the skills and confidence needed for challenging projects and initiatives (Yukl, 2013).
6. **Celebrate courageous acts:** Recognize and reward employees who take courageous actions in their work, reinforcing the significance of this trait within the organization (Kouzes & Posner, 2017).

Conclusion

Courage is an essential leadership trait that enables leaders to face and overcome the most demanding challenges, pursue a greater purpose, and inspire others to do the same (Covey, 2004). In today's complex and uncertain world, courage is more important than ever, as leaders must navigate ambiguity, make difficult decisions, and adapt to changing circumstances (Yukl, 2013). By embodying the qualities of courage and fostering a culture that encourages and supports courageous actions, leaders can positively influence their organizations and the broader community, leaving a legacy of resilience, innovation, and purpose-driven leadership (George, 2007).

References:

Covey, S. R. (2004). The 8th habit: From effectiveness to greatness. Simon and Schuster.

George, B. (2007). True North: Discover your authentic leadership. John Wiley & Sons.

Kouzes, J. M., & Posner, B. Z. (2017). The leadership challenge: How to make extraordinary things happen in organizations (6th ed.). John Wiley & Sons.

Northouse, P. G. (2019). Leadership: Theory and Practice (8th ed.). SAGE Publications.

Thunberg, G. (2019). No one is too small to make a difference. Penguin Books.

Yousafzai, M. (2013). I am Malala: The girl who stood up for education and was shot by the Taliban. Little, Brown and Company.

Yukl, G. (2013). Leadership in organizations (8th ed.). Pearson.

CHAPTER 29: THE LEADERSHIP TRAIT OF EMPATHY

Empathy is a crucial leadership quality that enables leaders to understand and connect with others' emotions (McKee et al., 2008). In their book, "Becoming a Resonant Leader," A. McKee et al. examine empathy from the perspective of a resonant leader, who they describe as being attuned to both their own and their followers' needs, desires, and dreams (McKee et al., 2008).

Components of Empathy

Empathy includes several key components that allow leaders to connect with their followers on a deeper level:

1. **Perspective-taking:** Placing oneself in others' shoes to grasp their experiences and challenges (Davis, 1983).
2. **Emotional resonance:** Recognizing the circumstances others are experiencing and sharing their predicaments, fears, anxieties, and worries (Goleman, 1995).
3. **Shared understanding:** Being in sync with followers fosters a sense of unity and collaboration (Uhl-Bien et al., 2014).
4. **Emotional connection:** Sensing the heartbeat of followers and team members allows leaders to inspire and motivate them toward a shared vision (George, 2003).
5. **Emotional intelligence:** Capacity to demonstrate self-awareness, social awareness, organizational awareness, and environmental awareness to navigate complex interpersonal dynamics (Goleman, 1995).

Empathy as a Deliberate Leadership Quality

Empathy is an essential leadership trait that enables leaders to connect more deeply with their followers, fostering trust, collaboration, and a shared sense of purpose. By relating to their followers or team members, empathetic leaders can better understand their needs, aspirations, and challenges, enabling them to tailor their leadership approach to address their team's unique needs (George, 2003).

Insights from Case Studies

These biblical figures exemplify the trait of empathy in their leadership:

1. **Abraham:** In Genesis 18:22-33, Abraham pleads with the LORD not to destroy Sodom and Gomorrah for the sake of a few righteous people, demonstrating his compassion for the innocent (Genesis 18:22-33, New International Version).
2. **Moses:** In the book of Exodus, Moses intercedes for the Israelites, who frequently rebel against the LORD, demonstrating his empathy and compassion for his people (Exodus 32:11-14, New International Version).
3. **Esther:** In Esther 7:3-4, Esther requests the king to spare her life and the lives of her people, who had been marked for destruction by Haman, demonstrating her empathy and courage in the face of adversity (Esther 7:3-4, New International Version).
4. **David:** In 2 Samuel 24:17, King David begs God to spare the people from punishment, recognizing his faults and showing compassion for those, he leads (2 Samuel 24:17, New International Version).
5. **Daniel:** In Daniel 9:1-3, Daniel intercedes for the Jewish people held captive in Babylon, showing

empathy and concern for their well-being (Daniel 9:1-3, New International Version).

6. **Paul:** In Romans 9:1-3, Paul conveys his deep sorrow and anguish for his fellow Jews who have rejected Christ, wishing he could be accursed for their sake, which showcases his profound empathy and love for his people (Romans 9:1-3, New International Version).

Empathy in the Context of Today's Leadership Environment

In today's rapidly changing and complex business environment, empathetic leaders are crucial for navigating challenges and seizing opportunities. These leaders embrace current difficulties and future possibilities, using their emotional intelligence to tap into their own and others' passions (McKee et al., 2008). They use emotions, relationships, and vision to drive followers toward a better future, creating environments where people can thrive and reach their full potential (McKee et al., 2008).

The Impact of Empathy on Leaders and Organizations

Empathy is a transformative trait that profoundly impacts leaders and their organizations. By demonstrating empathy, leaders can cultivate a culture of trust, collaboration, and psychological safety, which enables their teams to take risks, innovate, and reach their full potential (Edmondson, 1999). Empathetic leaders are better equipped to understand their followers' needs and aspirations, enabling them to tailor their leadership approach to address their team's unique needs (George, 2003). This, in turn, results in higher levels of employee engagement, job satisfaction, and organizational performance (Harter et al., 2002).

Examples of Contemporary Leaders Embodying this Trait

These contemporary leaders exemplify empathy in their leadership:

1. Indra Nooyi, former CEO of PepsiCo: Nooyi was recognized for her empathetic approach to leadership, which involved connecting with employees on a personal level and understanding their needs and aspirations (George, 2003).
2. Jacinda Ardern, Prime Minister of New Zealand: Ardern has received widespread praise for her empathetic response to the Christchurch Mosque shootings, demonstrating her ability to connect with her citizens and provide comfort during a tragic time (BBC News, 2019).

Strategies for Fostering Empathy in Organizations

Organizations can cultivate empathy among their leaders and employees through several strategies:

1. **Listening:** Creating an environment that fosters consultation, feedback, and teamwork enables leaders to gain a deeper understanding of their followers' perspectives and needs (Uhl-Bien et al., 2014).
2. **Caring, appreciating, and serving others:** Encourage leaders to demonstrate care and appreciation for their followers while acting as role models for empathy and compassion (George, 2003).
3. **Reflection, meditation, and journaling:** These activities provide leaders with opportunities for self-reflection and personal growth, enabling them to improve their emotional intelligence and capacity for empathy (Goleman, 1995).

Conclusion

Empathy is a crucial leadership quality that allows leaders to connect with their followers on a deeper level, fostering trust, collaboration, and a shared sense of purpose. By exhibiting empathy, leaders can navigate the challenges and opportunities of today's rapidly evolving business landscape, thereby creating conditions in which people can flourish and reach their full potential.   Through examples of both biblical and contemporary leaders, we observe the transformative power of empathy in action. By cultivating this trait within organizations, leaders can build more resilient, innovative, and successful teams.

References

BBC News. (2019, March 17). Christchurch shootings: New Zealand PM Jacinda Ardern praised for response. https://www.bbc.com/news/world-asia-47603854

Davis, M. H. (1983). Measuring individual differences in empathy: Evidence for a multidimensional approach. Journal of Personality and Social Psychology, 44(1), 113-126.

Edmondson, A. (1999). Psychological safety and learning behavior in work teams. Administrative Science Quarterly, 44(2), 350-383.

George, B. (2003). Authentic leadership: Rediscovering the secrets to creating lasting value. Jossey-Bass.

Goleman, D. (1995). Emotional intelligence: Why it can matter more than IQ. Bantam Books.

Groysberg, B., & Slind, M. (2012, June). Leadership is a conversation. Harvard Business Review.

https://hbr.org/2012/06/leadership-is-a-conversation

Harter, J. K., Schmidt, F. L., & Hayes, T. L. (2002). Business-unit-level relationship between employee satisfaction, employee engagement, and business outcomes: A meta-analysis. Journal of Applied Psychology, 87(2), 268-279.

McKee, A., Boyatzis, R. E., & Johnston, F. (2008). Becoming a resonant leader: Develop your emotional intelligence, renew your relationships, sustain your effectiveness. Harvard Business Press.

Uhl-Bien, M., Riggio, R. E., Lowe, K. B., & Carsten, M. K. (2014). Followership theory: A review and research agenda. The Leadership Quarterly, 25(1), 83-104.

CHAPTER 30: THE LEADERSHIP TRAIT OF INTEGRITY

Northouse (2019) defines integrity as honesty and trustworthiness. Integrity involves the consistency between an individual's actions and their values, reflecting honesty, ethical conduct, and reliability. It is a vital factor in establishing interpersonal trust (Yukl, 2010).

Components of Integrity

Integrity comprises several key components that contribute to its overall meaning and impact:

- o **Trustworthy:** Individuals with integrity can be relied upon to act by their stated values and principles.
- o **Honest:** Honesty is a fundamental aspect of integrity, as it involves being truthful and transparent in one's actions and communications.
- o **Credible:** People with integrity are perceived as credible, as their actions align with their words, thereby fostering trust and confidence in their leadership.
- o **Authentic:** Integrity involves being genuine to oneself, which helps build authentic relationships.
- o **Believed:** When leaders demonstrate integrity, their words and actions are more likely to be believed and trusted by their followers.
- o **Back words with action:** Leaders with integrity follow through on their promises and commitments, demonstrating that their words are backed by action.
- o **Promise keeper:** Keeping promises is a crucial aspect of integrity, as it shows a leader's dedication

to their word and willingness to uphold their commitments.

- o **Ready and willing to sacrifice at their own expense:** Leaders with integrity are willing to make personal sacrifices for the greater good, even if it means putting their interests aside.
- o **Courteous and respectful:** Integrity involves treating others with courtesy and respect, which helps to foster positive relationships and a healthy work environment.

Integrity as a Leadership Quality with Purpose

Integrity is a key leadership trait that guides decision-making and actions. Leaders who prioritize integrity are more likely to make ethical choices, even under challenging situations. They recognize that their actions set the tone for their organization and that upholding integrity is crucial for building trust and credibility with their followers.

Insights from Biblical Case Studies

Biblical figures demonstrate the importance of integrity in leadership:

- o **Abraham:** In Genesis 15:22-24, Abraham declines the king of Sodom's offer of goods after defeating his enemies, opting to uphold his oath and preserve his dignity instead of letting the king claim that he had made Abraham rich.
- o **Moses:** Moses did not leverage his position for personal gain; instead, he led an ordinary life, demonstrating his commitment to serving others rather than pursuing personal benefit.
- o **David:** Despite his role in Uriah's death during the Bathsheba incident, David expressed remorse, repented, and humbly accepted correction when

confronted by the prophet Nathan, demonstrating his willingness to acknowledge his mistakes and strive for personal growth.

- o **Esther:** Esther had the opportunity to leverage her position as the king's wife to persuade him to halt Haman's wicked scheme, but she opted to act with integrity and bravery, prioritizing the needs of her people over her safety.
- o **Daniel:** When King Belshazzar offered Daniel lavish gifts in exchange for interpreting the writing on the wall, Daniel declined the offer, illustrating his integrity and refusal to be influenced by material wealth.
- o **Paul:** In 1 Thessalonians 2:9, Paul sought to support himself rather than burden his followers, thereby demonstrating his integrity and dedication not to exploit others.

Integrity in the Context of Today's Leadership Environment

In today's complex, fast-paced leadership environment, integrity remains vital to effective leadership. Leaders encounter numerous challenges and ethical dilemmas, and those who prioritize integrity are better prepared to navigate these situations with honesty, transparency, and a commitment to doing what is right. Integrity is essential amid increasing scrutiny and public demand for accountability from leadership.

The Impact of Integrity on Leaders and Organizations

- o   Leaders who possess integrity inspire confidence in their followers and team members because they can be trusted with responsibility (Northouse, 2019).
- o   Research by Kouzes and Posner (2017) shows that honesty is the most critical factor in the leader-follower relationship and the primary quality followers seek in leaders. Integrity enhances team cohesion, encourages collaboration, and drives high performance.
- o   Organizations led by individuals with integrity typically enjoy a more positive work culture, higher employee engagement, and improved overall performance as trust and credibility permeate the organization.

Strategies for Developing the Trait of Integrity in Organizations

- o   **Lead by example:** Leaders must model integrity in their actions and decisions, setting the tone for the entire organization.
- o   **Establish clear values and ethical standards:** Organizations should develop and communicate clear values and ethical frameworks that guide employee behavior and decision-making.
- o   Provide training and development: Offering training and development opportunities that focus on ethics, integrity, and leadership helps employees understand the significance of these traits and how to embody them in their work.

- o **Encourage open communication and transparency:** Fostering an open dialogue and transparency builds trust, encouraging employees to speak up when they witness unethical behavior.
- o **Hold individuals accountable:** Organizations must hold individuals accountable for their actions and decisions, ensuring that those who demonstrate integrity are recognized and rewarded, while those who violate ethical standards face appropriate consequences.

Conclusion

Integrity is essential for effective leadership, incorporating honesty, trustworthiness, and ethical behavior. Leaders who emphasize integrity inspire confidence, cultivate trust, and promote positive organizational outcomes. By analyzing biblical case studies and modern examples, we can observe the lasting significance of integrity in leadership. Organizations can nurture this quality by setting a positive example, establishing clear values and ethical standards, providing training and development opportunities, fostering open communication and transparency, and holding individuals accountable.

As leaders navigate the complexities of today's business landscape, integrity remains a fundamental principle for making ethical decisions and fostering strong, trusting relationships with their followers.

References

Kouzes, J. M., & Posner, B. Z. (2017). The leadership challenge: How to make extraordinary things happen in organizations. John Wiley & Sons.

Northouse, P. G. (2019). Leadership: Theory and Practice. Sage Publications.

Yukl, G. (2010). Leadership in organizations. Pearson Education.

CHAPTER 31: THE LEADERSHIP TRAIT OF INTELLIGENCE

Intelligence in leadership includes the ability to think critically, relate to others effectively, collaborate to accomplish tasks, and manage emotions appropriately. Justin Menkes defines executive intelligence as the capacity to achieve objectives through teamwork and demonstrate suitable behavior in various situations (Menkes, 2006).

Components of Intelligence

- **Conceptual or Cognitive Aptitude**: This includes analytical and logical thinking, concept formation, and skills in inductive and deductive reasoning (Yukl, 2010).

- **Interpersonal Intelligence**: It involves how individuals within an organization interact and how these interactions affect outcomes, including emotions, attitudes, motives, and effective communication.

- **Emotional Intelligence**: This is the ability to be attuned to one's and others' emotions, integrating emotion and reason to enhance cognitive processes and manage emotions logically (Yukl, 2010).

- **Social Intelligence**: It entails understanding the needs, challenges, opportunities, and diverse behaviors of teams to adapt to various situations.

Intelligence as a Trait of Purposeful Leadership

Intelligence is essential for leaders because it enables them to navigate complex situations, make informed decisions, and inspire others toward a common goal. Leaders with high intelligence can effectively analyze issues, generate innovative solutions, and communicate their vision clearly to their teams (Menkes, 2006).

Insights from Biblical Case Studies Demonstrating Intelligence

- **Abraham (Genesis 18:23-33):** Abraham's negotiation for Sodom highlights his discernment, astuteness, and insight, qualities that are valuable for today's leaders. environment when negotiating and advocating for their teams or organizations.

- **Moses (Acts 7:22, Exodus 24:12-18):** Moses' intelligence enabled him to write, interpret, and teach the law, while also establishing effective administrative structures and processes. In contemporary leadership, this translates to the capacity to create and implement policies, procedures, and systems that foster organizational success.

- **David (1 Chronicles 22-29):** David's comprehensive preparations for the temple construction illustrate his ability to see the bigger picture, plan ahead, and exhibit exceptional stewardship. Today's leaders can learn from this by focusing on long-term objectives, managing resources efficiently, and fostering sustainable growth.

- **Esther (Esther 5-7):** Esther's thoughtful, methodical, and strategic approach to confronting Haman's plot emphasizes the importance of tact, diplomacy, and strategy in leadership. These skills are critical for navigating complex political landscapes and resolving conflicts in modern organizations.

- **Daniel (Daniel 1:4, 7)**: Daniel's wisdom, quick learning, and talent for interpreting dreams exemplify the essence of visionary leadership. Modern leaders can draw inspiration from Daniel's example by leveraging their intuition and intellect to craft transformative visions for their organizations.

- **Paul (Acts 26:24-26, Acts 22:3)**: Paul's expertise in various subjects, persuasive communication, creative problem-solving, and cross-cultural effectiveness highlights the significance of ongoing learning and flexibility in leadership. These skills are essential for guiding diverse teams and maneuvering through multicultural environments in today's globalized world.

Intelligence in the Context of Today's Leadership Environment

In the current dynamic and complex business landscape, leaders must exhibit:

- **Conceptual (Cognitive) Skills**: These encompass sound judgment, foresight, intuition, creativity, and the capacity to discern meaning and order amidst ambiguity and uncertainty.

- **Analytical and Logical Reasoning**: These skills are essential for planning, organizing, identifying complex relationships, and devising creative solutions. They encompass systems thinking and require an understanding of how various components of an organization interact and influence one another (Yukl, 2010).

- **Interpersonal, emotional, and social intelligence: These are crucial** for effective leadership in today's diverse and demanding environment. They empower leaders to build strong teams, foster cohesion, and encourage effective collaboration (Yukl, 2010).

Intelligence is essential in today's diverse and demanding environment. It enables leaders to build strong teams, foster cohesion, and promote effective collaboration (Yukl, 2010).

The Impact of Intelligence on Leaders and Organizations

Intelligence in leadership has a significant impact on both leaders and their organizations. Intelligent leaders are better equipped to:

• Make informed decisions based on data analysis and critical thinking.

• Develop innovative solutions to complex problems.

• Communicate effectively with diverse stakeholders.

• Build strong, cohesive teams that work toward a common goal.

• Adapt to changing circumstances and navigate uncertainty.

• Inspire and motivate others to reach their full potential.

Organizations led by intelligent leaders tend to be more agile and innovative, and they thrive in the long run. They can better anticipate market trends, capitalize on opportunities, and overcome challenges (Menkes, 2006).

Examples of Contemporary Leaders Embodying this Trait

- **Indra Nooyi (PepsiCo)**: Nooyi's strategic thinking and foresight enabled the successful diversification of PepsiCo's product portfolio, with a focus on healthier options. Her intelligence and leadership have significantly contributed to the company's long-term success.

- **Jeff Bezos (Amazon)**: Bezos's intelligence and customer-focused approach have driven Amazon to become one of the world's most valuable companies. His ability to anticipate market trends and drive innovation has been crucial to Amazon's ongoing growth and success.

Strategies for Promoting the Trait of Intelligence in Organizations

- **Encourage Continuous Learning**: Offer employees opportunities to participate in ongoing education and skill development through workshops, seminars, and online courses.

- **Foster a Culture of Curiosity**: Encourage employees to ask questions, challenge assumptions, and explore new ideas. Foster an environment that values experimentation and learning from failure.

- **Promote Collaboration and Knowledge Sharing**: Promote cross-functional teams and knowledge-sharing platforms to enhance the exchange of ideas and insights throughout the organization.

- **Develop Critical Thinking Skills**: Offer training and resources to help employees enhance their analytical and problem-solving abilities. Encourage them to address challenges using a data-driven and evidence-based approach.

- **Emphasize Emotional and Social Intelligence**: Offer training and development programs designed to enhance employees' emotional intelligence, communication skills, and ability to collaborate effectively in diverse teams.

- **Write and Create Knowledge**: Encourage employees to share what they have learned, insights, and best practices. This approach fosters the capture and dissemination of knowledge across the organization.

- **Teach and Mentor**: Offer experienced employees an opportunity to teach and mentor others, sharing their knowledge and expertise to help cultivate the next generation of leaders.

References

Menkes, J. (2006). *Executive Intelligence.* HarpperCollins Publishers.

Yukl, G. (2010). *Leadership in organizations*. Pearson Education.

PART 7: NAVIGATING INTERCONNECTED DYNAMICS: PURPOSEFUL LEADERSHIP IN A COMPLEX WORLD

In this pivotal section, we highlight the complex interplay among climate change, the rapid advancement of artificial intelligence, and the enduring impact of faith in leadership. We examine how these factors are profoundly connected and how thoughtful leaders can navigate these challenges to foster meaningful change.

1. **Interconnectivity of Dynamics:**
    o Evolving Dynamics: Discuss the shifts and trends in the environment – climate change, AI, and faith.
    o Highlight the complex relationship between climate change, artificial intelligence, and faith in the context of leadership.
    o Describe how these dynamics interconnect and impact one another.

2. **Proactive Leadership**

    o Emphasize the proactive role of purposeful leaders in shaping a sustainable future, utilizing systems thinking as a foundation for leadership, and recognizing the interconnectivity of climate change, AI, and faith. It is organized into the following sections:
    o Defining Systems Thinking

o Purposeful Leadership in the Context of Systems Thinking
o How Purposeful Leadership Can Aid in Developing AI Ethical Frameworks Aligned with Climate Change Mitigation

3. **Leveraging AI for Environmental Solutions:**
   o AI as a Tool for Good: Emphasize how AI can tackle climate change challenges.
   o Explore practical applications (e.g., predictive analytics, resource optimization).
   o Ensure that AI-driven solutions are accessible and beneficial for everyone, especially marginalized communities.
   o Partner with tech innovators dedicated to sustainability.

4. **Ethics and Responsibility:**

   o Explore the ethical implications of AI and climate action, urging leaders to create ethical frameworks that steer their organizations.

   o Discuss the risks associated with AI and the necessity of mitigating them.

   o Formulate and enact an AI Ethical Framework to direct decision-making.

5. **Empowerment Through Education and Build Adaptive Organizations**
   o Emphasize the crucial role of education and continuous learning for leaders and their teams.
   o Foster a culture of continuous learning and adaptation.
   o Encourage ongoing education about climate issues, AI advancements, and the principles of ethical leadership.

- o Promote a culture of curiosity and open-mindedness to facilitate learning and adaptation.
- o Build adaptive organizations: Cultivate resilience to thrive in a constantly changing world.
- o Embrace innovation and adaptability as core organizational values.

CHAPTER 32: INTERCONNECTIVITY OF DYNAMICS

Evolving Dynamics: Current and Future Shifts in the Environment

This chapter explores current and emerging trends related to climate change and technological advancements, particularly in artificial intelligence (AI). It presents the rise of AI technologies and their potential opportunities and risks for society. Additionally, it discusses the concept of faith and its foundational role in addressing ethical dilemmas, especially in AI and climate change mitigation.

1. Climate Change Trends

Rising global temperatures have increased the frequency, intensity, and duration of extreme weather events, resulting in record-breaking wildfires, hurricanes, and heat waves. These changes are causing socio-economic and political disruptions and potential crises. Climate change threatens food security by affecting production and supply chains. If current trends persist, it may lead to significant internal and external migration, with up to 216 million people displaced by 2050. Furthermore, climate change poses a substantial public health threat, potentially causing millions of additional deaths by 2050 due to malnutrition and diseases worsened by warmer temperatures and pollution.

2. Technological Trends

The emergence of artificial intelligence (AI) technologies presents both opportunities and ethical challenges for society, requiring thoughtful consideration and robust regulatory frameworks.

Artificial Intelligence – Definitions

AI is a broad field focused on developing machines that can replicate human behavior, including perception, reasoning, learning, and problem-solving (Mori L. et al., 2024; Blumberg S. et al., 2024). Michael Dell views AI as a technology with cognitive and thinking capabilities. With these abilities, AI utilizes available knowledge on a given subject and distills it into accurate outcomes and new understandings.

Types of AI

Machine learning is an AI that can adapt to various inputs, including large sets of historical data, synthesized data, or human contributions. Learning machines equipped with specialized algorithms are created to identify patterns (deep learning) and generate predictions and recommendations by analyzing data.

Generative AI is a branch of deep learning that utilizes extensive neural networks known as large language models (containing hundreds of billions of neurons) capable of learning abstract patterns. Language models for interpreting and creating text, video, images, and data are categorized as generative AI (Mori L. et al., 2024).

Artificial general intelligence (AGI) refers to systems with human-like cognitive abilities, including reasoning, problem-solving, perception, learning, and language comprehension. We have not yet achieved this advanced level.

3. Faith

Faith has long been a guiding force for leaders, providing a sense of purpose and direction. It represents a transcendent spiritual element that transcends the physical realm.

Faith offers a profound sense of purpose, empowering leaders to navigate complex ethical dilemmas and make decisions aligned with higher moral standards. It fosters integrity, compassion, and altruism, essential for effective and ethical leadership (Herrity J., 2024). Faith inspires leaders to prioritize the welfare of others and engage in practices that build community and nurture positive relationships (Herrity J., 2024). Moreover, incorporating faith into leadership encourages personal growth and self-awareness.

Leaders become more attuned to their values and the impact of their actions, enhancing their ability to lead authentically and empathetically. This spiritual foundation enables leaders to foster ethical organizational cultures and promote moral behavior within their teams (Elsayed K.G. et al., 2023).

Understanding the Interconnectedness of Climate Change, AI, and Faith

Leaders should develop a curious mindset defined by probing, questioning, and thorough exploration. This mindset is crucial for navigating the increasingly uncertain, ambiguous, and fluid environment influenced by the interplay of climate change, AI, and faith. By delving deeper and uncovering hidden connections, leaders can gain a better understanding of the complex relationships between these forces and make more informed decisions.

To understand the full extent of these dynamics, it is essential to explore their interconnections over time:

- **Past:** Socio-economic and technological advancements have greatly influenced the environment, leading to climate change.
- **Present:** Society faces urgent threats from climate change that require immediate solutions. While AI provides potential tools to tackle these challenges, it

also presents risks and ethical dilemmas. Leaders must navigate the present by learning from the past while embracing the future.

- **Envisioned future:** As a guiding force, faith helps leaders move beyond past constraints and envision a purposeful future. It inspires shared values and provides a moral compass for addressing the ethical dilemmas posed by AI while leveraging its potential to combat climate change. The intersection of these dynamics underscores the need for leaders to navigate complexities with purpose and foresight. By integrating faith, ethical leadership principles, and innovative AI solutions, leaders can steer society toward a sustainable and equitable future. This holistic approach empowers leaders to address environmental challenges while upholding ethical integrity effectively.

Diagram: Interconnectivity Illustration

The diagram below illustrates the relationships among faith, leadership, AI, and climate change, depicting how these elements influence one another within the framework of purposeful leadership.

```
                              +----------------------+
                              |  Faith               |
                              +----------------------+
           |
           v
+------------------------+   +----------------------+   +----------------------+
| Leadership             |   |  AI Framework        |   |  Climate Change      |
| Principles, Traits,  | |   | (Guided by Faith)  | |   |                      |
| and Mindsets           |   +----------------------+   +----------------------+
+------------------------+              |
                                        v
                              +----------------------+
                              |  Ethical Guidelines  |
                              +----------------------+
```

Explanation of the Diagram:

- **Faith:** Positioned at the top, representing the foundational element guiding leadership and decision-making.

- **Leadership Principles, Traits, and Mindsets:** Essential qualities and frameworks leaders embody, influenced by beliefs.

- **AI Framework (Guided by Faith):** This framework highlights AI's role in leadership, emphasizing its alignment with faith and ethical considerations.

- **Climate Change:** This represents a pressing global issue that leaders must address, and it is interconnected with AI and leadership principles.

- **Ethical Guidelines:** Positioned beneath the AI Framework, emphasizing the importance of ethics in applying AI to tackle climate change.

Leaders can create strategies that ethically and sustainably address urgent global issues by emphasizing the interconnectedness of faith, leadership, AI, and climate change. By integrating these elements, leaders can design frameworks that align AI with ethical standards and development goals, ensuring a balanced approach to tackling global challenges. Adopting a curious mindset allows leaders to navigate the complexities of our time with greater clarity and purpose, ultimately contributing to a more sustainable and equitable future for all.

References

Blanford, G. (2009). R&D investment strategy for climate change. Energy Economics. 31. 27-27. 10.1016/j.eneco.2008.03.010.

Bevan, O. et al. (2024). Implementing generative AI with speed and safety. McKinsey Quarterly.

Elsayed, K. G., Lestari, A. A., & Brougham, F. A. (2023). Role of Religion in Shaping Ethical and Moral Values Among the Youths in Athens, Greece. Journal of Sociology, Psychology & Religious Studies, 5(1), 11–20. https://doi.org/10.53819/81018102t5153

Herrity, J. (2024, January 26). *How to incorporate faith into leadership for success*. Indeed Career Guide. https://www.indeed.com/career-advice/career-development/faith-in-leadership

CHAPTER 33: PROACTIVE LEADERSHIP

In this chapter, we highlight the proactive role of purposeful leaders in shaping a sustainable future. We explore how systems thinking, a holistic approach to understanding the interconnectedness of systems, serves as the basis for intentional leadership. This leadership style is essential for navigating the complex interplay among climate change, artificial intelligence (AI), and faith, steering us toward a more balanced and ethical future.

Defining Systems Thinking

Systems thinking is a holistic approach to analysis and problem-solving that emphasizes understanding the interconnectedness and interactions within systems. This discipline allows us to perceive the whole, recognize patterns and interrelationships, and learn how to structure these interrelationships more effectively and efficiently (Morganelli, 2024). A system comprises intricately interconnected parts, each with its own dynamics, forming a complex entirety. These parts may serve different functions but complement one another, resulting in a compelling, efficient whole.

The power of systems thinking lies in the synergy of its parts, driving the whole and creating a complexity that reflects the dynamics of each part. This concept is fundamental to systems thinking, as it highlights the interconnectedness and interdependence of system components. The idea that the whole is greater than the sum of its parts and that complexity emerges from the interactions among these parts is a key aspect of systems thinking (Arnold & Wade, 2015).

Furthermore, the art of systems thinking involves navigating the intricate complexity of the underlying structures that generate change (Rountree, 1977). This aligns with the notion that systems thinking necessitates understanding the underlying structures and relationships that influence system behavior and change (Arnold & Wade, 2015).

Purposeful Leadership in the Context of Systems Thinking

Our analysis in Chapter 8 highlights purposeful leadership as a transformative process that guides individuals and organizations toward meaningful goals by embodying stewardship, authenticity, and value-driven decision-making. It aligns vision and actions with a higher purpose, fosters an inclusive and ethical environment, and draws from inner wisdom to inspire care, creativity, and resilience. Purposeful leadership transforms leaders and empowers others to pursue collective betterment, positively impacting individuals and the broader community.

This definition of purposeful leadership aligns well with systems thinking, emphasizing the interconnectedness of individuals, organizations, and the broader community. Purposeful leadership, with its focus on stewardship, authenticity, and value-driven decision-making, inherently considers the broader system in which it operates. By aligning their vision and actions with a higher purpose, fostering an inclusive and ethical environment, and drawing on inner wisdom, purposeful leaders are better equipped to navigate complex interactions within systems.

How Purposeful Leadership Can Help Create AI Ethical Frameworks Aligned with Climate Change Mitigation

A purposeful leadership approach establishes a robust foundation for creating an ethical AI framework to address climate change, considering the interconnectedness and relationships between climate change, AI, and faith. The focus on purposeful leadership, including stewardship and value-driven decision-making, aligns with the need for responsible AI development and deployment that prioritizes environmental sustainability. Emphasizing authenticity and inner wisdom can help leaders navigate the ethical challenges posed by AI, ensuring that decisions are made with integrity and a deep understanding of the potential impacts of climate change.

Moreover, the commitment of purposeful leadership to nurturing an inclusive and ethical environment is vital for tackling the intersection of AI, climate change, and faith. By fostering an atmosphere where diverse perspectives are respected and ethical considerations are paramount, leaders can encourage meaningful dialogue and collaboration among stakeholders from various backgrounds, including those with religious beliefs that may affect their views on climate change and technology.

The transformative essence of purposeful leadership, which empowers others to pursue collective improvement, is crucial to driving the systemic changes needed to mitigate climate change through AI. By inspiring care, creativity, and resilience, purposeful leaders can unite individuals and organizations to collectively pursue the shared goal of environmental sustainability, leveraging AI as a catalyst for positive impact.

References

Arnold, R. T., & Wade, J. P. (2015). A definition of systems thinking: A systems approach. *Procedia Computer Science, 44*, 669–678.

https://doi.org/10.1016/j.procs.2015.03.050

Morganelli, M. (2024). What is systems thinking? Retrieved from

https://www.snhu.edu/about-us/newsroom/business/what-is-systems-thinking

Rountree, J. H. (1977). Agricultural systems: Systems thinking—Some fundamental aspects. *Agricultural Systems, 2*(4), 247-254.

https://doi.org/10.1016/0308-521X(77)90019-1

CHAPTER 34: LEVERAGING AI FOR ENVIRONMENTAL SOLUTIONS

AI offers unprecedented opportunities to tackle climate change and environmental challenges. This chapter delves into how AI can drive innovation and address our most urgent environmental issues. We explore AI's role in mitigating climate change, discuss practical applications, showcase case studies of smart grids, and describe the types of AI employed.

AI's Role in Climate Change Mitigation

AI's role in climate change mitigation is complex, as it consumes significant energy while also offering the potential for substantial energy savings. Training an AI model can emit as much carbon as five cars over their lifetimes, underscoring the environmental impact of AI's energy consumption (Gexa Energy, 2024).

Nevertheless, AI can yield significant energy savings across various sectors, such as buildings and transportation systems. For example, AI-powered devices in modern households, such as thermostats and demand response systems, can learn from residents' patterns and adjust energy settings to optimize conservation, resulting in up to 20% energy savings in buildings and 15% in transportation systems (Gexa Energy, 2024).

AI's capability to monitor, gather information, control, evaluate, and manage energy consumption in buildings and factories enhances its potential for energy savings. AI can prevent energy waste and reduce maintenance costs by lowering energy use during peak hours, identifying and signaling issues, and detecting equipment failures before they happen (Gexa Energy, 2024).

Additionally, AI controls are used to conserve energy, and the universal workflow concept, which stems from machine learning (ML), helps users select learning, optimization, and control tools to achieve this goal (Da-Sheng Lee et al., 2022). Research indicates that the universal workflow can result in substantial energy cost savings across various sectors, such as 35% in buildings, 25% in heating, ventilation, and air conditioning systems, 50% in artificial lighting, up to 70% in information transfer and communication power, and a consistent output of 30% peak power from renewable energy technologies (Da-Sheng Lee et al., 2022).

AI's most significant contribution to combating climate change is its ability to enhance energy efficiency by optimizing energy usage and reducing waste and costs in buildings and data centers (Brant J., 2024). AI-powered smart grids and advanced electrical systems that feature two-way communication between energy providers and consumers showcase AI's potential, especially in cities where they have been implemented with notable success. These smart grids can boost energy efficiency and reduce carbon footprints by intelligently predicting energy demand, optimizing supply, and integrating renewable energy sources such as solar and wind into the grid (Brant J., 2024).

As AI continues to evolve, its role in addressing climate change will likely grow increasingly significantly.

Types of AI Used in Climate Change Mitigation

1. **Machine Learning (ML):** ML is the most widely used type of AI in climate change mitigation, owing to its capacity to process extensive datasets and recognize patterns. ML models are applied in several areas, including climate modeling and forecasting,

energy optimization, industrial process enhancement, and urban planning (Hao, 2019).

2. **Deep Learning (DL):** DL models are essential for predicting and modeling climate change. They enable researchers to forecast future changes in vegetation growth across various climate scenarios and to understand ecological impacts (Iglesias-Suarez et al., 2024). Furthermore, DL models are applied in remote sensing to monitor and predict changes in critical regions impacted by climate change, such as the Arctic and ocean environments (Johns Hopkins, 2024).

3. **Computer Vision:** Frequently powered by deep learning algorithms, computer vision significantly contributes to environmental monitoring. It monitors deforestation, supports precision agriculture and improves natural disaster preparedness (Hao, 2019).

4. **Generative AI:** While less common in climate change applications, generative AI shows promise in several areas. It is used in building decarbonization to optimize energy consumption, thereby reducing energy costs and emissions. Generative AI also plays a role in supply chain optimization, boosting efficiency and minimizing waste and emissions in the retail and agriculture sectors (Kaufman et al., 2024). Moreover, generative AI models are applied in climate modeling and simulation, enabling researchers to analyze and simulate complex environmental scenarios (Infosys BPM, 2024).

Case Studies of Cities Implementing AI-Driven Smart Grids

These case studies demonstrate AI's transformative potential to reduce carbon emissions, optimize energy use, and enable the transition from traditional to intelligent energy systems.

1. **Barcelona**: The city has successfully integrated AI-driven smart grids, which include solar panels, wind turbines, and energy storage systems. AI algorithms analyze real-time data to optimize energy consumption and reduce carbon emissions (Brant, 2024).
2. **Singapore**: By incorporating AI into its smart grid, Singapore has realized a 15% decrease in energy consumption. Key applications include predictive maintenance and demand response, highlighting AI's role in improving energy efficiency (Brant, 2024).
3. **New York**: The city's Distributed Energy Resources (DER) program employs AI to manage electricity distribution and effectively integrate renewable energy sources. A key aspect of DER is microgrids, which can operate independently or in parallel with the primary grid. AI also enhances analytics, with machine learning algorithms analyzing consumption data to optimize energy use further (Brant, 2024).

Integrating AI into smart grids reduces carbon emissions and lowers energy costs. It also enhances the reliability of the energy supply and supports the transition to renewable energy sources, highlighting the technology's crucial role in urban energy management.

To fully leverage AI's potential to revolutionize the energy system and achieve significant carbon emission reductions, it must be thoroughly integrated into the socio-economic fabric, requiring extensive learning, adaptation, and deliberate leadership.

References

Gexa Energy. (2024). AI and energy efficiency: Consumption, management, and impact. Retrieved from https://learn.gexaenergy.com/article/impact-of-ai-and-energy-efficiency

Da-Sheng Lee, et al. (2022). Universal workflow for energy saving. Energy Reports, 8, 1602-1633. doi.org/10.1016/j.egyr.2021-12.066. Retrieved from https://www.sciencedirect.com/article/pii/S23524847 2105055

Brant, J. (2024). AI-powered energy efficiency and smart grids: The future of urban energy management. Retrieved from https://www.linkedin.com/pulse/ai-powered-energy-efficiency-smart-grids-future-urban-jess-brant-xwjhc/

Hao, K. (2019). Here are 10 ways AI could help fight climate change. MIT Technology Review.

https://www.technologyreview.com/2019/06/20/13486 4/ai-climate-change-machine-learning/

Iglesias-Suarez, F., et al. (2024). Causally-Informed Deep Learning to Improve Climate Change Models and Projections. AGU

Johns Hopkins. (2024). Artificial Intelligence for Climate Action.

Johns Hopkins University Applied Physics Laboratory. https://jhuapl.edu/work/projects-and-missions/artificial-intelliegence-climate-action

CHAPTER 35: ETHICS AND RESPONSIBILITY

As a guiding force, faith shapes leaders' values and principles, influencing their approach to the interconnected dynamics of climate change and AI. It helps leaders transcend past constraints and envision a purposeful future. It inspires shared values and provides a moral compass for addressing the ethical dilemmas posed by AI. It guides leaders in ethically leveraging technology to combat climate change, prioritizing the welfare of others, and engaging in practices that build community and foster positive relationships. Therefore, faith influences moral frameworks and ethical leadership, providing a foundation for responsible decision-making.

Ethical Implications of AI and Climate Action

Recognizing the risks posed by AI technologies is crucial for understanding the ethical implications of AI and climate action, as well as the necessity for leaders to establish an ethical framework to guide their organizations.

AI's Potential Risks

The risks posed by AI generally apply to all organizations, regardless of their specific use cases. According to Bevan O. et al. (2024) and Kremer A. et al. (2024), these risks include:

- Risks associated with infringing intellectual property rights include unintentionally publishing copyrighted content on public platforms.
- Inaccurate outputs and biases embedded in the underlying training data, along with the inability to explain model outputs or inaccuracies appropriately,

could lead to factually incorrect or outdated answers and hallucinations.

- Fraud and cybersecurity issues related to AI's inability to secure biometric systems, including facial recognition software, and vulnerabilities in generative AI systems, such as payload splitting, circumventing safety filters, and the manipulability of open-source models.
- Concerns about disinformation, such as biased, gender-related, racial, offensive, erroneous, and harmful content, can negatively impact society and individual well-being.
- Privacy violations may involve the illegal use or disclosure of personal or sensitive information.
- The risks of noncompliance with standards or regulations, societal risks, and reputational risks.
- Concerns about people losing jobs to AI and robotics.

AI Ethical Framework

This framework integrates purposeful leadership principles discussed in Part 4 of the book with a commitment to combating climate change and addressing ethical challenges in AI while acknowledging the interconnectivity of faith, technology, and environmental stewardship. The framework establishes guidelines for safe implementation, reduces risks, and incorporates faith and interconnectivity dynamics to tackle climate change obstacles, guided by a long-term vision that unites the diverse needs of stakeholders.

A. Understanding the Times and Envisioning the Future

Effective leadership starts with a keen awareness of the current environment and the ability to anticipate future challenges. This includes:

- **Contextual Awareness:** Understanding contextual changes and trends is essential for effectively anticipating challenges and opportunities. This awareness is crucial for creating a vision aligning with long-term goals and a broader purpose.

- **Visionary Planning:** Articulating long-term, clearly defined goals rooted in a higher purpose that directs responses to immediate and future challenges.

- **Data-Driven Solutions:** Enhancing intelligence gathering and data synthesis capabilities while leveraging AI-assisted forecasting to align strategies with emerging trends, transforming complex information into actionable strategies within a turbulent, ambiguous environment.

B. Serving and Empathetic Leadership

Focusing the framework on service and empathy ensures that AI benefits the greater good.

- **Humility and Authenticity:** Leaders model genuine behavior—prioritizing empathy and authenticity over personal accolades.

- **Empowerment:** Inspiring and developing others so every team member reaches their full potential.

- **Self-Sacrifice:** Emphasizing the importance of placing collective welfare above personal ambition.

- **Community Building:** Establishing vibrant relationships and fostering a sense of belonging based on shared values and goals.

C. Partnership and Collaboration Among Stakeholders

Considering the interconnected dynamics of climate change, AI, and faith, strong partnerships are essential:

- **Collaborative Structures:** AI developers, data centers, and application providers must establish protocols that distinguish between enterprise and public tools, safeguard proprietary data, and protect consumers.

- **Mutual Benefits:** These strategic partnerships protect investor interests and promote further investments, ensuring ethical considerations remain paramount.

D. Governance Structures

Strong governance mechanisms are essential for accountability and safe practices:

- **Strict Standards:** Governments and regulatory bodies must view AI systems as consumer products by enforcing legal and regulatory frameworks. Providers should supply detailed user manuals and be held responsible for compliance with safety standards, reliability, and accuracy.

- **Continuous Monitoring:** Creating monitoring systems to track compliance, report deficiencies, and implement real-time corrective actions.

- **Education and Training:** Encourage broad education on the safe use of AI—aimed at employees and the general public—to ensure informed and responsible deployment.

E. Accountability

Establishing a culture of accountability is essential for upholding trust and ethical integrity.

- **Feedback Systems:** Develop strong channels for stakeholders to share input and report on AI applications, fostering continuous improvement.

- **Transparent Reporting:** Commit to fostering open communication about successes and challenges, building trust among all parties.

- **Ethical Stewardship:** Integrate accountability into the organizational culture to guide decision-making and strengthen ethical practices at all levels, now and in the future.

F. Communication

Clear and effective communication is vital for bridging differences and uniting stakeholders.

- **Active Listening:** Active and empathetic listening to understand diverse perspectives.

- **Clear Messaging:** Use relatable stories and analogies to clarify complex concepts and ensure messages remain clear—even in crises.

- **Performance Benchmarks:** Regularly evaluate and enhance communication strategies to ensure clarity and foster trust among diverse audiences.

G. Adaptability and Continuous Learning

Being adaptable and committed to lifelong learning is essential in our fast-paced world.

- **Change Leadership:** Leaders should embrace change, serve as catalysts for transformation, and continually adapt their strategies to meet new challenges.

- **Growth Mindset:** Foster a culture that values learning from failure, embraces diverse perspectives, and views challenges as opportunities.

- **Organizational Learning:** To promote innovation, invest in ongoing education, and establish safe environments for experimentation and risk-taking, including cross-cultural learning.

H. Skillful Hands and Integrity of the Heart

Technical proficiency should be balanced with strong ethical integrity.

- **Practical Competence:** Continuously enhance technical expertise and problem-solving abilities to tackle complex issues effectively.

- **Moral Compass:** Guide decision-making with unwavering honesty, fairness, and respect for human dignity.

- **Emotional Intelligence:** Stay attuned to personal emotions and lead with passion and conviction to inspire others.

I. Faith and Hope

Faith and hope form the inspirational foundation that brings the community together and fosters progress.

- **Perseverance:** Maintain unwavering confidence in pursuing long-term, aspirational goals.

- **Resilience:** Build mental fortitude to overcome challenges and inspire optimism even in times of uncertainty.

- **Community Unity:** Strengthen communities by aligning them through shared values and a common vision for a sustainable future.

- **Optimism:** Inspire followers to remain optimistic in adversity.

J. Appreciation and Thanksgiving

Gratitude promotes an inclusive and supportive culture while reinforcing ethical practices.

- **Acknowledgment:** Regularly recognize and celebrate the contributions of individuals and groups.

- **Cultivating Gratitude:** Develop a culture of thankfulness that unites stakeholders and drives collective improvement.

This framework encapsulates the principles of responsible AI deployment while integrating the dynamics of climate change and the motivational power of faith. Through transparent governance, effective communication, and a commitment to continuous learning and ethical integrity, the framework seeks to guide leaders in navigating the complexities of our interconnected world.

CHAPTER 36: BUILDING ADAPTIVE ORGANIZATIONS TO ADDRESS THE CHALLENGES OF INTERCONNECTIVITY DYNAMICS — EMPOWERMENT THROUGH EDUCATION

As we conclude our journey from the timeless teachings of Jesus to a future propelled by AI and global challenges, we recognize that adaptive organizations must be built upon not only innovation and continuous learning but also ethical integrity and shared values. In today's era, characterized by rapid digital disruption, climate change, and ethical dilemmas in technology, adaptive leadership is essential. By integrating the moral compass provided by faith, along with the principles of the AI Ethical Framework, leaders can build resilient organizations that are both visionary and responsible.

Building Adaptive Organizations in the 21st Century: Key Pillars

1. Adaptive Leadership & Ethical

Vision A Timeless Example:

Jesus' approach to leadership—raising individuals with humility, authenticity, and integrity—serves as a timeless model. He empowered His disciples to address fundamental issues immediately and for future generations, emphasizing personal transformation over rigid systems. In our context, this means that a 21st-century organization must cultivate a vibrant mindset and ethical leadership traits to tackle challenges such as climate change and AI disruption effectively.

Faith & Moral Guidance:

Faith plays a crucial role in shaping leaders' values, helping them transcend past constraints and envision a purposeful future. It provides a moral framework for addressing ethical dilemmas posed by AI and for leveraging technology responsibly. This ethical foundation reinforces adaptive leaders' commitment to community welfare and environmental stewardship, guiding them in making responsible decisions in a complex world.

2. Critical Mindsets & Leadership Traits

Drawing upon insights from our earlier discussions and the AI Ethical Framework, adaptive leaders in the modern era must cultivate both robust mindsets and practical personal qualities:

Critical Mindsets

- **Forward-Looking & Visionary Planning:**
  Leaders must develop clarity, discipline, and resilience. By integrating contextual awareness and data-driven insights (AI-assisted forecasting), they can anticipate emerging challenges and opportunities in a turbulent environment. This aligns closely with the imperative for visionary planning outlined in the AI Ethical Framework.

- **Curious & Asset-Based Thinking:**
  Embracing inquisitiveness and focusing on strengths rather than limitations enables leaders to navigate complexity effectively. This mindset encourages experimentation with novel ideas and promotes personal and organizational growth.

- **Growth & Believing Mindsets:**

  A willingness to embrace challenges, learn from mistakes, and see failures as opportunities is essential. Coupled with steadfast faith and optimism, this mindset fuels the perseverance needed to overcome obstacles and drive continuous improvement.

- **Intuitive Mindset:**

  In environments marked by uncertainty and ambiguity, combining logical analysis with heart-led wisdom offers clarity and creative solutions.

Effective Leadership Traits

Informed by both timeless teachings and contemporary ethical imperatives, today's leaders must exemplify:

- **Humility & Empathy:**

  Effective leaders listen, acknowledge their limitations, and prioritize the welfare of their community. This empathy is vital in times of burnout and widespread workplace disengagement.

- **Courage & Accountability:**

  Courage drives leaders to confront risks and overcome obstacles despite potential misunderstandings. A culture of accountability—supported by transparent reporting and robust governance—is essential for maintaining trust and ethical integrity (Kouzes & Posner, 2017).

- **Integrity & Intelligence:**

  Integrity, the cornerstone of trust, must guide every decision (Kouzes & Posner, 2017). Leaders also require strong analytical and conceptual skills, which can be enhanced through AI-assisted data analytics, to steer adaptive organizations amid increasing complexity.

- **Service & Authenticity:**
  Inspired by the principles of serving and empathetic leadership, modern leaders must empower others, foster community unity, and model authentic behavior that transcends personal ambition.

3. Governance, Partnerships, & Ethical Infrastructure

Building adaptive organizations requires robust structures that ensure accountability, collaboration, and ethical practices:

- **Collaborative Structures & Community Building:**
  In recognizing the interconnected dynamics of climate change, AI, and faith, organizations must foster strategic partnerships. Whether between AI developers and application providers or within internal teams, collaboration protects stakeholders' interests and strengthens ethical oversight.
- **Governance & Continuous Monitoring:** Establishing and enforcing strict legal and regulatory standards is imperative. Organizations are required to implement regular monitoring, clear feedback systems, and transparent communication channels, ensuring compliance with guidelines for safety, reliability, and accuracy.
- **Clear Communication & Active Listening:** Effective communication—characterized by active listening and clear messaging—connects diverse perspectives and brings stakeholders together during times of crisis and change. Highlighting relatable stories and performance benchmarks fosters trust throughout the organization.

4. Empowerment Through Education & Continuous Learning

Empowering adaptive organizations starts with fostering lifelong learning and self-reflection.

- **Ongoing Education Initiatives:**
  Invest in programs that cultivate ethical leadership, cross-functional expertise, and the technical know-how necessary in an AI-driven landscape. A well-rounded education must combine technical knowledge with the development of emotional intelligence and a strong moral compass.
- **Self-Reflection & Organizational Learning:** Historical exemplars, such as Marcus Aurelius, who utilized self-reflection to navigate the challenges of leadership (Badaracco, J.L. Jr., 1997)[1]Innovative leaders who have harnessed reflective practices underscore the importance of personal growth. Creating routines for self-assessment, whether through journaling or weekly reviews, reinforces a culture of continuous learning and adaptability (Carnegie, D., 1981)[2].

---

[1] Historical examples illustrate the power of adaptability through self-reflection and continuous learning. Marcus Aurelius, a Roman emperor and philosopher, utilized his journal "To Himself" to examine his heart, uncover hidden motives, biases, and impulses, and renew himself after demanding days filled with activities (Badaracco, J.L. Jr., 1997). His practice of reflection enabled him to adapt to the challenges of leading his army through long campaigns against invading enemies. Marcus Aurelius's advice to today's leaders underscores the importance of creating moments of serenity, slowing down, reflecting on ways to enhance one's knowledge, and managing restlessness.

[2] A prominent Wall Street bank president with limited education created a self-improvement system that led to remarkable success. Every Saturday evening, he withdrew to a quiet room with his engagement

- **Adaptability & Growth:**

    A commitment to ongoing education fosters an environment where innovation thrives. Embracing change, learning from diverse sources, and encouraging risk-taking are pivotal for organizational resilience.

Conclusion

Integrating ethical responsibility with adaptive leadership is the cornerstone of building adaptive organizations for the 21st century. By uniting timeless values—exemplified by Jesus' leadership—with the pragmatic guidelines of the AI Ethical Framework, today's leaders can craft dynamic organizations capable of navigating the complexities of climate change, AI disruption, and shifting global paradigms. Embracing critical mindsets, effective leadership traits, robust governance, and continuous learning not only honors our shared moral heritage but also equips us to confront the challenges of an interconnected future head-on.

---

book, reflecting on the week's interactions and posing critical questions about his mistakes and areas for improvement (Carnegie, D., 1981).

References

Badaracco, J.L. Jr. (1997). Defining Moments: When Managers Must Choose Between Right and Right. Harvard Business Review Press.

Carnegie, D. (1981). How to Win Friends and Influence People. Simon and Schuster.

Kouzes, J. M., & Posner, B. Z. (2017). The Leadership Challenge: How to Make Extraordinary Things Happen in Organizations. Wiley.

Schulze, J. H., & Pinkow, F. (2020). Leadership for Organisational Adaptability: How Enabling Leaders Create Adaptive Space. Administrative Sciences, 10(3), 37. https://doi.org/10.3390/admsci10030037

CHAPTER 37: CONCLUSION OF THE BOOK

For This Reason: The Quest for Purposeful Leadership

"Leadership from the Heart, Illuminating Lives, Inspiring Organizations."

My journey toward purposeful leadership began with the profound declaration of Jesus:

"For this reason, I came into the world."

This timeless message shaped His ministry and inspired me to explore how emerging forces—such as artificial intelligence and modern adaptive practices—can redefine leadership today. Just as Jesus' words illuminated His path in a bygone era, they resonate with us, providing clarity in an ever-changing landscape.

Leadership from the Heart

Reflecting on Jesus' profound declaration and the potentially transformative role of AI in our future, I reached a powerful conclusion: purposeful leadership originates from the depths of our hearts. When we embrace this inner source of leadership, it radiates outward, illuminating the world with love and compassion.

Purposeful leaders are characterized by humility and a genuine commitment to service, enabling them to transcend selfish ambitions and guide their communities toward a shared destiny that extends beyond mere material gain to encompass the spiritual and the eternal.

Bridging Ancient Wisdom with Modern Realities
The declaration, "For this reason, I came into the world," serves as a bridge between the ancient and the modern. Today's leaders, much like Jesus, are called upon to:

- **Teach and Train:** Impart knowledge and wisdom with clarity.
- **Develop and Empower:** Create environments that foster continuous learning, growth, and innovation.
- **Lead by Example:** Embody qualities such as courage, empathy, integrity, and humility.

As we face the challenges of the 21st century—from climate change and artificial intelligence to evolving societal expectations—adaptive organizations must foster a range of mindsets, including forward-thinking, curious, and growth-oriented approaches. This adaptability is crucial not only for survival but also for driving transformative change.

A Call for Collaboration

No leader can make a lasting impact in isolation. Collaboration across sectors and communities is key. By building networks and partnerships that leverage diverse expertise, we can develop innovative solutions to address today's multifaceted challenges. Whether addressing environmental shifts, technological advances, or questions of faith, working together is imperative.

Closing Inspiration

In a world where everything is deeply interconnected, the call to purpose remains as urgent as ever. Purposeful leaders are like masterful weavers, interlacing strands of technology, the environment, and humanity into a tapestry that envisions a brighter future.

As we conclude this journey, let us reaffirm our commitment to leadership from the heart. May the enduring message of purpose serve as a beacon—guiding you, inspiring those you lead, and catalyzing a legacy built on unwavering integrity and compassion. In embracing our collective destiny and fostering organizations that embody purpose, we transform leadership from a role into a transformative force for good.

Together, let us light the way to the future with our common purpose, building communities and organizations that genuinely inspire and empower.